a love story

by

gina noelle daggett

2010

Bella Books, Inc.
P.O. Box 10543
Tallahassee, FL 32302

Printed in the United States of America on acid-free paper
First Edition

Editor: Katherine V. Forrest
Cover Designer: Gina Daggett
Photographer: Derek Brouwers

ISBN 13:978-1-59493-212-0

Dedication

Jukebox is dedicated to Nana—my No.1 fan and soul sister—and my generous, devoted parents, Bill and Jennifer. Thank you for supporting me every step of the way, for passing on fierce determination and for setting the bar so high in life and in love.

And to all the young Graces and Harpers out there...
May you find the strength to stand
in the truth of who you are, no
matter the cost.
This one's for you.

Acknowledgments

Jukebox has been a decade-long journey that includes seven drafts, five states, four countries, one marathon, three hard drive meltdowns, nineteen pairs of running shoes, one writing program, five moves, two writing retreats, four laptops, a small forest, a handful of all-nighters, three iPods, innumerable sticks of Nag Champa, a trail of dead babies, (beloved words/scenes) tears, laughter, frosty pints of Hefeweizen, a deskful of black Uni-ball Vision pens, drums of candle wax, hundreds of sunrises, bottles of wine, weeks of music, vats of coffees, and enough sushi to fill a Japanese fishing boat.

At a young age, I learned the importance of surrounding myself with good people—those who are loyal, reliable, sincere, funny, inspiring, and, when possible, those who are wiser than myself. If this is the measure of success, I've done pretty well in life and as it relates to the evolution of this novel.

Two women in particular who fit this bill: my literary agent, Holly Bemiss, and Bella Books' Contributing Editor, Katherine V. Forrest. These two gems (both of whom, I believe, I manifested into my life) gave much of themselves to *Jukebox*, ensuring that it not only ended up in your hands, but also, now that it is, that you won't put it down.

Holly: Thank you for your leap of faith, for working hard, for taking such good care and for your repeated, insightful feedback. You were just what I needed, right when I needed it. And continue to be. I deeply appreciate you and our alliance.

Katherine: No one has gotten closer to Grace and Harper than you and no one has taught me as much about the craft. Stuff you can't learn in school. That pencil you hold is golden, as is your prolific career as an award-winning author. Thank you for your time and for everything you gave.

Thank you POWER UP and Stacy Codikow/Lisa Thrasher/Chris Thrasher for my 2004 Filmmakers Fund grant, which *Jukebox* received as a work-in-progress. I've since adapted the novel into a screenplay and plan on going into pre-production on the film in 2011. You can follow its progress here: chateauentertainment.com.

Thank you Linda Hill at Bella Books for publishing this little love story and for allowing me to design the cover. Also, thank you Belgian photographer Derek Brouwers for your stellar jukebox cover photos, both of which were taken at a bar in Barcelona, Spain. (A link to his work can be found at jukeboxnovel.com.)

Beyond those generous souls, there are other fingerprints all over this novel—so many who've contributed to *Jukebox* or supported me in my career along the way.

Kelly Staley, thank you for the music and for your enduring friendship.

Patricia McKenny, thank you for the beautiful place that is your soul and that is my home. With boundless love and gratitude, I will cherish you and the CN forever.

Billy Daggett, my brother and spiritual twin, thank you for everything, which includes your design brilliance, donating so many hours to my websites, and for being an amazing friend.

Big thanks also go out to: Shea Steel (who was there at beginning and gave so much for so long), Kathy Belge (Dipstick—I've loved our years of collaboration), Lanie Whittle-Daggett (sissy), Shanna Germain, Andrea Carlisle, Christina Scott (Minxy), Tina Hoogs, Diane Anderson-Minshall, Frances Stevens (Daddy), Professor Doyle W. Walls, Professor Kathlene Postma, Jourdan Fremin, Thalia Zepatos, Barbara Nelson, Mary Foulk, Stacy Bias, The Posse (Lina, Marblez, Pinion, TW, Shan, Gwendolyn, Junta, Bitty), Lucy Jane Bledsoe, my senior thesis group at Pacific University (Aimee Ault, Rachel Smucker, Cera Varvaro), Professor Lorelle Browning, Veronica Russell, Scott Dillinger, Marc Acito, Floyd Sklaver, Sarah Schulman, Jill Bendziewicz Tracy, Jessica Tracy, Harper Jude, Nicky Forsman, Mick Krizaj, Magali Gillon, Ryan Page, Jennifer Polci, Tara Pisciotta Flannery, Staci Grevillius Kruse, Heather Bennett Weber, The McKenny Clan (Weeness, Miga, Big B, Pearl, Pameeeela, Tiny B), Cameron Grant, Zeljka Carol Kekez, Michelle Kne, Ryan Ketchum, Jason Stall, Bonnie Ste-Croix, Ashleigh Flynn, Maggie Parker, Wade McCollum, Noah Jordan, Colin O'Neill, my family at *Curve* Magazine (where I got my first big break with Lipstick & Dipstick), the folks at *Just Out* (where I published my first word), Heather Findlay (who assigned me my first cover feature at *Girlfriends*), Suzanne Westenhoefer, Emily Nemesi, Shoshana Oppenheim, Walker Macy, Lisa Town, Jeffrey Selin, Sara Jane Keskula, Tara Cowell-Plain, Char Power, Christine Havrilla, Gina James, Caron Parker, Janice Dulle, Dawnie Grubstein, Jason Frank, Stacy Forrester Kelly, Julie Hunter Ballesteros, Devida Chacon, Beth Gaughan, Roland Arnold, Courtney DeMilio, Kelly Martin and Mindy Shotwell.

To any I may've forgotten—please forgive me.

If you'd like to buy the songs which are the melodic bones of this story, visit: jukeboxnovel.com. While you're there, sign up for the mailing list and I'll keep you apprised of all-things-*Jukebox* and let you know when I'm in your neighborhood for a reading.

I hope you enjoy this story. It's a paradigm of persistence and determination and, truly, a labor of love.

Cheers,

Gina Noelle Daggett

PLAYLIST

We've Only Just Begun	The Carpenters
Wishin' And Hopin'	Dusty Springfield
You Are My Lady	Freddie Jackson
If Only For One Night	Luther Vandross
Hello Again	Neil Diamond
I Kissed A Girl	Jill Sobule
Let's Get It On	Marvin Gaye
Secret Lovers	Atlantic Starr
The Lady In Red	Chris De Burgh
Private Eyes	Daryl Hall & John Oates
My Boyfriend's Back	The Angels
Pressure	Billy Joel
The Carnival Is Over	Dead Can Dance
Fire	The Pointer Sisters
Hold On	Sarah McLachlan
Gone Too Soon	Babyface
Alone	Heart
I Shall Believe	Sheryl Crow
Hangin' By A Thread	Jann Arden
Love Bites	Def Leppard
Somewhere In My Broken Heart	Billy Dean
Missing You	John Waite
Again	Janet Jackson

Thinkin' About You	Trisha Yearwood
Reunited	Peaches & Herb
Why	Annie Lennox
You Still Move Me	Dan Seals
Against All Odds	Phil Collins
Guilty	Barbra Streisand & Barry Gibb
I Just Fall In Love Again	Anne Murray
We're All Alone	Crystal Gayle
Look What You've Done To Me	Boz Scaggs
The Old Songs	Barry Manilow
Late For The Sky	Jackson Browne
Hallelujah	Jeff Buckley
Love Is Everything	k.d. lang
You Had Time	Ani DiFranco
The Glory Of Love	Bette Midler

As Harper Alessi walked the dark stairs, crimson blood dotted each step. The rag, wrapped tightly around her hand, was saturated.

Howling gusts rattled the old windowpanes as she entered the bathroom. The lights flickered. At the pedestal sink, she cleaned the cut and used a tourniquet on her finger, which hadn't stopped bleeding since she sliced it open. Her wavy chestnut hair, twisted into a clip, was a mess, halfway fallen, and she couldn't have cared less.

Before leaving the safe confines of the washroom, Harper turned off the light. Alone, she stood in the dark and let herself cry. And it wasn't about the wound. Slouched over against the linen cabinet, she couldn't hold it any longer; the ripping and tearing in her chest made it difficult to breathe.

She took one final breath before entering her bedroom again, knowing the attic door was still wide open. So was her hope chest inside. And all the secrets it held.

Sprinkled like blue confetti, broken glass littered the rough floor panels of the low-ceiling attic. Woolly insulation, folded like heaps of cotton candy, still partially encircled the chest even though it had been pushed aside by the intruder, who'd clearly known what they were after.

Amidst the debris, items from Harper's past were strewn about, in piles here and there—a teetering stack of 45s was covered in bits of torn photos like fallen cherry blossoms.

A solitary utility light swung as a beacon above as she approached the trunk, careful where she stepped. The ornamental cedar chest had been in her family for three generations. It was her grandmother's and had crossed the Pond by boat in 1952, when she arrived from Italy.

Tentatively, Harper knelt down beside it.

As she surveyed what was left behind, her grief slowly galvanized into anger.

A strand of pearls, given to Harper the night of her debutante ball, was curved like a millipede on the floor. Beside it were several worn cassette tapes with handwritten song titles. Letters Harper collected that European summer, partially bound in string, were picked apart.

All that was left of the antique pickling jar from Uncle Alvaro was the rusted handle and mouth. The rest was scattered like a booby trap now, shards misted with blood.

For Harper, the most alarming discovery was under one of her sorority sweatshirts, open and face down. The stained and ragged journal from her night of revelation on the mountain.

She closed her eyes and took in its familiar scent. The smell—her body's most acute sense—gently opened up cavities in Harper's soul, ones better left sealed.

She hadn't touched it in twelve years. Hadn't wanted to. Hadn't been ready.

There were thousands of places Grace Dunlop would've rather been than in Jack Stowe's office. There was one in particular and it had her on the edge of a panic attack.

Even before Stowe began reading her great grandfather's will, Grace was already staring at the ceiling, worlds away from his downtown Phoenix law office.

Grace's mom, Cilla, sat to her left. They were the spitting image of each other, she and Grace—the same flushed apple cheeks, loose blond curls and a delicately feminine body despite the hours spent at the gym.

Other Dunlop heirs were seated around the expansive

conference room table, which had a silver bowl of Granny Smith apples at its center. Stowe was at the head. Grace's foot tapped steadily as Stowe, the decrepit lawyer who'd been the executor of James Warden Dunlop's will since he died, cleared his throat.

"All right, let's get started," Stowe said, adjusting his western belt buckle. He nodded to one of his assistants, who fiddled with a tape recorder before he began.

Grace had never met her great-grandfather, JW, as he was known to his inner circle, but he was a man whom Grace had been—along with the rest of the family—living her life for since she was eighteen, the age each heir was brought into the abundant Dunlop Trust.

Grace never looked at Stowe when he read the will, which happened every August. Per JW's wishes, each year they'd gathered as a family, put their hands on a King James Bible and sworn their lives away.

Stowe started reading: "This is the last will and testament of me, James Warden Dunlop, of sound mind"—Grace let out a caustic laugh—"and body." Cilla shot her a look, as she always did. It was like clockwork.

Stowe sped up when he got to the next section, since they'd all heard it so many times.

"I hereby revoke all wills and testamentary dispositions of every nature and kind whatsoever by me hereto before made..."

Rubbing her temples, Grace tried to tune out Stowe, a man she'd hated her entire adult life. The only man she loathed more than JW. They were cut from the same cloth, Stowe and her great-granddaddy.

JW had unabashedly controlled every member of the Dunlop clan since the day he made his first million. The hundreds of millions that followed only dug the claws deeper.

"I give, devise and bequeath annual installments to all heirs, beginning at their eighteenth birthday, the dividends and interest accrued in the established trust split equally among able beneficiaries who meet these set forth conditions." Stowe pulled a handkerchief from his pocket and coughed out a lung into it.

Grace cringed. She hated this part the most, the list. She took a deep breath, fighting back tears, as Stowe continued.

"All heirs to retain family name, regardless of sex. All heirs to marry white-skinned persons of European descent," Stowe said. "All heirs to be circumcised at birth."

Sitting in the leather swivel chair, Grace closed her eyes and shut out the rest of the list; she couldn't hear the most painful parts again. Instead, she floated off to her favorite place—the Italian countryside, where she chased fireflies through a maze of grapevines. Distant laughter. Booming beats of thunder. The night sky veined with lightning.

"Grace?" Stowe barked.

Despite being startled, Grace slowly opened her eyes.

"Do you comply?" Stowe asked.

Hesitating, Grace took a long hard look at Cilla before answering.

Grace's glare moved to Stowe as she put her hand on the Bible.

Part One

“We’ve Only Just Begun”
The Carpenters

1984
Paradise Valley
Arizona

The scalding sun baked Harper Alessi’s head as she stood outside the pro shop looking at the tennis tournament draw. She took a deep breath when she saw the name next to hers.

Grace Dunlop vs. Harper Alessi.

She knew she was in trouble.

Beside Harper was Sloan Weasle, her pudgy classmate and nemesis.

“I got lucky,” Sloan said. “I’m playing April Cohen.”

They both looked at her name, two brackets down.

Above them, a fiberglass sign that said NO CHEWING GUM was fastened to the green chain-link fence.

“You have to play that new girl,” Sloan said. “I hear she breaks a racquet every time she plays.”

Sloan breathed down Harper’s neck. “She’s going to kill you.”

The private club where they were playing that day, Camelback Country Club, was nestled between two mountains in Paradise Valley, Arizona, a ritzy enclave of Scottsdale. Homes surrounding the club were two and three acres with multimillion dollar price tags.

Harper’s grandmother, Nonna—a proper, polished woman

of sixty—walked up to Harper and put her hand, dripping in diamonds, in front of her mouth. Reluctantly, Harper spit her wad of bubblegum into her cupped hand.

"Your parents just called from Milan. They wanted me to give you this," she said, hugging Harper and squeezing tight. "And wish you luck. We're supposed to call afterwards no matter how late."

It was at this very moment, as Nonna had her arms around Harper, that she locked eyes with Grace for the first time. The golf course's driving range was the backdrop as Grace wiped her forehead and looked Harper's way.

Quite developed for her age, Grace didn't seem athletic, Harper thought. The grunts coming from the court as she warmed up with her coach, however, said otherwise.

With her tennis bag, Harper walked to a nearby table and sat down. T-minus five minutes, she counted, sipping on her cold cup of water.

Finally, it was game on.

As Harper walked toward the court, she kept her head down until she got to the gate. A row of girls was lined up against the fence, including Sloan, who was on the end making a face.

From the court, Harper saw Nonna in the stands sitting a comfortable distance from a guy who looked like the lead singer of Duran Duran. Next to him was an amazingly beautiful woman who looked a lot like her opponent, Grace, Harper thought. She was wearing a straw hat and fanning herself with an issue of *The New Yorker*.

Grace spun her tennis racquet on one finger as Harper approached with a can of tennis balls. Walking slowly down the alley, Harper prayed she'd take at least one game.

Although they'd never met, Harper was curious about Grace. From afar, before this day, she'd watched her play other girls. She had textbook form and was known for the power in her backhand. The energy behind her strokes was remarkable. Harper heard coaches talking about it behind the dusty fence when she moved in to retrieve a ball during their warm-up.

Everyone, including Harper, also knew about Grace's competitive temper. Sloan was right. Just like the winners she hit down the line, it was as predictable as summer monsoons in the desert. After she'd missed a shot, from a court away Harper had seen Grace slam her racquet so hard the graphite splintered into pieces.

Grace chewed bubblegum and took a few steps in her direction as Harper got closer.

"Are you Harper?"

"Yeah."

Harper was surprised by Grace's accent. And she was also surprised by the question; she figured Grace knew exactly who she was, they just hadn't met yet. Grace was relatively new to town, but they went to the same grade school after all.

Focused on Grace's dangling gold cross cradled in her young cleavage, Harper avoided her eyes as they shook hands.

"I'm Grace," she said, blowing a bubble.

Harper looked to Nonna, who gave her thumbs-up.

As Harper bent over to tie her shoelaces, she wondered where Grace was from. From her own world travels, Harper was sure she'd heard the accent before. She took extra time with the double knot. Was she from Scotland? Somewhere else in the UK?

From under the bill of Harper's hat, she could see Grace's hands flat on the ground as she stretched her Achilles tendon. Growing up on the tennis court, Harper had learned the hard way about the importance of stretching. Once you've heard someone's tendon snap, even if it's from several courts away, it never escapes your memory; it sounds like a gunshot when it coils from the bone.

Physically, they couldn't have been more opposite. Grace, who already had the bosom of a teenager, was like a picture from a magazine. She looked like a model, Harper thought, completely put together; her hot pink skirt even matched the grip on her tennis racquet. Grace's blond hair, long relaxed golden ringlets, was pulled back into a loose ponytail.

A full-blooded Italian, Harper had hair of dark chocolate with a hint of red—*cioccolato*, her Aunt Amelia said—done up in a tight French braid that fell to the middle of her back. Harper was starting to get hips. She'd always been rail thin and lanky, but she was quickly developing. And faster than she liked.

Grace, on the other hand, seemed quite comfortable in her stretching skin. You could see it in the way she carried herself, the way her tank was a V-neck, accentuating her newly forming womanhood. Standing about two inches above Harper, Grace looked down at her after they finished stretching.

"So, do you go to Carlyle?" Harper asked, unzipping her tennis bag, digging out a racquet. She was already playing Grace's game.

"Right."

"Me, too."

"Oh yeah?" Grace said, pounding her strings before walking toward the baseline, leaving Harper at the bench.

In between sets, Harper tried to strike up conversation again. "Where is your accent from?"

Grace finished her water and crushed the paper cup in her hand. "England," she said, and left it at that.

Harper wanted to tell Grace that she'd been to England, had been on every continent, even Antarctica, but decided to just retie her shoelaces instead.

Their warm-up was almost as long as their match, which Grace won 6-0, 6-1. Harper got her game.

Afterward, while Grace stood at the net waiting for a handshake, Harper fumbled with the balls at the fence, accidentally kicking one into the adjacent court.

"Good game," Grace said, even though it wasn't.

Quickly, she loaded up her racquets and left the court.

Carlyle, the grade school both girls attended, was an expansive ranch-style building that fanned out onto a shaded lawn like a deck of cards spread on an evergreen tablecloth. The five-acre campus was nestled into an orange grove at the base of Camelback Mountain. Each night, it was flooded by an irrigation system that kept that part of town ten degrees cooler than the rest of Scottsdale. Carlyle was ultra private and ultra posh. Students had to live in a certain zip code to get in and there was a steep tuition; the administrators even looked at parents' financials for admission.

Around campus, there were always maintenance men working furiously, planting fresh flowers and painting things that didn't need paint. Near the parking lot was an Olympic-size pool kids swam in at lunch. It was the perfect blue. There, too, men were always skimming leaves, fussing with colored water gauges and measuring chemicals.

Less than a week after their first match, Harper had just asked the lunch lady for her sandwich to go when she spotted Grace sitting at a table near the back doors. The hot new girl, she was surrounded by boys and their raging hormones. Jamie Simons—a pompous, popular boy with a pretty face—was sitting closest, bending her ear, flexing his young muscles.

As Harper slid her tray down the line, they caught eyes. Grace smiled first.

Sloan slammed her tray up against Harper's. "I told you Grace would whip you on Saturday," she hissed. "Neaner. Neaner."

Harper chose a pint of chocolate milk, a cold one near the bottom. "How bad did she beat you in the last tournament?" she asked.

"I had the flu," Sloan sniffed, "it didn't count."

Harper shook her head as she grabbed her lunch, packed in a brown bag to go.

"Helping Miss Jensen again?" Sloan asked.

Miss Jensen, a young fetching teacher carrying a messy stack of papers, waited near the exit for Harper.

"She asked for help," Harper said, paying for lunch. "She's behind on grading."

Sloan immediately stuck her fat tongue out—it had bits of bread on it—and pretended like she was French kissing the air.

"Oh Miss Jensen, I love you. Oh Miss Jensen, I want to kiss you."

"Screw you," Harper said, throwing her change, a few pennies and a nickel, at Sloan. Just as quickly, she turned and walked away, rolling her eyes as she always did at Sloan and her torment.

Harper was headed toward Miss Jensen when she caught Grace staring again. Making her way through the cafeteria, Harper opened her chocolate milk and held the carton up to Grace.

"Cheers," she said.

Grace did the same with her apple juice.

Maybe they'd be friends one day, Harper thought.

During afternoon recess, Harper was on top of the jungle gym swinging from her knees, upside down like an orangutan. Through the web of crossbars, she could see Grace on the swing across the yard. Grace was huffing, pointing her toes to the sky as hard as she could. If there were gears on the swing set, Grace had hit full speed.

Nearby, Sloan was playing four square with a group of classmates. Even from upside down, Harper could tell she was arguing about a miscalculated point.

"Nu-uh," Sloan fought. "Five!"

Sitting on the park bench under the old Palo Verde tree, Miss Jensen was still grading papers. Harper watched her for a long time—she loved the dress she was wearing, wanted one just like it.

From hanging this way, Harper's face looked like a plum, blood draining into her head at an alarming rate. She felt dizzy and decided it was time for a dismount. She'd run over to help Miss Jensen some more.

Reaching up, Harper was unhooking her legs from the monkey bars when Jamie appeared out of nowhere. He stood above her on top of the webbed dome like the king of the playground.

In mid-swing, Harper didn't have time to right herself before Jamie stepped on her bent fingers. Harper screamed before her fingers involuntarily released their grip and gravity took over. In a sort-of somersault, Harper was flung to the earthen floor beneath the bars.

She heard her collarbone snap before she felt the pain, which immediately filled her body with adrenaline.

The first thing Harper saw once she hit the ground was

Jamie, about ten feet above her, with a smile on his face. Once he saw the teachers coming, he jumped off like Spiderman.

Miss Jensen was on her way; Harper heard the jingle of her whistle on a lanyard around her neck. She would save Harper.

"Are you okay?" Miss Jensen asked, taking Harper's hand. Beyond the excruciating pain from her back, blood ran down her leg. "We're getting help."

Rolling to her side, Harper saw a worried Grace slowing the swing with her sandal. She dragged it through the soft dirt until she stopped completely.

Harper tried to move her arm, but the stabbing pain along her left clavicle made it impossible.

"Nurse Umble is coming," Miss Jensen said.

Through her tears, Harper saw Grace walking slowly, cautiously in her direction along with a cluster of other students surveying the scene.

Even though the bell rang, Grace, with clear, genuine concern, waited until Harper was placed on a stretcher and taken to the nurse's office before she went back to class.

Jamie was called to the principal's office immediately. As Harper sat in the nurse's chair waiting for Nonna, a bag of ice taped to her shoulder, she could hear Principal Wagner yelling. In between his booming voice, Jamie defended himself. "It was an accident. I didn't mean to hurt her."

At the urgent care clinic, the x-rays were telling—Harper had broken her collarbone in two places, both on her left side. The blood was from a pencil that had been in her pocket; it had torn a gash in her leg the size of a caterpillar. Seven stitches. The point of the pencil had wedged itself in her flesh so she'd had a tetanus shot, too, for lead poisoning.

"Even at your age," the doctor said, "the damage done here may be irreversible. We'll see how it heals. You won't be able to play tennis for some time. Maybe never again."

"What do you mean?" Nonna asked, as upset as Harper, who was crying into her Carlyle Cougars sweatshirt.

"What about pom and cheer?" Harper wept. "Can I still be a cheerleader? Once I'm better?"

"Eventually."

"I need to call your parents," Nonna said later as she and Harper arrived home, parking in the circular driveway of their family's sprawling estate. "They'll want to be on the next flight."

Even though her day had been awful, Harper worried about the call to her parents; she hated being the reason they had to cut an assignment short and fly home.

Grace was the last person Harper expected to see a week after surgery. It was mid-afternoon and Harper was in the game room, with more ice on her shoulder, lying on a couch, watching a *Gilligan's Island* marathon when Grace, accompanied by her mother, came around the corner carrying a gallon of ice cream and a card.

At first, Harper didn't know what to say. Quietly, she watched Grace sit down on the leather ottoman and smile.

"Hi," Grace said, tucking her hair behind her ears.

Grace's hair looked different when it was down. Harper almost didn't believe it was Grace Dunlop. Her hair was clean, bright and thick, but the same watercolor yellow. Feathered. As if she'd been on her own desert island, Harper stared like she'd never seen another human.

After they each said hi, a good ten seconds went by before anything else was said. Grace smelled of orange blossoms and was giving off heat. Their mothers could be heard chatting in the foyer.

"How are you feeling?"

"Better." Harper paused. "I think. The doctor says I'm better. I saw him today."

Grace handed Harper a get well card with the tub. "I brought you some ice cream. I hope you like Rocky Road."

Harper didn't like nuts, but she said Rocky Road was her favorite.

"I am sorry for what happened. Jamie's a jerk."

"He did it on purpose you know."

"I know." Grace touched Harper's arm. She was on her side. "He got suspended."

It wasn't long before Nonna, who'd stopped by to check on Harper, brought the girls two bowls and an ice cream scooper. Grace reached for the spoon and did the dirty work.

In silence, they watched Ginger flirt with the Professor on TV while they ate their ice cream. Harper kept her bowl at an angle so Grace couldn't see the heap of nuts she was collecting at the bottom. She put her napkin on top when she finished.

Out of the corner of Harper's eye, she could tell by the shoes Grace was wearing that she hadn't come from tennis practice.

"What did you do today?" Harper asked.

"I had piano."

"I play piano," Harper said. "I'm sure you're better. I only know one song. 'Lean on Me.'"

They smiled and watched Gilligan and Skipper argue.

"How do you like Carlyle?" Harper finally asked.

"Fine. How do you like it?" Grace asked quickly, nervous.

"It's all right."

After a few minutes, Harper asked Grace if she wanted to see her stitches. Grace paused before she said sure. Harper pulled up her pant leg and leaned back onto the arm of the couch.

"You can lift the gauze."

While Harper waited, staring out the window at the crew of Hispanic men working in the yard, she wondered when Grace had decided to be her friend, if coming over was her idea.

"Is this blood?" Grace asked, tentative.

"No, it's Betadine. It's gross, huh? It's for the germs, I guess."

"It's not gross."

Harper could tell by the way she said it that she thought it was.

Coming over had been Grace's idea. As Harper and her mom, Ana, made dinner that night, they discussed it. "I don't get it," Harper said. "She was so mean to me when we played. I tried to be nice."

"I remember you saying she was bitchy," Ana said, standing a few feet away, towering over Harper, her premature gray hair sloppily wound into a bun.

As Harper sat at the counter doing homework, she wondered if she was allowed to say *bitch*, too. She was eleven and had already gotten her period; perhaps she was old enough. They'd been working on becoming friends. It felt weird, but she tried it out.

"Yeah, she was bitchy."

She glanced at Ana, who wore an African stone around her neck and was chopping Maitake mushrooms. Ana smiled. And so did Harper. It worked.

Ana wasn't like other moms in Paradise Valley; as an international photographer for *National Geographic*, she was cultured, worldly and open in a way others simply weren't. Harper yearned to spend more time with her mom. Each time she and Harper's dad were home in between assignments, it was never enough.

A soft-spoken feminist, Ana had somehow escaped the conservative trappings of the Valley and her wealthy upbringing. Since college, where she'd left midstream to join the Peace Corps, she'd bucked every tradition. Something inside her had changed and never went back.

"How do you like your pottery class?" Ana asked, drying spinach in the salad spinner.

"I like it. Nonna thinks I should be in ballet instead, so I might switch classes."

"But you love art. You don't love ballet."

Harper chewed on the green crazy straw leftover from her afternoon milkshake. "I like ballet, Mama. Grace takes ballet." Over her glasses, Ana looked at Harper and then dumped a pile of mushrooms into the sautéing onions on the stove. Harper added, "Maybe I want to take ballet, too."

"Whatever you want, baby, is fine with me."

After Grace stopped by to see if Harper was okay, it seemed that overnight they were best friends. Inseparable. They made a pact and did all the things best friends do, securing their place in each other's lives. At the mall, they bought a best friend charm and each wore half around their neck—BE FRI and ST ENDS. They sealed the deal after overturning the Dunlops' golf cart. Both girls were catapulted onto the gravel path. "Blood Sisters Forever," they said, swearing on it, pressing their wounded knees together.

That same summer, they started planning their futures. "I'll be your maid of honor and you can be mine," Grace said, bouncing on her trampoline.

"Okay," Harper agreed after she did a backflip. "And we'll be neighbors. And live on the same street."

"The two houses perched above the lake," Grace added, always specific, knowing exactly what she wanted.

As they spoke, they bounced up and down opposite each other, speaking mostly in midair.

"And we'll have two kids each, maybe three."

"And we'll plan it so we can be pregnant at the same time."

"And our kids can all grow up together."

"I want a dog. And a cat."

"And a fish tank. I love fish," Harper said.

"Our husbands. They'll be handsome and successful."

"They'll drive nice cars and play golf."

"And they'll always be away on business trips, so we can still have slumber parties," Grace added. "You, me and all our kids."

Beyond specific childhood experiences—activities which revolved around the country club and the private golf course they grew up on—the soil Harper and Grace sprouted from was quite different.

Grace's home life was structured and conservative. They lived in an eight-bedroom Tudor-style home, a mansion to some, that was always spick-and-span; the live-in housekeeper, Ophelia, made sure of that. Their Arizona address was one of many around the world.

Harper always knew it was time to split when she heard Cilla yell from the back door at dinnertime. Seven sharp. "Gra-a-ce." She always carried the "a."

Beyond their ordered house, the Dunlops, without fail, attended Mass each Sunday. A full Mass, too. Not just an in-and-out-Hail-Mary quickie. Sleepovers on Saturday nights were always tricky for this reason. Harper hated to get up early.

Highly-educated, Grace's parents both had doctorate degrees and had begun their love affair at Oxford. He was studying law, she, English Lit. On their anniversary one year, Cilla told the girls how he proposed.

"The summer we met," she explained, her British accent even stronger than Grace's, "we traveled the Mediterranean by boat. On the top of Mount Etna, Daddy asked for my hand." She was still whimsical about it.

Cilla had kept her maiden name: Dunlop. It was a commandment of Cilla's granddaddy's will, along with a number of other strange conditions. Harper didn't remember all the details, even though Grace shared them one day, but she thought this alone was crazy. Women were supposed to take the guy's name.

An eccentric man who wanted things how he liked them, Grace's great-grandpa was an empire builder and had invented the first pneumatic tire. Generation after generation reaped the benefits. Following his quirky, peculiar dogma was the price they had to pay for wealth.

Harper could tell it bothered Benson, Grace's father, who was born Benson James Mulroney III. Had the circumstances been different, he would have been unequivocally set on Grace taking the family name. The Mulroneys were as traditional as the Dunlops sans the loony patriarch.

In contrast, Harper's family was a juxtaposition of her artistic parents, laid-back and fluid, and her old-money grandparents, with whom Harper had lived with during large patches of her childhood. Their home, her parents' home, looked like it was designed by Frank Lloyd Wright. It had been featured in *Architectural Digest* one summer. Modern. Clean edges. Lots of contemporary art. Interesting stone water features.

Harper's parents, both professional photographers, had met

in Africa on assignment, when her mom was twenty-two and her dad was forty. A considerable age difference, but Ana was an old soul. You could see it in her baby pictures; the eyes of a ninety-year-old in an infant's body. Wise beyond her years.

Of Harper's father, "He was a rogue photographer," Ana would say, sitting at her easel painting watercolors of the desert.

"I saw her through the brush in Kenya," her dad, Blue, explained, "and I hunted her like she was a gazelle."

They had a beautiful love affair, were always dancing.

During Harper's youth, her parents traveled a lot and had become a packaged deal, working exclusively together, capturing exotic places and people. While each had their own collection of photography, they had published three coffee table books together.

"Life is to be lived, Popina," they said, both fierce dreamers, infusing Harper with an intrepid, entrepreneurial spirit.

They called Harper *Popina* because, even though it was more information than she wanted, it was the name of the island where she was conceived. A part of Romania, Popina Island was a small game reserve where they were working on a piece about Shelducks.

Despite her parents' good intentions, Harper's grandparents, Nonna and Papa—the two who'd really raised Harper—experienced most of the important moments of her youth: lost teeth, broken bones and her transition into womanhood. With thoughtful orchestration, her folks had been around for other significant, planable milestones like senior prom, graduation and Harper's debutante ball.

Even though Paradise Valley was Ana's hometown, both of Harper's parents struggled with its pretension.

When Ana got pregnant, they had moved here from Manhattan to put down roots for Harper.

Harper overheard her parents talking about it one night during a dinner party.

"We did it for our baby," Blue said. The table, full of artsy, academic friends in town for a conference, toasted the sacrifices her parents had made.

"She needed stability in her life," Ana said.

"And we sleep a lot better in those pop tents in Africa knowing she's well taken care of by her grandparents," Blue added.

A witty, commanding man, Blue was handsome and well-proportioned. A force. On most days, he pulled his sandy hair into a ponytail and wore khaki cargo pants. Not exactly country club fashion. It drove Nonna crazy.

Every weekend when he was in town, Blue made his Sunday gravy. A big stewing, bubbling pot of Alessi marinara with special fennel sausage balls. It was something he and his brother, Alvaro, both did on Sundays. Growing up, they'd learned the secret recipe from Harper's grandmother, Gemma, whom Harper had never met because she died of polio in her forties.

In addition to the Sunday gravy, Blue also made homemade pastas to pair with them. Depending on his mood, it could be sun-dried tomato linguini, spinach fusilli, pappardelle, simple angel hair or ravioli, Harper's favorite.

And he always let Harper help. At a very young age, she learned how to make the perfect ravioli. On a step stool, she'd stand by her dad and mimic everything he did. He taught her how to build a volcano with the flour and crack her eggs right in its caldera. Like a children's book, he broke everything down for her.

"And then justa pinch of Fleur de Sel," he added, pinching her too. "And a dash of Alessi oil." The olive oil was from the Alessi vineyard in Italy, where Uncle Alvaro and Aunt Amelia still lived.

After the oil, Blue taught Harper the proper way to knead. "You want it to feela like baby skin," he'd say, showing her carefully. Together, they filled each pocket. The final touch, Harper sealed them with the fork.

Although her parents went against the grain, Harper realized early on what they did for a living was envied. Understanding this candy-coated their sacrifices, somehow made them worth it.

During the holidays, if they were on assignment, one of them would fly home and pull Harper out of school, whisking her off to a tent in the Serengeti Plain, or to a green canopy in the Madagascar rainforest. It infuriated Nonna, like so many things; she'd gotten used to having Harper around and thought a traditional holiday—a traditional anything—was more suitable.

No matter, wherever they were, Blue would decorate a tree and turn on his satellite radio while they opened gifts. Harper worried that the reindeer would overheat and it wowed her that Santa could find them in Tanzania or along the banks of the Amazon.

Even though Harper and Grace came from different soil, over time they grew into one family because Harper spent so much time at the Dunlop house. Gymnastics in the grass and monthly piano concerts. At a young age, Grace was already an amazing pianist. A near prodigy. She taught Harper how to play Beethoven's "Fur Elise" and "Danny Boy."

Every week there were slumber parties and pool parties, where they dove onto the Slip 'n Slide and ate Otter Pops in the hammock. It was under the old cottonwood tree in the Dunlops' backyard where they both first kissed a boy. Jimmy Sachs for Harper. Kip Kelly for Grace. It was the same afternoon.

Throughout their summers, Harper and Grace spent nearly every day at the local country club. It was a safe haven, a spot where parents could drop kids off and not worry.

By sweet-talking the coach, Grace and Harper managed to get into the same swim group every June. One year it was the Dolphins, the next the Porpoises. Each day they swam hard, preparing for the big swim meet at the end of summer, where, after the competition and the awards were handed out, they dumped hundreds of goldfish into the pool for the kids to catch. This became the real competition for Grace and Harper, even though they were two of the oldest who still participated in the Goldfish Plunge.

With sunscreen on their faces, the swimmers teetered on the water's edge. Grace, in her suit, swim cap and goggles, was always the first to jump. Water sloshed as bodies disappeared into the pool, and Harper screamed as she surfaced with her first fish. As high as she could, she held a flimsy cup up for her nanny, Mariana, who was standing nearby with a plastic bag. Easily excitable, Mariana, along with the other nannies, cheered, her black hair wild with Medusa coils, her sagging arms swinging in the sun like she'd just won bingo. Ana and Blue had met Mariana in Ecuador. She'd been living in a dire, abusive situation, so they saved her, bringing her back to America. Kids fought for each fish, swimming erratically, dodging cups and ingesting chlorine, until few remained.

When it was over, Grace and Harper tallied their catches side by side on the lip of the pool. In a wide hat, Cilla sat next to them on the cool deck, dipping her long legs into the water. "How'd you girls do?"

"I won," Grace said, the fierce competitor.

"No. We haven't finished counting."

Cilla grabbed their bags and inspected them. "Looks like a tie to me." She was a mom, a regular peacemaker who liked things neat and orderly with no surprises. Grace was full of surprises.

In the shade, Cilla's skin was perfect and looked too young for her years spent in the sun. Sisley face creams, she said. "I swear by them." Her stomach was flat, almost as if she'd never had Grace.

Standing on the edge of the pool in his blue Speedo, Grace's Uncle Dean stood over the girls. His legs were bony and hairy, much different than his muscular, hairless upper half.

"Look out!" Dean said, stepping back a few feet. "Captain Chlorine incoming."

Grace, still recounting, stopped and watched him jump over their pruned bodies in a cannonball. She was the first one to push off the cool deck and join him.

Taking turns, Harper and Grace climbed on Dean, a hip, aspiring actor living in Los Angeles. By their ankles, he would launch them across the lane dividers and into the deep end, where they would do swan dives and belly flops.

"My turn," Harper said, getting into position on his shoulders.

"I'm next," Grace would say.

Twenty years older than Grace and Harper, Dean was a kid at heart and always ready to roughhouse. It was something both girls could always count on. They loved Deano.

After Dean tired out, the girls practiced their synchronized swimming routine. In the sun, they hooked their legs together and spun like a propeller.

"Faster," Grace said, tightening her legs around Harper's. She was intense. Focused. "Faster."

As they twirled around, Harper liked the way Grace's skin rubbed against hers when it was wet; it was different than it felt when they had sleepovers, and their legs touched under the covers.

Dean and Cilla looked on. Harper could overhear them.

To Dean, Cilla said, "I don't like it when they do that windmill thing. The way they wrap their legs around each other."

"For crying out loud, sis, let them play," Dean snapped. "They're kids."

From her lounge chair, Cilla studied Grace and Harper in the pool. "Girls," she barked. "Come dry off. It's time for dinner."

The sun was setting, so Harper, wrapped in a towel like a burrito, dropped down onto a lounge chair next to Dean. He was staring at the mountain in the distance.

"Doesn't it look fake?" Dean asked.

From the country club, they had a perfect view of Camelback Mountain. As the light of day melted into the horizon, the head of the camel looked less like a pile of enormous rocks and more like the inside of an abalone shell, its sprays of color dissolving with the falling sun from scarlet to purple to deep violet.

Lazily, Dean rolled over to Harper. "You did great today," he said. "Let me see that ribbon."

Digging in her bag, she pulled out her red second-place ribbon.

He admired it. "Nice work. I bet your parents are sorry they missed it. Where are they this week?"

Harper envisioned their shooting schedule, taped to her bathroom mirror. Each morning she checked off where they were.

"Rackavajeck. I think," she said, doing her best to pronounce the name.

Dean smiled, knowing she meant Reykjavik, Iceland. "I'd kill to have their job," he said, looking back to the mountain.

"Being an actor is cool. You were on that soap opera. And in that movie. When you played the security guard."

Pulling his glasses down, Dean said, "I've got another spot on *The Young & the Restless* coming up."

"Rad!"

Ever since she'd visited him with Grace the summer before, Harper was easily excited by all things Hollywood. Dean was a movie star!

"But I've always loved photography," Dean said, still dreaming. "And *National Geographic*. That's got to be like the top place to work."

"Yeah," Harper said, recalling off the cuff what she'd read. "It has a subscriber base of five million. And they not only have magnificent photography, but also captivating storytelling."

"Impressive," Dean said, charmed.

The evening light cast a blue hue on the pool area and all the families eating around it. From the west, one sharp ray of sun burned through the indigo dusk like a laser.

After dinner, Harper dared Grace to jump off the high dive. It wasn't the first time the high dive gauntlet had been thrown down, nor the first time Harper would chicken out.

Each day, it was the same story: Grace, who always went first, would dive straight into the cold water without pause, sometimes even backwards. The occasional flip. Harper, on the other hand, would stand on the diving board for fifteen minutes sometimes, trying to muster the courage as she let other kids go by.

In the pool below, Grace always egged Harper on. Taunted her. "Sissy!" Grace yelled.

And she was.

Grace was the real daredevil; she jumped every time.

“Wishin’ And Hopin”
Dusty Springfield

Grade school blew by for Harper after she met Grace. So did junior high, which both girls finished at Carlyle. It wasn’t until their freshmen year in high school that they entered a public school. Many of their friends were in the Scottsdale School District, but it was still a transition.

So much was different. New faces, clubs, activities, choices. Privilege and exclusivity was all they’d ever known. And the public school system did not play favorites, nor did they get to work on their tan poolside at lunch. This put a small crimp in their style, but they learned to adjust.

At their high school there were fistfights, drugs used in the bathrooms and lots of people having sex. Much different than Carlyle.

Grace, who by this time was the number one tennis player in the southwest region, was already being recruited by universities. Even when she was a freshman, they all had their eye on her. Each summer, she went to the Nick Bollettieri Tennis Academy for a month, where she’d play with some of the best coaches and upcoming players in the world.

For Harper, whose collarbone eventually healed, she continued cheering from the sidelines. Junior year, she made varsity cheer and was selected as the captain senior year. But, like the doctor said, there was no more tennis for Harper.

Harper had been born a debutante. At least that's what Nonna used to tell her. "One day," Nonna would say when Ana wasn't around, "you'll be a debutante just like your mother."

The Valley Debutante Ball had been transplanted by a southern family who moved to Scottsdale from Texas in the early Sixties. At first, people were leery of such a production. "It'll never fly in Arizona," natives said, turning up their noses. "Let the South stay in the South."

Sloan's mom, Mary Bell Weasle, a Southern, sagging, sun-worshipping gossipmonger who Grace and Harper called *The Bitch*, was head of the selection committee that year and had been presented, along with Ana, back in the day. Some thirty years later, right before graduating from high school, at their respective front doors, Grace and Harper were both greeted by a barrage of women with flowers.

"Congratulations," they squealed, rushing into the house. "You're a debutante!"

That afternoon, standing in the doorway in her cheerleading uniform—her hair coifed into a bob—Harper listened to The Bitch share details of the upcoming event: "Debutante classes start next month and then, after some good ole southern training, ya'll be presented onstage at the Valley Debutante Ball in December," she explained.

Harper and Grace already knew the routine, had watched their older friends from the country club go through the elemental right of passage. It was just part of the PV culture.

They talked about it the next day after their golf lesson.

Swinging her putter, Harper asked Grace a question that had been on her mind since they opened their invitations. "Who are you gonna ask to the ball?"

"I don't know," Grace said, zeroed in on her ball, intently calculating the angle of the grass. "Maybe Jamie."

Harper sighed. "I was afraid of that."

"Who should I take? Who else is there?"

"I don't know. Just not him."

"Harp," Grace said, still analyzing her shot. "Do we have to have escorts? Maybe we could go stag."

"Rich would be devastated," Harper said, leaning onto her putter. "He's really excited."

Grace hit her ball and ignored Harper's comment about Rich. She often dismissed altogether that she even had a boyfriend.

Harper had been dating Rich Caldwell for nearly two years, ever since she'd spotted him on their high school campus and decided he was hers. His 90210 chops and tan biceps stopped Harper at her locker—he was cute, she thought—and she spun the lock's wheel for good measure before saying hello.

Even before they spoke, Harper could tell Rich hadn't spent much time around other teenagers; he wasn't interested in the popular patch of grass or the meatheads tossing footballs in the cafeteria. And even though it was the crowd she and Grace ran around with, she liked that he was different. He was complex. As Blue used to say, like a great glass of wine.

Before high school, Rich had been homeschooled and had grown up without juvenile toxins. The other boys wanted to drive fast cars and drink beer at desert parties. Rich wanted to see the latest independent film and sail his parents' thirty-six foot boat, *Capricious.*

The jocks called him a *fag*, but Harper knew better, could tell by the way he kissed her that it wasn't true. Not only was he hopelessly handsome with his chiseled features and dark hair, he had a personality and sense of humor to match. Harper was smarter, more attractive on his arm.

Later that afternoon, after sharing a soft pretzel at the club's snack bar, Grace dug a small embroidered purse out of her golf bag as they walked to her car.

"Let's have a ciggie before we go," Grace said.

Swiftly, Grace grabbed Harper's hand and pulled her toward the thicket of oleanders encircling the country club grounds. Smoking in Grace's new sports car was strictly forbidden. Cilla had the nose of a hound.

Harper looked both ways as they stepped behind the bushes. It wasn't the first time they'd smoked, but Harper was still nervous, afraid someone would see. "Did you bring gum?" she asked, still glancing around. The tight space in between the shrubs and the fence was littered with half-smoked butts.

"Yes." Grace slid one cigarette from the crushed pack. "Hold it like this," she said, stylishly putting it to her lips. "And then blow it out"—she paused, puffing it alive—"like this." Smoke rings curled near Harper's face. She made it look so cool, Harper thought, like Rizzo in *Grease*. She felt like Sandy.

As she tried to mimic Grace's technique, Harper wondered if Brits were natural born smokers. Like Irish men were natural born drinkers.

During those summer months leading up to their freshmen year in college, the girls were thrown into debutante training, a series of classes that began soon after they were selected.

Quickly, it was clear Grace and Harper were the bad seeds in the crop of debs. It couldn't have been a surprise to the women in charge, who'd known both girls through their teenage years.

One morning, Harper and Grace had been abnormally raucous with one another. It had started the night before when they were making cupcakes and Grace smeared chocolate mix across Harper's face. That alone had resulted in an all-out chocolate cake war in the Alessis' gourmet kitchen. When they were done, mix was on the ceiling, all over the thick wood island and matted in both girls' hair and clothes. Fortunately, no one was home at the time.

In the end, Grace won the cake war, pinning Harper to the floor, her slippery, chocolate-covered knees restraining Harper's arms until she conceded defeat. Grace pushed buttons inside Harper, buttons she enjoyed having pushed.

The next day, The Bitch, standing at the front of the room talking about proper curtsies, was showing the eager debutantes how it was done when Harper loaded her spoon with a ball of butter.

"Knees bent. Head up," The Bitch commanded, a drill sergeant with a headset. "Knees bent. Head up." Jazzy elevator music played in the background.

Even before Harper pulled the spoon back, cocking it into position, she knew she might get caught, but it was worth the risk.

It was slow going as it sailed over the table. Harper saw The Bitch catch its movement above the tulip centerpiece.

There was nothing she could do at that point, even though she put the spoon down as quickly as possible. Harper missed Grace's head, but hit her shoulder with some velocity—the butter, soft from being on the table for hours, spread out like a well-salivated spitball on her silk sleeve. The look on Grace's face was priceless and well worth it, Harper thought, even though she'd been reprimanded in front of the whole room.

Later that night, while Grace and Harper were watching young Jay Leno do his monologue—a University of Arizona pendant hanging above Grace's dresser—Harper asked: "Do you think they'll kick us out for what happened today?"

"*Us* out?" Grace said, turning to her side, propping her head up. "You're the one who got caught."

"Seriously."

Grace smiled. "I read the bylaws and there's no way they can 'legally' kick you out for what happened," Grace—the aspiring lawyer—explained.

"Okay," Harper said, somewhat relieved.

"Don't worry. Like The Bitch said, it was just a warning."

"Nonna would kill me."

As freshmen at the University of Arizona, Grace and Harper lived in dorms nearby one another on campus. On a full-ride tennis scholarship, Grace was forced to shack up with a fellow teammate. Her name was Chauncey and she was from Cape Town, South Africa.

Even though Grace had her pick of universities around the country, she'd ended up in Tucson with Harper. She chose U of A because it was close to home, but not too close, and, so she said, because it was close to Harper.

A month into school, they both went through rush and pledged the same sorority. Harper moved into the house almost immediately and their life quickly became all about Gamma Kappa. Sorority mixers, meetings, dinners, movie nights, weekend fraternity parties, their innumerable sisters.

For both girls, that first college semester went quickly. Finals were a blur and so were the days, as they packed for winter break. With the chaos of moving back home for a month and getting settled again, there wasn't much time to prepare for their debutante ball.

The morning of the event, two days before Christmas, the streets were packed with enthusiastic shoppers and irritated procrastinators.

Together, Harper and Ana were getting gussied up with Nonna at Tint, a trendy Scottsdale salon. Around them, women were getting waxed, foiled and primped for the biggest social event of the season: the Valley Debutante Ball. All the dryers, strung together with silver tinsel and blinking lights, were on high. Sitting in between Nonna and Ana, Harper was wearing a white shirt with her sorority letters embroidered across her chest.

"I can't believe it's finally here," Nonna said, watching the technician file her nails.

"It came so fast," Harper said, excited.

"I'm sorry I've missed all the prep," Ana said. "I know you're going to be great tonight. Mrs. Weasle said you're one of the stars in the group."

"She did?"

"Yep. I ran into her at the mall yesterday."

"Did you and your father practice this morning?" Nonna asked.

"Yes. I think we're ready."

"He acts so nonchalant like he doesn't care," Ana said, inspecting her nails. "But he does. He's nervous."

Nonna pursed her lips before she spoke. "Well, Anastasia"—she was the only one who called Harper's mom by her real name—"you should tell him that this is a big deal for Harper. And to be more..." Nonna thought about this before she finished her sentence. "Enthusiastic."

Ana rolled her eyes. "Don't start, Mother. We're lucky we got him to agree to this at all."

As two of the celebrated debs, the girls had to arrive early that afternoon, so Grace picked up Harper on her way to the resort. From the house, Rich carried Harper's dress to the car while she lugged her bag of beauty tricks: duct tape, Vaseline, Band-Aids and a lint roller.

"Hi Grace," he said, carefully hanging Harper's gown in the backseat.

"Rich."

Harper took a double-take at Grace, who was staring straight ahead; something about her was off.

Rich kissed Harper through the open window. "See you at six."

"What's different about you?" Harper asked once they were alone in the car.

"I've got an inch of makeup on. The stylist has been at our house since noon." Grace looked dramatically at her watch.

"But you always wear makeup."

"Not this much."

"Let me see you."

"I'm trying to drive."

"Look at me."

Harper studied Grace's face. "It's your eyes."

"My eyebrows. Mummy wanted me to have them shaped for tonight."

"They look great."

They were stopping at a light, so Harper grabbed Grace by the chin and pulled her face closer. She stared into Grace's eyes for a while, not saying a word. A wave of indefinable feeling rolled through Harper, as Grace met her eyes with an intense gaze of her own.

"They're sexy. Sophisticated," she finally said. "Speaking of sexy and sophisticated, look what Rich gave me." Harper offered her arm.

Grace glared at the new bracelet. "Wow. Very nice"—her white-knuckled hands firm on the steering wheel—"I saw those on clearance at Neiman's."

Earlier that afternoon, when Harper and Ana arrived home from their pampering, Rich was waiting in the living room watching the History Channel with Blue. He'd brought a bouquet of calla lilies and a small box wrapped in pink paper. He and Harper had gotten into a fight the day before—one that Grace had played a hand in—but Harper thought they'd smoothed things over.

"What's all this?" she had asked Rich, leading him down the hall to her bedroom.

He kissed her before she opened the box.

Inside, a David Yurman cuff was tied with a velvet ribbon. It was one she'd pointed out in the store. Sapphires on each end.

"Rich. My God! You can't afford this." She immediately regretted her reaction; it was boorish, un-debutante. She tried to recover. "I love it!"

He reached for the curved bracelet. "It's to serve as a reminder of how much I love you."

"Thank you," Harper said, watching him gently slide it on her wrist. "It's amazing."

Harper tried to focus on Rich and his generous gift, but it was difficult, for she couldn't get the picture of Grace out of her mind.

The night before, Grace had tried on her debutante dress for Harper in her parents' walk-in closet. Barefoot, Grace stood on a small stool and twirled around several times in the octagonal room of full-length mirrors; a hundred Graces from different angles, each one more unreachable than the next.

"I love you," Rich said before kissing her.

"I love you, too," Harper said.

She meant it.

Sort of.

"You Are My Lady"

Freddie Jackson

The resort where the ball would be held was lavish, five star. Backed up against Camelback Mountain, it was on the flipside of the mountain where both Harper and Grace had grown up less than a mile from each other. With nine cascading pools throughout the property and one of the best golf courses in Arizona, the Phoenician attracted the elite. Stars from Hollywood stayed there, so did dignitaries and international businessmen.

The night of the Valley Debutante Ball, Harper, with a rehearsed smile and a freshly-waxed lip, walked out on the arm of her father to a crowd of people she'd known her entire life. They were all there. As the band played an aria from *Madame Butterfly*, Harper focused on her breathing and her poise—just as she'd been taught in debutante training—as she curtsied to Blue, whose white gloves matched his pale face.

Unlike the other dads, all wearing jet-black, Blue was in a pinstriped tuxedo. Even though he thought the whole debutante tradition was "antiquated and far too patriarchal," he seemed to enjoy the moment.

"Harper Evangeline Alessi."

Her name had never felt so large, so important, as it came through the speakers.

"Daughter of Mr. and Mrs. Blue Alessi."

From the stage, the sea of tuxedos, designer dresses and tables—draped in stark linen—twinkled with a thousand tiny flames reflecting off the wine goblets.

Staring at the light beam in her face, Harper smiled as big as she could. The Vaseline on her teeth really worked; it tasted like medicine, but it gave her a sparkling smile.

She'd been on a stage before as a cheerleader, many in fact, and was used to performing in front of crowds, but this was different. This was her big debut and had to go off without a hitch. For so long, she'd imagined this moment, almost obsessively, seeing it all play out in the spotlight.

And just like she'd visualized, she nailed it.

Her curtsy was perfectly executed. Not a wobble.

After her presentation, like a lady, just like she'd been trained, her arm through her dad's, Harper waited on the dark dance floor for the others to be presented.

Her hair in a tight, fussy bun, The Bitch stood at the podium in the corner of the packed ballroom, a brass lamp illuminating her notes. As the debs submissively bowed before their fathers and then to the crowd, she was the one reading snippets about each girl. Beyond announcing who their parents were, she also read what they did for a living, where each girl went to school and her plans after college.

Aside from her anxious curtsy, Harper's most vivid memory from that night was Grace, standing on the stage with her father, Benson, a tall, stately lawyer possibly headed to the mayor's office.

When they called her name, Grace Anne Dunlop, Harper's face flushed; like a magnet, Grace's beauty pulled all sorts of things out of Harper, things she didn't understand.

The whole room watched as Grace, practically floating, walked to her father at center stage. And it was there that she gave him her hand, covered in a long white glove to the soft bend at her elbow. She smiled as she went into her curtsy, she and her newly sculpted eyebrows.

Standing with her knees locked, Harper studied Grace liked she'd never studied her before, totally in awe of the way the chiffon bunched around her breasts, the way the satin clung to her torso, seamlessly tailored to her voluptuous figure.

Harper memorized every curve, every line, every stitch of her strapless gown.

Grace was elegant.

Confident.

The highlight.

After Grace joined the rest of the debs, she looked down the row of girls until she found Harper standing at the end. They winked at each other.

As the debut continued, Harper searched the darkness around her as the last girls were presented. Faintly, zigzagging through the crowd, she followed her roots. Her grandparents tried to get her attention and Harper waved even though she wasn't allowed. Shimmering in the light, Nonna was wearing more eye shadow than she'd dared before. Papa, his white hair gelled back, was wearing a slick Armani tuxedo and Harper's favorite airplane cufflinks, the ones that matched the plane he bought when he made Chief of Staff at the hospital.

"That's my girl," she could hear her Papa saying, his thumb up. Nonna held a tissue to the corner of her eye.

Scattered around the ballroom sat everyone who'd shaped Harper's childhood—Dominic, the club's former tennis pro now married to one of the rich ladies he used to teach; Minnie, her piano teacher who lived around the corner and always smelled like Bengay; and Mariana, who'd morphed from a nanny to a glorified housekeeper to an extended family member.

The last person Harper saw was Dean. As if they shared blood, he shook his head in disbelief when they caught eyes. Even from the stage, she could see tears welling as she read his lips.

"I love you," he said, tapping his heart.

Dean had been there for Harper through it all—especially during the tumultuous teenage years when her parents were gone all the time and she didn't have a rock to hold on to.

After all the girls were presented, they turned up the houselights so the crowd could applaud the newly-minted debutantes.

When the ovation trailed off, Harper and Blue got in position. He acted cool, but his hands were clammy.

This was it.

They'd practiced their routine in class and in the living room the day before, but they were still nervous. Just like they'd rehearsed, they waltzed around as a cello and an acoustic guitar serenaded them. Keeping pace. Counting time.

"My precious Popina," Blue said as they finished, choking up. "Look at you." He kissed her on the cheek before taking his seat.

After the father-daughter waltz, Harper waited, watching Rich in his tuxedo, along with the other escorts, move into his choreographed position.

As Rich and Harper danced, he told her that seeing her on stage was powerful, stirring his imagination—someday he hoped she'd walk down the aisle toward him in a similar white dress. It was a bold statement, one she wasn't quite ready to hear. She listened as he continued on about their future, musing about how attractive their kids would be. She smiled, but didn't add much, just concentrated on his lead and ignoring the blister on her toe.

Even though the debutantes and their cronies were underage, the wait staff served them alcohol all night. When you pay enough money, laws don't always apply. Sitting at their respective tables, Grace and Harper picked strategic chairs allowing only a slight drift in their gaze to make contact.

When the waiter topped off Harper's wine, she watched Grace and Dean as he talked wildly with his hands. Grace responded with building peals of laughter, something that always made Harper smile. Even though Grace was across the room, Harper could hear it like she was sitting beside her.

Jamie-the-bastard-Simons sat on the other side of Grace and flashed a cocky smile at Harper when he caught her staring.

She'd never forgiven him for the jungle gym.

With a fresh scotch, midway through dinner, Dean approached Harper's table.

"I can't believe how beautiful you look tonight," he said, crouching at her chair. "I had to come over and tell you." Then,

Dean stood. "And I wanted to finally meet this fella." Rich also stood. "Hey there old sport. I'm Dean, Harper's bodyguard." He smiled. "I don't know how I've missed you each time I've been in town, but I've heard nice things about you."

Rich blushed. "Thanks. I've heard a lot about you, too."

Squeezing Rich's shoulder in a chummy sort of way, Dean leaned in close. "Hurt her," he whispered. "And I'll kill you."

"Got it," Rich said before sitting back down.

As he walked away, Dean offered another big smile to the table.

"Cheers," he said, raising his glass.

As dinner progressed, it didn't take long for Harper to spill cabernet on her white dress. She'd always been a bit clumsy. Even with her refined social graces, she was a whirling dervish at her core.

Rich snickered as he tried, unsuccessfully, to wipe it with his napkin.

"You're no help," Harper huffed. "I'll be back."

Stopping at Grace's chair was all Harper had to do. When Grace saw the dribble, she stood before Harper even asked for help.

"We can dress you up," Grace began.

"But you can't take me anywhere," Harper finished.

In the restroom, at the marble sink, Grace knelt down and slid her hand under Harper's dress to where the stains were. "How did it go up on stage?" she asked.

"It's all a blur, really, but I think well."

"Some slaggy waiter was in my way," Grace complained as she dipped the linen towel into the soda, "so I could only see half of you get presented. The top half." She looked up, smiled. "You were beautiful."

"So were you," Harper said. "Yikes, your hand's cold!"

Grace grabbed her leg and Harper screamed.

As she rubbed soda into the porous fabric, Harper watched her every move: the delicate lace along her cleavage and the tulle bustling around Grace's legs. In her mind, she saw snapshots of Grace on stage, getting lost as the wave moved through her again.

Grace's arm suddenly sizzled, was now like hot metal against her thigh, a branding iron.

"What are you thinking about?" Grace asked, focused on the stains. It was just the two of them. "You seem. I don't know. Lost in something."

"Nothing," Harper said. "Just"—she thought for a moment—"nothing."

Grace finally fluffed Harper's dress. "I think I got it all."

Looking down, Harper pointed to a small red dot and Grace went back to work.

Harper wanted to stay in the bathroom forever, pour a whole bottle down the front of her gown and let Grace work on it all night.

The room exploded into movement after dinner. Rich, dancing with the girls, was the best dancer at the ball. He was smooth and flexible, scuffing the wood floors with his steps.

During a break, as Harper stopped to take off her shoes, Cilla came up from behind. "Our little Harper," she said, hugging her. "All grown up. You're just gorgeous."

"Thanks."

"Tell me"—Cilla put her arm around Harper as she whispered—"are you going to marry that Rich? He's so handsome."

Was she crazy? Harper thought. She was only nineteen. What was with everyone?

"I don't know. We'll see."

"He's a great catch. You ought to scoop him up while you can. Good ones are hard to find." Benson pulled her away as a slow song started.

Harper walked slowly and watched them join the dance floor until she spotted Rich, who, like a suitor, was across the room with his hand out. Grace stood next to him. As if they'd rehearsed it, she approached Rich and he twirled then lifted her off the ground.

While Rich and Harper swayed to the music, the Glenn

Miller classic *Moonlight Serenade*, he told her he wanted to make amends with Grace. "Do you think she'd dance with me?"

Even though she wasn't sure, Harper said, "Of course."

"I know I'm not her favorite person."

"That's ridiculous," Harper said. "Believe it or not, there was a time when I didn't think she liked me either." Harper flashed on their first match, the way the tennis ball whopped against the fence each time Grace aced a winner.

Harper danced with Dean when Rich made his conciliatory move.

"So that's your boyfriend," Dean said.

While they waltzed, Harper kept a curious eye on Grace and Rich. "What do you think?" she asked Dean.

"He seems nice."

Unexpectedly, Dean dipped Harper backward. Still in the dip, he said, "Does he treat you well?"

"He does. He gave me this earlier today."

Dean looked at the bracelet. "Very nice." His approval was fleeting. "If he's such a great boyfriend, why did he want to dance with Grace?"

"Oh that's nothing. He's got this idea she doesn't like him." Dean let his gaze go back to Grace and Rich across the dance floor. "He's trying to make amends."

"Grace doesn't like him?"

"I don't know"—Harper was fixated on them again, too—"Not really. I guess."

"Why?"

"I'm not sure. She's never liked anyone I've gone out with. She doesn't think anyone's good enough."

"Well, I agree with that," Dean said with a smile.

A saxophonist played a solo and time passed as they both enjoyed it. "How's your date going?" Harper asked.

Together, they both looked at the woman talking with Cilla at their table. "Fine," Dean said. "She's in the Junior League with Cil." He smiled. "Not really my type."

Later that night, as Harper ate dessert with Rich at their table, she continued watching Grace, who danced with various admirers throughout the evening. When Jamie wasn't around, they lined up.

As *You Are My Lady* began, Jamie, who'd been drinking gin and smoking cigars with his dad at the bar, cut in and took back what was his.

In the small of Grace's back, with his hand, Jamie kept their bodies close together as they danced, his face flush with hers.

By this time, some of Grace's hair, golden and soft, had escaped her pearled clip. Harper closed her eyes, imagining Grace's perfume, how careful she was with the wine stains, the way Grace's hand had singed the inside of her thigh.

For a moment, sitting in her debutante dress amidst the Scottsdale elite—the governor, CEOs, and her parents—Harper wished she were him.

"If Only For One Night"

Luther Vandross

After the ball, the limo driver dumped Grace, Harper and Dean, along with their dates, at Ernie's Bar.

Still in their gowns and tuxedos, they overran the neighborhood dive, which was filled with regulars. It was somewhere Grace and Harper had been before, a safe refuge where they could escape the usual clubs and social outlets.

At the bar ordering the first round, Harper and Grace slid their fake IDs to the bartender with attitude. "Two pitchers," Grace said before throwing down her money, tipping well.

"And a pack of Camel Lights," Harper added, trying to stand as tall as Grace, with as much chutzpah. The balding, perspiring bartender wasn't sure what to make of the faux wedding dresses.

Under a bright humming Coors sign, the jukebox waited, giving off an impatient energy as the girls delivered the drinks to where the boys waited, grinning. Harper wasted no time making her way to the music. In her clutch bag, next to her lipstick case, was a small pocket she'd filled with quarters. It wasn't the first time the jukebox had called out to her, nor the first time she'd suggested Ernie's so she could play DJ all night—they had the best jukebox in town. The glass was smudged, finger and nose prints, and the "u" in Wurlitzer was missing, but the speakers worked fine.

Holding her quarters, Harper read the titles carefully, flipping through album after album. Its metal siding was cold against her shoulder as she rested against it. Before she played her first song, she glanced back at her group, gathered around two high bar tables on the other side of the room. It was Grace she was looking for and Grace she caught eyes with as Grace pulled darts from the board and handed them to Jamie.

B12, Harper told herself before punching in her request—Debbie Gibson's "Lost In Your Eyes."

After it started, Harper looked again. This time, Grace was talking to Dean and his date, a woman drinking white zinfandel who looked very uncomfortable at Ernie's. As Debbie Gibson hit the bridge, Grace looked over at Harper again. A wink.

Cutting the line in between them, Rich walked up and blocked her view. "Things are better with Grace," Rich said, rattling the ice in his glass.

"So it seems."

"You were right," he added, crunching a cube. "She doesn't hate me."

"I told you," Harper said, distracted. She continued scanning the music. "Did she actually say that?"

Instead of answering the question, Rich said apologetically, "I'm sorry if I suffocate you. I don't mean to overpamper you." He looked at Harper's new bracelet, as if embarrassed.

"What...are you talking about?" Harper stopped, got serious. "Grace said that you're nomadic and that I shouldn't dote on you so much. She said I should play harder to get."

"Did she?" Across the room, Grace was throwing darts again. "Did you find that helpful?"

Jamie called Rich's name from the pool table; they were up for doubles.

"Yes," he said.

"I bet you did," Harper said under her breath as he walked away.

Getting back to business, Harper picked up where she left off and continued searching the jukebox albums.

Lenny Kravitz.

Bruce Springsteen.

Carole King.

Luther Vandross.

Luther, Harper thought, scanning his album. That one song…

And there it was—number four.

"If Only for One Night."

She put in the right combination of letter and number and waited for the familiar song, one she'd first heard after rifling through Grace's CDs that summer.

Harper closed her eyes when it started. As Luther sang, something stirred deep within her. The wave was back, rolling through her slowly this time with his soulful beat.

The song was in its second verse when Grace approached from behind. Her eyes still closed, Harper sensed Grace's energy before she spoke.

"Nice choice," Grace whispered, getting even closer, her chin against Harper's shoulder. "Didn't know you knew that one."

"There's a lot about me you don't know," Harper said.

"Really?"

The bass drum kicked in. And so did the alcohol.

Grace—still behind Harper, the two of them swaying together—sang softly in Harper's ear about not telling a soul and no one knowing.

Stepping to the side, Harper opened her eyes quickly to see Grace and then closed them again as she slowly reached for her hand. Rich and Jamie were busy with the pool game.

Grace sang some more, twirling Harper like Rich had on the dance floor, and then pulled their bodies together. Harper closed her eyes again as Grace continued singing even more softly about eyes saying what she didn't hear. She delivered several more lines, steamy blasts that scorched Harper's skin.

For Harper, Luther ended too soon. Like their moment in the bathroom with the wine stains, she wanted it to last forever.

On Luther's final note, they stopped moving and stood for a moment together, both still locked in.

When Harper opened her eyes, the first thing she saw was

Dean. He was standing at the bar, another scotch in his hand, watching them at the jukebox.

It was late when Rich finally dropped them off. Grace, sitting on a stone bench at the Alessis' front door, waited while he and Harper said good night.

"Took you long enough," Grace said, holding her shoes.

"Sorry." Harper stepped into the light and searched for her keys.

"What were you doing out there?"

"Saying good night."

"Did you kiss him?" Grace asked.

Harper looked at Grace. It was a crazy question.

"Is he a good kisser?"

"Yes, Grace," Harper said, sliding the house key into the hole. "He's a good kisser."

"Are you?"

Harper paused. "Am I what?"

"A good kisser."

Flummoxed, Harper said, "I don't know," and pushed open the glass door.

Grace smiled and followed her inside. "Oh I bet you are."

In her room, Harper threw off her dress and dove onto her four-post canopy bed. She was in her gartered pantyhose and bra, her hair still fixed into place.

"I'm so tired," she whined.

"I know." Grace unzipped her gown and tossed it onto the chair. "I can't believe it's over," she said, flopping next to Harper in her slip.

Lying on their sides facing one another, they both exhaled a breath of exhaustion. A spray of fleur-de-lis—their sorority flower—was in a vase by the bed.

Grace put her leg over Harper's body. "What was your favorite part of the night?"

Harper thought for a moment, staring at the ceiling fan. "Getting to Ernie's."

Grace laughed. "Me, too. Although seeing you get presented was pretty awesome."

"You couldn't even see me," Harper said, tucking her hands under her head. "That waiter was in the way."

"I could see enough."

Harper's eyes were heavy as Grace asked, "Was Rich mad he couldn't spend the night?"

"Kind of," Harper sighed. "Not mad. Disappointed. Why did you tell him I don't like to be pampered?"

"You don't."

"Yes I do."

Grace played with Harper's hair for a spell before either of them spoke again.

"Do you think you'll marry Rich?"

Harper paused. "You sound like your mother. She asked me the same thing tonight. I don't know. Maybe. We've got a lot of living to do before then. You and me. Like that B & B we want to open in Napa and that trip to the moon."

"Right, the moon," Grace said.

"Are you going to marry Jamie?"

"Jamie isn't even my boyfriend."

"Yes he is," Harper said. "Why won't you admit it?"

"Because he's not my boyfriend. He was just my escort tonight. That's all." Grace sat up, pulled the clip from her hair and launched it across the room. Harper watched her hair come down all the way. She could smell the Aveda. "But who needs guys anyway. We should both be single. We're in the prime of our lives."

A run in Harper's pantyhose caught her eye and she lifted her leg to inspect it.

Grace—sliding her finger down Harper's thigh—stopped at the small snag. "Uh-oh," she said.

"I'm so white trash."

Grace touched the hole with her finger, and then tore it even bigger.

Hysterically, they laughed as Grace pulled harder. Harper wrestled her off the bed, and they knocked over the small side table on their way down, ripping the alarm clock out of the wall.

They struggled until Harper restrained Grace against the chair.

"Truce," Grace finally said, though not giving up easy.

Back in bed, Harper, missing an entire leg of hose, rolled over and turned out the lamp. In the stillness of the room, Grace began scratching Harper's back in slow circles.

"I miss you when you're asleep," Grace whispered.

Harper reached back and gently touched the sway of Grace's hip. "I miss you, too," she said, letting her hand rest there in the dark.

Together, on top of Harper's duvet, they drifted off to sleep against one another, skin-to-skin, Grace's arm looped around Harper's waist.

"Hello Again"
Neil Diamond

Harper and Rich lasted only another six months. It was Rich who'd taken Harper's virginity, and it was she who'd broken his heart for reasons she still couldn't pinpoint.

She genuinely loved Rich. But in all the wrong ways. She simply wanted to be friends. For much of that summer, at least until she went back to the university, late at night, Harper would wake up to Rich knocking on her French door. She'd let him in, guilty over his pain, and they'd talk and talk about how she just didn't love him the way he loved her. He'd cry, she'd cry, and then he'd leave. It was a vicious cycle.

Harper and Grace both dated a string of fraternity guys during their sophomore and junior years. Nameless, faceless men.

Harper had been waiting—patiently, she thought—for the big bang, the fireworks everyone talked about.

Harper had orgasms, and so, she confessed, did Grace, but not at the hands of the men of whom they'd pleased. The girls had had to ring that bell on their own.

By their senior year, Harper and Grace were living in Europe for the summer, several countries apart. Grace had signed up for a Spanish immersion program in Barcelona, and Harper was living in Dusseldorf, learning German photography techniques from one of her parents' colleagues at an art college.

Harper knew about the lax drug laws in Holland. She also knew that Dusseldorf was close to the Dutch border, but she was still blown away when she walked into her first coffee shop and saw the giant Tupperware containers full of the greenest, almost iridescent, marijuana she'd ever seen. In high school she'd tried it a couple times at parties, but this was a whole new deal. It was legal. It was even taxed. Just like coffee shops in America, the bar—where patrons sat and ordered eggs and bacon—was instead packed with people of all walks of life getting stoned.

Shortly after her summer program started, Harper and the other students would take the short train ride to Venlo, Holland to study each afternoon in the coffee shops. Drug tourism, it was called, and it was very popular with surrounding countries.

Harper soon discovered that her favorite variety was Northern Lights, and a few puffs gave her the shiniest, most colorful daydreams of her life. Sitting at her table, she'd often forget about exposure, filters and darkroom techniques, and drift into another world. A world where Grace was always waiting.

In her psychedelic dreams, she was often flying, and flying across city after European city until she reached Spain. She'd sail over Luxembourg, Lyon and Montpellier before she reached Barcelona. She imagined, through the vivid details Grace was giving her on the phone, the four-bedroom Mediterranean apartment where she was living in an old village called Barceloneta. If it was after dark, she'd see Grace sleeping, curled up next to the stucco wall her bed was pushed up against. Letters Harper had written were stacked on her night table, so were books by John Grisham and a bottle of Kiehl's grapefruit lotion, her favorite.

That's why she loved Northern Lights; it was a channel—a secret wormhole—to Grace.

The first letter Harper got from Grace said she missed her terribly, more than she thought she would. *My bed's lonely without you*, Grace wrote. Harper read it three times before fumbling it back into the envelope as her roommate, Barb Hanson, approached. Barb, a bleached blond sorority sister with whom Harper was not close, had coincidentally signed up for the same program that summer. Barb was best friends with Harper's still archenemy Sloan Weasle, although they'd learned to tolerate each other socially.

Grace's message stayed with Harper all week—*my bed is lonely without you*—haunting her, keeping her up at night. It burned in places Harper wasn't ready to acknowledge.

Every day, the words Harper scribbled in ballpoint pen were much different than the ones she whispered through the phone lines at night. And the calls increased with every joint Harper smoked. Harper had it down to a science: when the other students were amply faded, she'd slip out the door and walk twenty steps to the corner *telefoon*.

In her wood clogs, Harper talked to Grace for hours. Leaning against the weathered wall of a hardware store, she bored her finger into a corroded hole where the bolts met the plaster. Bits of white powder crumbled to the sidewalk until Harper's finger fit all the way inside. They discussed what they'd do when they got home—drive-in movies, long dinners, endless games of pool. They'd find every jukebox in town.

At that payphone, Grace told Harper about Spanish wine, her days in Madrid and the family with which she was living. Harper mused about the strudel, the German architecture and the remaining strip of the Berlin wall.

One weekend in Paris, as dusk settled in over the city, Harper made one of her calls. She'd been traveling with Barb and a few others when she passed a circle of local Parisians playing music near the Arc de Triomphe. She stopped, pulled out her 35mm camera and began swapping lenses. As Harper adjusted her shutter speed, she saw the other students disappear into a restaurant.

Barb stopped and waited at the door. "I'll meet you inside," Harper said, waving her off.

After Harper captured shots of each performer—including a man lighting his tongue on fire—she walked to the corner phone booth before joining the others for dinner. She dialed a flurry of numbers and then someone answered in Spanish.

"*Puedo hablar yo con Grace?*" Harper asked.

With a husky voice, the man of the house yelled Grace's name.

"*Gracias* Marco," Grace said, taking the receiver. "I've been waiting all day. Where have you been?"

"The Louvre. It's like five hundred million miles long," Harper said, still watching the musicians. "I tried to get away earlier. But—"

"Nobody understands why we need to talk three times a day?" Grace asked.

"Exactly."

"Tell me about it. Marco and his wife think you're my sister."

A woman, who sounded just like Edith Piaf, began singing with the band. Her dress, adorned with intricate silk weaving, looked like vintage Hermés, Harper thought.

"I miss you extra today," Grace said. They sat with this for a moment. "I sent two letters this morning. And there may be others waiting. I've lost track."

"I mailed one yesterday," Harper said. "And I've been carrying a postcard around all afternoon. I've yet to find a mailbox."

"Where are you? It's loud."

"I'm on the Champs-Élysées," Harper said, shutting the booth's door. "I can't believe the summer's nearly over. Just three weeks and I'll see you in Amsterdam."

"It's not soon enough," Grace said. "Call later to say good night."

At the end of the long weekend, when Harper returned to her hotel in Dusseldorf—a place called the Tulip Inn near the university—several of Grace's letters were waiting.

Still wearing her overstuffed backpack, Harper grabbed the pile of mail and tore the first letter open. She read it as she walked to the lobby cafe, where she also read the others before returning to her room.

Later that night, after Barb was asleep, with a flashlight, Harper reread them in bed:

I'm going insane. The way I miss you is mad!

You're the first thing I think about in the morning and the last thing at night. Why are you all I think about, my silly Harp?

I can't wait to sleep next to you again. I've never wanted anything more.

Harper read the last lines several times as she lit a cigarette, the words delighting her. *I can't wait to sleep next to you again. I've never wanted anything more.*

Harper began writing Grace back, her second letter of the day.

My darling, she wrote.

From the darkness, Harper heard rustling. She quickly smothered the light.

"What are you doing?" Barb grumbled.

"Just journaling," Harper said, still in the dark.

"It's like four in the morning."

"Sorry," Harper said, clicking off the flashlight.

On her last night in Germany, after the school program had come to a close, Harper organized the mail hidden under her bed when she was alone. There were over a hundred letters stacked in three piles. Nearly all from Grace. Before she bound them in string, she reread some of her words:

This will be the last time we'll ever be apart, I've decided. I can't handle not having you each day. You're a drug. And I'm an addict.

With fewer brain cells, longer hair and a new belly button ring, Harper traveled to Amsterdam to meet Grace the next day.

Harper's well-traveled parents had set them up at their favorite hotel in the city, a five-star jewel on the Amstel River. Harper got an early start, called ahead and arranged for a morning pedicure and massage, hoping the bodywork would calm her nerves.

In the afternoon, Harper flitted around town while Grace, who was impressively fluent in Spanish by then, rode the train from Barcelona. After a long weekend in Amsterdam, they would travel to Italy for several days before heading home. Harper's aunt and uncle were expecting them in Bologna.

Harper rented a scooter, and in a half-shell Snoopy helmet, she stopped at one market after another before ending up at the Van Gogh museum. She'd already visited earlier that summer, but his painting *A Pair of Shoes* was calling her back. When Harper got to the self-inspired 1886 canvas, she must've stood there for a half hour, consumed, again, by his strokes, the rabid bend in the laces, the darkness—darkness which resonated somewhere inside her. There was such acute fear and sorrow in his work, she thought.

After lunch, on the steps of Central Station, Harper smoked a cigarette and thought again about Grace's letters. What would it be like between them?

I've never wanted anything more.

And what did this all mean, the connection between her and Grace? This weird dance. This strange, unspoken conversation they'd had all summer.

Aside from her nerves, for the most part Harper felt normal, just like she always had. She was aware, however, of the intensity of her feelings for it had kept her awake many nights writing poems and rereading Grace's letters. She'd never felt such a strong connection with another person before.

It was just their friendship, Harper decided, that had reached an intimacy of epic proportion. They were the best of best friends.

Soul mates.

Harper found a café on the water near their hotel, an old

skiff painted in lollipop colors that rocked when she stepped in. From her square table, she could see all the way down the canal. Amidst the mildew and coffee, Harper tapped her pen, searching for words to finish her European memoir, a soft leather journal Grace had given her. A Celtic symbol representing the bonds of friendship was burned into the front. The pages were nearly full. That summer, Grace was carrying the same one.

Staring at the sheet, Harper had no idea where it ended or where it began. Even in a different country, Grace was the largest, most vital artery of her trip, the life force, what she remembered most. How could that be? As she thumbed through it, Grace's name was on every page.

Harper's chest was tight as she watched the clock ticking toward Grace's arrival. Thinking about the things Grace had said, the things she'd written, Harper remembered Grace's frustrated delight, her inability to articulate the depth of her void. *I can't sleep some nights*, Grace wrote, *wondering if I'll get a letter the next day.*

It had been the same for Harper.

She couldn't quite place it then, but somewhere silent and deep, anger simmered beneath the surface. And it was fueling her anxiety. Van Gogh's painting had set it off.

In a dark corner of her soul, Harper knew she was betraying herself, slowly breaking an unconscious pact she'd made years earlier—right around the time she stopped beating boys in PE and, instead, began kissing them in the baseball dugouts after school.

"I Kissed A Girl"

Jill Sobule

It was early evening when Harper strolled back through the lobby. On her way to the elevator, she told the front desk to give Grace a key when she arrived.

In the center courtyard, chefs in tall hats snipped herbs and guests gathered for happy hour. Harper checked her watch. Grace was two hours away and would arrive just in time for dinner.

While she waited, Harper unpacked some of her things. Their three-bedroom suite was way more space than they needed. With a full view of the city, a baby grand piano, white linens and fresh orchids in a sparkling Waterford vase, it was much different than the hostels Harper had stayed in with classmates over the summer.

In the upstairs loft, the only bedroom with a king-size bed, Harper set out her clothing options for the night, two very different looks. A knit set she'd picked up in Cologne and a plaid miniskirt she'd found at Harrod's. The German schoolgirl or the English seductress? Who would she be?

When she pulled out the accompanying shoes, she tried to picture Grace's face. She couldn't; it was vague, a chopped mosaic of memory. Funny how time and physical distance did that.

Harper was putting her toiletries in the bathroom when she

heard the knock. She looked at her watch again; it was too early to be Grace.

With quiet steps, Harper walked to the glass door covered by a thin wine-colored panel. Through the cloth, she could see an outline on the other side.

She peeked. Her knees nearly buckled when she saw Grace, her tan the color of a hot cup of cocoa.

At that moment, something fractured inside Harper. She could feel it breaking apart.

Another knock, louder, almost forceful, startled Harper. She stepped back and looked at the silk robe she was wearing; there wasn't time to get dressed.

After a measured breath, she finally pulled back the curtain, leaving the door between them.

Despite her own fear, the rich anticipation in Grace's eyes—wistful, but intent—made Harper feel safe.

Slowly, she lifted her hand to the glass. Grace mirrored with hers. Through the pane, Harper felt the warmth of her palm.

Grace held the room key in the other hand, but waited for Harper to let her inside. With one more teasing smile, Harper unlocked the door.

"I thought you'd never let me in," Grace said, reaching for her.

When their bodies came together, Grace's face against hers, everything came rushing back like no time passed. She'd missed Grace even more than she'd realized.

"I can't believe it's you," Grace said. "Is it really you?" She pulled away to get a good look.

"It's me!" Harper said. "You're early. Really early."

"I know. I took an express train through Paris. I couldn't stand the wait."

Harper grabbed Grace's heavy bag and set it on the luggage rack. "I can't believe how long twelve weeks was," Harper said.

"Twelve weeks was forever." From behind, Grace put her arms around Harper's waist. "I never want to be away from you again."

The concierge had made reservations at a small Spanish tapas bar near the Magere Brug, a narrow bridge that cut across the Amstel. "It will be perfectly romantic for you and your husband," the woman had said. Harper didn't bother correcting her.

Like Van Gogh's turbulent strokes, the sky swirled and twisted with wind. A swift gust almost knocked the girls over as they parked Harper's rented Vespa in front of the restaurant. The waiter mentioned a storm as they sat at their window table, the bridge illuminated in the distance.

Grace showed off her Spanish. From across the table, Harper watched her order and chat up the waiter—something about Almeria, his hometown. That much Harper understood. There was still so much she didn't.

After he walked away, Grace looked at Harper and continued in Spanish. "*Yo me moría lentamente sin usted, mi amor*," she said.

"What are you saying?"

Grace poured Tempranillo from the decanter. "I said I missed you"—Grace smiled—"a lot."

The night air had shifted during dinner. They could smell it when they walked out of the restaurant.

At the scooter, Grace straddled the seat first and inched back making room for Harper, who had chosen to be the English seductress. She bent over and dug the Vespa key from her knee-high boot.

"Hurry up," Grace said, pulling Harper in close.

After Harper fired up the engine, she leaned back and kissed Grace on the cheek. It surprised them both.

Once they started to move along the cobblestone, Harper could feel Grace's head turn and rest on her shoulder; Grace's hands were already clasped around Harper tightly. She felt Grace's breath, her body swell then deflate, her full breasts pressed flat against her back. Grace squeezed tighter, then gently kissed Harper's shoulder.

Like the night air, fundamental boundaries were shifting.

Through the tiny side mirror, Harper could see Grace's eyes close. She could also see a big storm moving in from the west, the clouds dark and ominous. Wet. Getting closer.

Harper slowed at a stop sign, and stole another peek at Grace in the reflection.

She was startled when she saw the white of Grace's eyes. Harper looked away quickly.

But then, like the kiss, instinctively, Harper's gaze returned. Grace hadn't looked away and let a confident, uninhibited smile come to the surface, one that sent the electricity in the air through her body.

No one was around when they stopped in front of the hotel. Harper's skirt, like Saran Wrap, charged and clingy, stuck to her legs when she put down the kickstand.

In the distance, the squall hanging in the atmosphere was a bag of water. Ready to break. Whether the heavy dampness was the impending storm or the magnitude of what was building between them, she'd never know. Was it all the years of unspoken dialogue through the jukebox, their knowing eyes in the mirror, how quickly they looked away? Or didn't.

Harper turned off the engine. When they locked eyes one more time in the reflection, a raindrop fell. The bag was breaking.

It was quiet in the lobby, only a plump man at the front desk. He watched as the girls passed. "*Goedenavond*," he said with a hand wave.

"*Dank u*," Harper said, wishing him a good evening back.

"Glad you got in before storm," he continued, his English stilted. "It's big one."

Harper watched her feet, her deliberate steps to the elevator.

Grace, a few strides ahead, pressed the button calling the elevator. In silence, they stood for a moment, both looking around as it made its way to the lobby. Harper could hear the old cables working behind the etched glass doors.

"Dinner was good," Harper said, swinging her purse, still looking down.

Grace turned to Harper, paused and said, "It was," with a hint of a smile. "Really good."

They pulled open and shut the elevator's gate together.

As it began its ascent, Grace leaned against the wall and crossed her arms. She was facing Harper, who was watching the numbers slowly increase, avoiding eye contact.

"It's crazy," Grace said. "How much I missed you."

Back in their room, Harper sat on the opposite end of the couch from Grace while they watched TV, her feet in Grace's lap. Rain beat the courtyard window and a mist blew through the screen, filling their suite with storm, stirring Grace's hair before lifting the magazine cover on the table.

Midway through a subtitled episode of *Friends*, Harper went upstairs to her shopping bags from the day and dug out a box of incense. She lit a stick of Nag Champa on the loft's ledge and headed back to the couch.

Harper was halfway down the spiral staircase when the first bolt hit. *Crack boom.* Lightning struck nearby—so close there was no time to prepare for the thunderous explosion—knocking out electricity.

"My God," Grace said from somewhere in the darkness.

Grace and Harper met in the suite's foyer where the tall windows towered over the river. In the dark, they watched the storm rip through Amsterdam, the town covered in an electric blanket.

Shoulder to shoulder, with only lightning illuminating the night, they looked at each other.

Grace lit a sconce in the bathroom so a soft light flickered against the porcelain sink while they got ready for bed. In the distant sparks of energy, Harper could see Grace step into her pajamas, an old Gamma shirt, while she brushed her teeth.

Her panties, pink paisleys, peeked from the back of Grace's shirt as she pulled back the bedding, which was already partially turned-down, a truffle on each pillow.

Harper took a moment, told herself to relax. What the hell was wrong with her?

After they slid into bed, incense layered the ceiling with smoke as Grace began tickling Harper's back, predictable and perpetual, her soothing way of putting them both to sleep.

Only it was different this time. And they both knew it.

As she carefully scratched Harper's back, their breaths deepened and the room heated as years of kindling went up in flames. It blistered Harper's skin and forced her, abruptly, to the sitting position.

"Do you want a glass of water?" Harper asked.

Grace rolled away.

"No. Thanks."

Harper shot from bed and headed downstairs. At the sink, she drank a full glass of water, wiped the sweat from her forehead and sucked on an ice cube before returning to bed.

In the light, Harper could see Grace's outline under the sheets as she approached, her curvaceous hips, her hair feathered on the sheets. Harper flashed on fantasies she'd had, her hand under the covers, Grace coming to her in the night, rocking Harper awake. In her dreams, Grace whispering, "I can't sleep." Then Grace holding out her hand and leading Harper from the sorority sleeping porch to her room. Grace locking the door, sliding her nightgown off, it falling to the ground.

This wasn't a fantasy.

Instead, a pivotal moment of truth.

Back in bed, Grace started scratching again, softer, slower. Harper tried helplessly to concentrate on other things—the new semester, the highlights of summer, the following week's sorority rush, anything but what was going on.

Harper imagined herself leaving the room. Barefooted, she ran out of the lobby and down the uneven cobbled streets. When she got to a payphone, there wasn't a receiver, just a dangling chord with jagged metal spewing from its mouth.

Crack boom.

Harper didn't see it coming. Grace slid her hand under the back of Harper's silk nightgown. With nothing between them, Grace's fingertips sent a frosty chill up and down Harper's spine; Grace hadn't gone under before, only over the pajamas. Harper didn't move, wholly focused on the burning incense, hoping to survive.

When the walls around them ignited, Harper refocused on the glowing speck across the room as Grace scratched careful circles. She lay still, pretending to sleep—it had worked in the past, when Grace's touch made her nervous. Harper tried to calm her body and fool Grace again; she closed her eyes and feigned sleeping noises.

But it didn't work. When Harper felt Grace's hot breath on her neck, she realized the only fool was her—climbing up the high dive stairs—unsure if she really could jump.

Dampness again beaded Harper's hairline, and she shivered. In her mind, or maybe out loud, she said her name.

Grace.

In their quiet space, Grace's brave fingers swooped near Harper's breast. An accident? Harper breathed deeply, bracing herself, as Grace moved closer with each pass. Harper couldn't run any longer.

Through the years—as they'd taken each step up the ladder—not a single word had been spoken, only the songs, only the words, the looks, arrows through the smoky bars.

Grace was ready.

She grazed Harper's breast.

Suddenly, Harper was standing at the top, her toes hanging over the edge of the high dive.

Crack boom. Lightning filled the room with a dangerous current as Grace came back for more, moving in a small circle around Harper's nipple. Grace's fingertips filled her body with a violent fever, causing sweat to seep from her skin.

Completely exposed, Harper turned her head—*crack boom*—and saw Grace's face.

The weakness in her eyes made Harper want her even more.

On the precipice, Harper bent her knees.

And then jumped.

Without committing to a kiss, their lips brushed in the darkness.

The moment was suspended as they each cautiously waited for body cues to bring them together again. Grace's lips, like the truffles, melted in Harper's mouth when they finally kissed. And when their tongues met, they fell into each other completely. It was everything Harper never knew she wanted, a softness, a sweetness she'd never known before.

As they pushed, their breathing escalated—an unknown animal was waking from hibernation, renewed and alive. Hungry.

Crack boom.

Thunder shuddered the old building, and Harper pulled away to see her. All she saw were shadows, but it was enough. It was real. It was happening. It was Grace.

Crack boom. Their eyes locked in the white light.

Harper hardly got the words out. "What are we doing?" In her veiled subconscious, she'd rehearsed them.

With an unfamiliar lilt, Grace whispered, "Don't think about it." She drew their bodies even closer together.

They giggled as Harper, slow and bashful, slid her hand under Grace's shirt. In her cupped palm, Grace's breasts were warm, erect, succulent.

Her whole life, she'd been starving for Grace. Her whole life, Harper had been underfed, emaciated without even realizing. Ravenous now, Harper wanted to put Grace's breasts in her mouth one by one, like the melons she ate in Mykonos, Grace's juice spilling down her face, her neck.

Crack boom.

"Let's Get It On"
Marvin Gaye

The piano woke Harper the next morning.

When she first opened her eyes, she wasn't sure that what she remembered from the night before was real.

Had it been another fantasy, an alcohol-induced illusion? They hadn't had sex—even though Harper didn't really know what that meant between two women—but it seemed they'd gotten dangerously close.

Not until Harper sat up and saw her nightie hanging from the lampshade did she realize the real weight of what had happened. She covered her mouth.

"My God," she whispered. "What have I done?"

For several minutes, she stared at the ceiling replaying their night.

With each note from *Lakme*, everything moved through her body again: the lightning, the way their lips came together. The grinding.

Like the storm, like the memory, the piano was thunderous, moving through the suite with counterpoint. The two of them had seen the tragic opera the year before with Grace's parents in New York, not realizing that less than a year later, lying alone in a foreign country thousands of miles from home, everything between them would take a sharp turn.

Before getting up, Harper watched the dancing drape still flirting with the wind, wondering what it would be like when she went downstairs.

In only panties, Harper wrapped the sheet around her body and walked to the stairs. From the top, she could see Grace at the piano; she was in Harper's robe, half of which had fallen off her shoulder.

As the song crescendoed, Harper made her way down the stairs and stood behind Grace as she hit the final keys.

"Bravo," Harper said, clapping before touching Grace's bare shoulder.

Grace grabbed Harper's fingers and brought them to her lips.

"Good morning," Grace said, turning around.

When she did, Harper felt, deep down inside, another bolt of lightning strike. It didn't rattle the building or knock out the power, but it filled the room again with desire as Grace ran her pinky down Harper's cleavage.

"How did you sleep?" Harper asked.

Grace brought Harper's hands to her face again and took in a full breath. "Did we sleep?"

For the next two days, the girls gallivanted around Amsterdam, taking in art, stopping at coffee shops and enjoying walks along the canals. Time passed like a snapshot.

At the end of the week, they hopped a flight to Rome, off to see Harper's aunt and uncle.

After going through customs, they met their driver on the curb. Giovanni, his nametag said. He wore a small hat and carried a sign that said "Alessi Party." It was fitting, Harper thought, the sign suggesting they were headed to a party. Every time she'd visited Uncle Alvaro and Aunt Amelia at the vineyard, it was just that: a party. Her memories—many from childhood, but some from adulthood—included endless pitchers of wine and balmy nights of laughter.

As they drove through the Tuscan hillside, the rise and fall of the sun-drenched mountains were another page from Harper's memory book. The serene countryside scattered with spears of ancient cypress and gently rolling hills of quiet farmhouses. The solitary monasteries and picturesque villages set as if time stood still.

After passing through Cortona and Carraia, the car pulled up to the familiar Alessi gates—an iron "A" at its center—leading into the vineyard. The property was just outside Bologna, a town in northern Italy, about an hour inland from the east.

Uncle Alvaro was first to blow through the worn stable door. The bottom swung open and hit the side of the farmhouse with a thud as he yelled Harper's name. He wrapped his chunky arms around her and picked her up off the ground. Aunt Amelia, who was right behind him, did the same.

With her hands to the sky, she said "*Ringrazio Dio*!"

They both lifted Grace, too, even before Harper had the chance to introduce them.

"Come kitchen," Alvaro said, leading the girls inside. Amelia clapped with joy.

As they stepped into the house, the kitchen timer went off for the ciabatta browning in the stove. Their home was full of childhood scents. A wave of bread, freshly-picked olives, the homemade lavender candle lit on the counter.

"Auntie!" Harper rubbed her belly for Amelia, who didn't speak English. "*Decadente*."

Spread on the linen-covered table were cheeses, thinly sliced prosciutto and olives, along with a bottle of their signature vintage, Alessi Glorioso, and one of their reserve, Angel Parti, or Angel Share. On both bottles, a black and white sketched image of their dog—Muffa, short for Muffa Nobile, which meant noble rot—was on the front.

"These are the best olives I've ever tasted," Grace said, reaching for another handful.

"Later tonight," Harper said, "I'll take you out to the olive grove."

"It where Harper play as *bambina*," Alvaro said, his gray hair receding, his stubby fingers calloused from years of grape picking. "She catch *luccioles*." His aquamarine eyes sparkled like the Caribbean on his leathered face.

"*Luccioles*?"

"Lightning bugs," Harper said, setting her glass down. She put her arms around a giggling Amelia and squeezed tight. "I used to chase them when I was little."

Grace seemed suddenly lost in Harper's story, enamored by it. "I've never seen a lightning bug."

"More wine," Alvaro offered, filling each cup.

"How long has the vineyard been in the family?" Grace asked.

"1843," Alvaro said proudly, his hand on his chest. "Grandpoppy. Those barrels"—he pointed to the cellar doors across the cobbled driveway—"he maked wine in same."

Even though the kitchen was bursting with bread, as Alvaro spoke, Harper could smell the mustard milled deep in the stone grinder on the counter. Bound by yarn in an urn, seed-packed mustard twigs were choked by a mass of dried leaves behind it. Harper lifted the grinder. "Smell this."

Grace took a hefty whiff and her eyes widened. "Wow."

Amelia giggled. A well-built, sturdy woman in her late fifties, Amelia was wearing an apron that said Kiss the Cook. Harper had given it to her as a gift and even though Amelia hardly spoke a lick of English, she wore it with pride. Amelia's hair, the color of sudsy dishwater, was partially pulled back with a simple gold barrette.

"Secret"—Alvaro held up the Angel Parti bottle—"old oak. Same barrels grandpoppy first maked chianti. On dis land." He stuck his flat Italian nose into the glass. "Mmmm."

"Really?" Grace inquired.

"Gooder every year." Alvaro swore on it.

Harper and Grace both knew a thing or two about wine. Even though they were barely twenty-one, they'd been to Napa twice together with the Dunlops. Usually the girls spent the days soaking up sun and chlorine at the pool while Cilla and Benson tasted, but occasionally they tagged along, especially on their most recent trip during their sophomore year in college.

It was at the Beaulieu Vineyards that they learned the older the barrel, the poorer the wine. It might explain why the Alessi wine hadn't won any awards. Oak didn't age like the juice; instead, the quality of wine actually declined with each vintage. That's why most wineries bought new barrels every year. Alvaro knew this, but still tried to justify it when he took the girls to the cave for a tasting.

You'd never know the Alessi wine cellar was actually a cave until you walked through the rustic entrance, Harper thought. You'd certainly know it once inside by the slick moss on the cave walls and the stairs leading down. Drops of condensation trickled on their heads.

"This barrel," Alvaro said, popping the portly, wine-stained cork, "signature vintage. It aged two year. Taste."

He dipped the wine thief into the barrel. Despite his best effort, red wine dribbled down the sides of each glass and onto the earthen floor when he filled the glasses.

While they tasted and toured the rows of barrels—catching a buzz quickly—the girls got increasingly affectionate in the cave. They kept their arms around each other; Harper's hand was in Grace's back pocket.

After an hour of trying every barrel, Alvaro finally hung up the thief and said: "You go *bassetto*. I show."

The sun exploded into the cave as he opened the doors, blinding them as they exited.

With a whistle from Alvaro, Amelia, in the kitchen working on dinner, flew from the stable doors. She was carrying fresh towels they'd seen flapping in the wind on a line when they arrived.

The bunkhouse, or "*bassetto*"—the name hand-painted on the archway leading to the spiral staircase—was hidden in the vineyard about an acre from the central estate. Like the main house, the *bassetto* had blue window shingles, weathered from the strong sun rays, and wrought iron details. The stucco finish was painted the same washed amber with fingers of ivy climbing its walls.

Getting to the top of the stairs, Alvaro stepped into the first guest room, the junior suite with two double beds. Through the open window, the view below was the side patio where a fountain with cherubs back to back, wing to wing, spouted water. Grace started to put her bag down until Alvaro said, "*Attendi*!" He then led them to the second room, the master suite, down the hall.

"Perhaps more comfortable here."

The grand room had a plush, sprawling king bed on one wall and an open, private, expansive balcony overlooking the vineyard and the quietly sloping hills beyond it. The ceilings, high and coved, came to a point in the center of the room, where an ornamental chandelier hung.

"*Grazie*, Uncle Al." Harper put her arms around Grace from behind. "*Merci* Auntie, *questo farà*."

An awkward moment followed when Grace stepped away from Harper.

"Dinner at seven," Alvaro said, closing the door behind him.

When they were finally alone, Grace turned to Harper. "What were you doing?" She paused. "Shouldn't we, you know, be a little more careful."

"Careful?"

"Discreet."

"Oh." The thought hadn't occurred to Harper. "Don't worry. They don't care."

"Well," Grace said, stopping again, "what about your parents?" She sat on the edge of the bed. "Aren't you worried they'll talk to your dad about it? Us. This thing. What's happening."

"What is happening?" Harper asked.

"I don't know." Grace smiled. "You tell me."

"It's fine. Don't worry. My dad only talks to Uncle Al a couple times a year. They wouldn't talk about stuff like this anyway. It's usually about the weather. Or the grapes. Or their sister in Sicily."

Grace was tentative again before dinner, but as the evening progressed she got more and more comfortable, especially after she saw the red rose placed in between them when they sat down at the old farmhouse table.

Dinner was served on the back deck, where grapevines sagged from the trellis. A swanlike decanter was filled at the center of the table, which was lit by a simple iron candelabra above and wide pillars amidst the steaming bowls of food. Amelia had made her famous Bolognese with crispy polenta, an heirloom caprese salad, blanched haricot verts and pesto pizzette.

As the four enjoyed dinner together, breaking bread and marveling at the sunset, Grace loosened up even more, occasionally stealing kisses between bites.

Seeing this, Alvaro raised his glass halfway through dinner. "*Ecco per amorè*!"

Amelia and Harper lifted theirs immediately. "To love," Alvaro toasted.

Having lived in Italy their whole lives, like most Italians, Alvaro and Amelia were in love with love; they didn't care who was giving or receiving, just as long as there was love.

"When Harper was Bambina," Alvaro recalled after he cleaned his plate, "she run through vineyard at night. We ate at same *tabella*." He pounded the table with his fist. "She was *timida*, or how you say?"

"Shy," Harper said, feeling it again as Alvaro spoke.

"Shy. But smart. And loyal. One summer, she cared for baby duck who lose his *mamma*. She called Johnny."

"*Non zio*," Harper interrupted, "*il suo nome è stato Jeffrey*."

"Jeffrey," he corrected. "Little Mallard thought she was *mamma*. Followed her everywhere. She put him in *lago* and"—he let out a rough laugh as big as his belly—"she go ten steps before he jump out. Come after her. Run toward house."

In the gold candlelight, Amelia and Grace sipped their wine and smiled at the story.

"She so sweet," he said, getting choked up. "Full of *amorè*."

"I loved that damn duck," Harper said, laughing, too, then gazing toward the pond, which was really no more than irrigation runoff at the bottom of the hill.

"I did never tell you. Jeffrey come back."

"He did?"

"For months. He was looked for you."

The fading twilight cast the perfect light on the pond's

water, which reflected the old vines growing close to its edge. In her mind, Harper saw Jeffrey waddling their way.

After they ate homemade tiramisu, Amelia suddenly spoke with excitement. "*Alvie, vai ottenere il vaso.*"

"What?" Harper asked Amelia. She'd spoken too fast. Alvaro immediately stood and disappeared into his nearby workshop.

She didn't answer, just giggled and winked.

Moments later, Alvaro returned carrying a jar.

"Your nightlight," he said. Harper immediately recognized it as the old pickling jar where she kept her captured fireflies as a child. The lid was rusted around the mouth and so were the holes Alvaro poked in the top so the captives could breathe.

"I clean for you," he said. "Now go. *Buona notte*!"

As the girls left the table, Grace said, "Are you sure?" about the dishes and the clean up. Alvaro already had the plates stacked and was headed toward the house.

"*Ciao! Divertiti*!" Amelia yelled collecting the glasses.

Harper grabbed Grace's hand and took off for the grove.

"Where are we going?" Grace asked.

"You'll see."

In the darkness, the stars burning through the black canvas sky in clusters, the girls made their way through the grapes toward the olive thicket. The closer they got to the grove, the warmer the glow, a glow so subtle you wouldn't necessarily notice if you weren't looking.

"Do you see?" Harper asked.

"See what?" Grace looked toward the sky and then squinted at the light.

"The light." She pointed. "Fireflies."

Grace slowed and then stopped. "Wow," she said.

"Come on!" Harper grabbed her hand and they took off running.

When she was young, Harper disappeared into the olive grove for hours, always within earshot of her parents. She caught fireflies and put them in the same old pickling jar Alvaro proudly unearthed. At bedtime, she placed her capture bedside and watched their glowing tails until her eyelids became too heavy.

Like the nineteenth century vines, the old olive growth was

dense and tangled. The branches—twisted and knotted like witch fingers—formed a green canopy above them as they hurried along. Their gait quickly turned into a skip and then suddenly they were kids again playing in the shadows the shadows, cast onto the ground like distorted fairytale characters.

Harper caught the first firefly in her hand and gently coerced it into the jar.

"I got one!" Grace hollered, her hands cupped together as she walked toward Harper.

This continued until they had at least twenty fireflies in their jar.

Wild bursts of laughter could be heard throughout the valley in the temperate motionless night, as Harper and Grace meandered through the grove back toward the *bassetto.*

They put the jar, glowing like a lantern, on the side table near the double chaise on the balcony. Easily, both girls fit onto the canvas chair—which was more like an outdoor bed—a centerpiece of the *bassetto*, jutting out into the grapes.

"Let's sleep out here tonight," Grace said, flopping onto the lounger, making room for Harper by her side.

Just as Harper nestled into Grace, a star burned across the sky.

"Did you see that?" Harper asked.

Grace closed her eyes. "Make a wish."

Harper closed hers too, and made a wish, a very important one: she wished things between her and Grace would always feel the way they felt that night.

"What did you wish for?" Grace asked.

"It won't come true if I tell you."

"I'll tell you mine if you tell me yours."

Harper didn't want to jinx it, so she refused.

"I wished we could stay here forever," Grace said. "And never have to go back home."

After midnight, Harper moved the lantern to the nightstand and cozied in beside it. Grace was busy in the bathroom.

Lying on her side, she watched the fireflies and reminisced

about her youth; she could hear her mom's laugh, smell her dad's aftershave.

Grace finally got into bed. "Did I miss anything?" she asked, looping her arms around Harper's waist.

"No."

Together, they watched the flies buzz around the jar, their glowing tails clustered together behind the glass.

"They're so beautiful," Grace sighed. "Why do they glow like that?"

"I don't know, but I think it has to do with sex."

"Sex?"

"It's like their way of attracting one another."

More time passed as they watched their lights slowly fade.

"Are they dying?"

"I'm not sure," Harper said, tapping the glass.

"I can't stand it," Grace suddenly said, leaving one hand on Harper's shoulder. "We have to set them free."

Harper agreed.

In her pajamas, red boy-cut undies, Grace grabbed the jar. Unscrewing the lid, she tilted it and let each firefly out. One by one, they flew to freedom. They were like little angels, the fireflies, taking off into the air above them, their tails quickly glowing even brighter than before.

"Go," Grace said, swinging her hands, palms up. "Go."

As they lay back down, the little *luccioles* hung out around the dark chandelier, perhaps mistaking the sparkling jewels as some of their own. They kept the ceiling illuminated—like their own constellation of stars—until both girls, wrapped around each other, fell asleep.

The morning songbirds serenaded them at dawn. The sun was just coming up when Harper made her way down the staircase through the winding vineyard trail to the main house for coffee. It was unlike Grace to still be snoozing—she was always the early bird—so Harper let her sleep.

In the kitchen, Alvaro was working on breakfast.

"*Buon giorno*," he said. Harper kissed him on the cheek before reaching for coffee.

"You is well-rested?" He dropped a piece of egg-drenched bread into the frying pan.

"I am," Harper said. "French toast?"

"*Italiano* toast." Alvaro smiled as he ground a cinnamon stick onto each slice. "I like Grace. *Lei è così delizioso*!"

"Perfect word, Uncle Al." Harper was caught in Grace's rapture too. "She is delightful."

"*Buon giorno*," Auntie said, joining them with her usual wink. "Gracie?" she said, typing on her apron.

"*Si.*"

"*Cosi delizioso*," she added.

They must have discussed her in bed after they'd said goodnight.

"How long you be in love," Alvaro asked, his bushy eyebrow up.

"I don't. I guess. A while. You won't tell Daddy." Harper looked up from the coffee press. "Will you?"

"No worry."

Harper took her coffee down to the pond and meandered its perimeter. She waved at the Cionis, neighbors nearby, eating breakfast on their veranda.

She picked up two rocks, smooth and even, and skimmed the first one on the water. It skipped six times.

As she started to throw the second, she heard Grace, still in her pajamas, call her from the *bassetto's* balcony.

"*Bella*!" Grace yelled. It was one of the only words she knew in Italian and what she would call Harper from then on. "Good morning."

Grace quickly joined Harper lakeside and threw a rock of her own.

"You know that runoff is horrible for the environment," Grace said. "All the chemicals people in the valley use to protect the grapes end up in their drinking water."

Harper shrugged and threw another stone.

Slowly, they walked the pond, watching a family of ducks gliding across until a cowbell from the main house called them for breakfast.

In true Alessi fashion, the spread was, once again, elaborate. Italians hardly do anything *cosi cosi* and Alvaro and Amelia were the real deal. Several different freshly-squeezed juices, sliced mandarins, pomegranates and loquats. Italian toast and poached eggs with shaved ham and bologna. And plenty of espresso.

"*Per favore prosciutto*," Alvaro said. And then almost in the same breath: "You take Giada for drive today. I has mechanic tune."

"Giada?" Grace asked.

"Their Alfa Romeo. It's awesome. Totally restored. Vintage. Nineteen sixty?"

"Sixty-one," Alvaro said, lapping up syrup with his last bite of toast.

"We make together lunch." To Amelia, Alvaro said, "*Le ragazze stanno andando a prendere Giatta. Faremo un picnic.*"

Amelia did a triad this time: giggled, winked and raised her fork.

When Alvaro fired up the convertible Spider's diesel engine, it ticked like a bomb. An Italian work of art, their red Alfa Romeo was in mint condition. Giada's curves were right out of an old movie—the round front lights like Sophia Loren's eyes taking in the Tuscan countryside. Slim and slender, the classy ride was spit-shined from bumper to bumper.

Amelia brought out a basket of goodies for their road trip. She tucked it into the backseat and then tied a scarf around each girl's head.

"*Molto carina*," she said, squeezing their cheeks.

"Go fun!" Alvaro yelled as they pulled out of the driveway.

They first drove the back roads outside Bologna toward the coast. Grace had never seen the Adriatic Sea, so they stopped for a picture at a viewpoint overlooking the Ravenna beaches, packed with bathers below. Against the railing, Harper took a series of photos of Grace who was leaning back and gazing into the sun.

After the coast, Harper drove south toward Florence. On the winding roads, Grace scooted against Harper on the leather bench seat. Harper kissed Grace's temple. The sun was high in the sky and it baked their shoulders.

She turned off the main highway onto a dirt road, where they drove for miles until they found the perfect shaded spot, under a blooming mimosa tree, for their picnic on the grounds of Villa Mangiacane. It was surrounded by poppies. In the distance, the ancient renaissance villa was impressively magnificent. Set on a hill overlooking Florence, the estate had been built by the Machiavelli family in the fifteenth century and still had many of its famous hallmarks. The rumor around town was that Michelangelo had played a role in its design.

The wicker basket was packed with mouthwatering treats. Homemade olive tapenade, fig spread, a wheel of brie and a crisp baguette. Not forgotten was a bottle of Angel Parti, a church key and two glasses.

"Do we have to go home tomorrow?" Grace asked as Harper poured her second glass of wine. "Can't we just send for our things? Finish school from here?"

Harper sighed. "Seriously."

"I'm so glad we came through Bologna. Your Uncle Al is such a charmer, just like you said. And that Amelia. Even though we can't have a conversation, she's so funny. Her little laugh and her winks."

"I know."

"You don't realize how lucky you are. They're so warm and loving. Their love is so unconditional."

She didn't say it, but both girls knew they were going home to conditions.

After the wine kicked in, Grace worked her way over onto Harper's side of the blanket.

Surrounded by a sea of poppies, Grace kissed her with a near rage. It was hot, sudden, Grace making her move.

As the sun set, there were nervous giggles when Grace unbuttoned Harper's shirt and then slid her hands down Harper's body, along her thighs, and across her stomach. Harper's skirt rolled up around her waist.

Suddenly, everything shifted into an old movie; even Harper's memory was in black and white. Slow and deliberate, Grace's hand moved up Harper's leg and over her panties. Harper couldn't believe the shock it sent through her veins, a physical reaction she'd never known. With one touch from Grace's hand, she almost had an orgasm.

Crack boom.

Harper pushed Grace away, shocked at her loss of control, her near climax. Grace looked at Harper carefully, trying to understand her resistance. Gently, Harper touched her face before kissing her with passion and resolve. Grace knew what it meant—they both did.

Not here.

They got back to the vineyard late. The *bassetto's* porch light was on, so was a small antique lamp at the base of the iron staircase.

When they walked inside, Harper's heart stopped as she shut the front door. She swallowed hard. She knew what was coming and it scared her.

In the bathroom, Harper took her time at the sink—flossing her teeth, washing her face and getting ready. Preparing for what would happen.

What if I don't like it?

What if Grace doesn't?

While she stalled in the bathroom, Grace put a music mix into the corner stereo. The room, with its vaulted ceilings, had the perfect acoustics for Al Green's groove.

Harper was putting away her makeup remover when Grace walked up and stood in the doorway, her eyes full of surrender. They reminded Harper of Grace's eleven-year-old eyes, the tub of ice cream, their rocky road since puberty.

Nearly ten years later, Grace asked softly, "Are you coming?"

With a deep breath, Harper said, "Yes," and took her hand. Just like in her fantasy.

Grace let Harper lead the way, standing back, watching Harper pass as she escorted Grace to the master suite. When Grace closed the door, in Harper's mind, the loud hardware sliding into place shook the walls of the bunkhouse. Standing in front of Grace, Harper imagined an earthquake, the *bassetto* beams buckling, its stucco crumbling, its two-by-fours breaking in half like toothpicks.

Harper let go of Grace's hand and walked to the opposite side of the bed.

She worried Grace would think it was ugly. Like every other woman, after seeing *Fried Green Tomatoes*, Harper had stood over a mirror to get a look at her vagina. She couldn't see much. She couldn't know what Grace was in for, but she hoped it was pretty.

With her knees pressed to the cold bedframe, Harper prepared herself for death. So, this is how it ends, my life as Harper Alessi, she thought. Everything she'd ever known, ever expected her life to be twisted and disappeared into a fated vortex she never knew was there.

Harper's panties were suddenly the epicenter, the hub of all feeling.

Like she'd been asleep all those years, tiny pins poked the skin between her legs as she awoke. Wind chimes on the balcony pealed, crashing into one another as the night air hissed into the room.

At a fork in the road, with five feet of mattress between them, Grace and Harper captured one last look at the sky as the clouds changed formation outside. The billowing sky opened for a harvest moon.

Grace kneeled first and reached across the bed.

Full of strange desire, Harper's chest ached, the pangs acute, but hushed and hidden. She trembled forward, took Grace's hand again and brought it to her face. Grace's skin was lavender and vanilla.

God, please forgive me, she prayed.

Harper's body fell and she was swimming, buoyant and fluid, until she was on her back, Grace above her.

Around the chandelier, one firefly still circled the room, its tail aglow.

Grace sprinkled Harper's ears with kisses, covering her, tickling her face with her long curls as she moved down. Grace licked the salt off Harper's body and explored her torso.

Where had Grace gotten her confidence? Harper wondered. Her unfolding experience was just the opposite. She felt insecure and fought welling tears as Marvin Gaye began "Sexual Healing."

Harper did what she could to keep her cool, reminding herself, again, to breathe, but once Grace passed her navel, Harper shifted strategies as a tear escaped—she had to survive—focusing instead on the aged ceiling, fractured like a hardboiled egg, like her mind.

As Grace's finger slipped inside, Harper closed her eyes.

Dear God.

A welcome intruder, it was overwhelming. When Grace's lips met the naïve skin below Harper's panty line, a heavy weight crushed the bones in her chest and Harper felt like she was suffocating. Her body, shaking out of control, had never been so alive, never felt so deeply.

Grace moved slowly. As she inched closer, Grace's tongue was against Harper's thigh and she fought off an orgasm. Purposefully, Harper stopped breathing. It was the only way. She had to hold on to the moment, couldn't blow it like an eighteen-year-old virgin on prom night.

When Harper looked down, all she saw were Grace's eyes, focused, devoted, determined. The bashful debutante, she couldn't believe it was real, and she quickly put a pillow between them. But Grace wouldn't have it—she grabbed it and threw it to the floor. Harper laughed nervously; she could feel Grace laughing, too.

Grace was soft and careful, doing things Harper didn't know a woman could do, and to her surprise, with a level of expertise Rich never had. She knew right where to be. Just what to do.

As Grace split Harper in half, she held onto the bed sheet with both hands, crumpling it like wads of paper.

Harper squeezed tighter, again, trying to make it last.

Until finally, she let go.

Somewhere deep below the surface, as Harper's young, fragile frame shook, her foundation gave way—just like in the earthquake—and everything about her crashed down the hill into the vineyard and olive grove. There was no more imagining. The big one finally hit.

When Harper smelled herself on Grace's face, something inside her released, popped open allowing all the fear which had consumed her to dissipate. With intention, she squirmed away from Grace and got on top; Harper was ready to dive into what she'd dreamed about since she was a teenager.

After the kiss, Harper traced Grace's nose and lips with her finger until Grace's tongue curled around it like a grape leaf.

She took her time with Grace's breasts, sucking her nipples until they were nearly raw. As Harper worked her way down, she didn't miss an inch of Grace's body, never worrying about the way she smelled, the way she tasted. All the fear washed away.

When Harper passed Grace's stomach, she looked up. Grace, too, stared at the ceiling, unsure where to put her gaze. She kissed above her panties and waited until intuitively, she knew Grace was ready. Outside, the clouds moved once more, forming something enigmatic, something not everyone could see. Just like the fireflies in the grove.

Harper stuck her finger in the top of Grace's G-string and teased the skin underneath. After a profound breath, she pulled them off with her teeth.

At last, nothing between them.

This was it, Harper thought, as she pulled Grace to the edge of the bed. Her real debut.

When Grace's pubic hair brushed her chin, Harper's blood pressure raged, expanding then retracting. She could feel her heartbeat in her fingers, in her temple, even her toes. When she finally got Grace into her mouth, it filled Harper with rich desire, sweet pearls of honey against her tongue. Grace's bouquet was familiar, but foreign, like spices from another country. And just like Grace, Harper instinctively knew what to do. It amazed and delighted her.

Harper swallowed drops of Grace as she melted in ecstasy, using the duvet to muffle her moans. Watching Grace's body, feeling her tremble was even better than her own pleasure.

As Grace crawled into her arms, Harper was overwhelmed; she'd never held love that closely.

"I love you," Grace whispered.

"I love you, too. I've wanted to tell you for days," Harper said. "I was afraid."

Grace covered them with the blanket. "You have nothing to be afraid of," she said. A silent moment passed as Harper tried to suppress her tears. But it was no use; she was too naked to hide anything.

As they lay together, deeply stirred, Harper unwrapped her heart and laid it before Grace. "You're everything," she whispered.

"You're my everything, too," Grace said, just as unguarded and vulnerable, "and you always will be."

These flowery words didn't come easy and neither did the others that night as they both revealed all they'd kept hidden, holding nothing back.

When Alvaro and Amelia rang the cowbell the next morning, up early again preparing another huge breakfast, the girls were pulled from a deep sleep. Both still nude, they were entangled in one another.

"We have to get up?" Grace asked, burying her face in the pillow.

"God. Really?" Harper agreed, groggily, but with a smile still on her face. It was their last day here.

In the kitchen, Alvaro met Grace and Harper with orange juice. He was in wine-stained jumpsuit. Each girl's hair was a mess.

It was a sad day for all, as nobody wanted them to leave.

"Come soon back," Alvaro said, as they hugged and kissed goodbye. In a black Mercedes station wagon, the driver waited patiently.

"We will," promised a crying Harper. "*Lo prometto.*"

"*Grazie.*" Grace also sobbed. "*Grazie mille.*" She held on as they embraced one last time.

"*Arrivederci*!" Harper shouted from the window as the gates closed behind them.

Their 747 took off from Rome's airport through a thicket of clouds. Together, Grace and Harper looked out the window with despair.

"I really do wish we could stay forever," Grace said.

"Me, too."

But school beckoned—their final year—and so did responsibility. Classes and labs. Clubs and sorority meetings.

Their evening flight to the states was a blink in time. Around them, businessmen were buried in newspapers and the stewardesses left Harper and Grace alone after they served dinner, a filet with béarnaise sauce and baby asparagus. Sitting in first class made it easy to kiss and cuddle as they chased the sun.

They extended their layover in Los Angeles overnight so they could stay with Dean before heading home. One final bright spot before it was back to reality.

It was supposed to be a surprise, but Dean had clearly been tipped off. No doubt by Cilla. They could tell by his warm, but casual reaction when they arrived in the cab. He was washing his Studebaker Avanti with a chamois in the shade of the Coral tree beside his garage.

Lying in the grass, Dean's greyhounds, Geisha and Boris, seemed to also be in on the secret. They hardly moved, lazy in the hot sun, as Harper and Grace pulled their luggage down his driveway. Of course that could've had something to do with LA's record-breaking heat wave, which had pushed the thermometer to nearly 100 degrees that day.

Even with his doors open, Dean's swanky Hollywood Hills

home was a sauna. His guest room, tucked into the hillside and covered by a dense web of Japanese maple, was a little better than the main house, which had fans propped in every window.

"Is this going to be all right?" Dean asked. "I'm sorry it's such a scorcher. I'd give you my room, but it's worse."

Hot or not, his place was just as Harper remembered. It always was. Since her youth, she and Grace had visited so many times they'd lost count.

Barely reinforced by the mountain, his crib, as they called it, was built on stilts and had a dramatic view of Hollywood. Throughout the house, there were pitched beam ceilings and bamboo floors with stainless steel accents. His living room opened onto a lush outdoor deck where they sat, trying to keep cool, into the afternoon listening to old records. Ella Fitzgerald. Nina Simone. The standards. The sun was intense, baking their skin, parching the brown mountains around them.

In her round sunglasses—nearly as big as the records playing—Harper was able to flirt with Grace without Dean knowing. At one point, Grace's feet propped up on the table, Harper could see Grace's panties; they were red, lacy, soaked.

Between cocktails, Dean recited a monologue on the second tier of his deck. He was growing his hair out for a role—a Caesar cut for a tough guy.

As she watched Dean, Harper thought back to the first time she met him at Grace's birthday party. He'd come as a clown, a cross between the Joker and Ronald McDonald, and made balloon animals before secretly taking off his makeup and showing up as Uncle Dean to join them in the pool.

The constant pillar, Grace had once said of her uncle, Dean was a bleeding heart dedicated to those he loved. Always there. The glue holding the family together. And steady he was—unless headed to an audition or out on the town—he was always dressed in khaki shorts, Polo collar up, and Sperry topsiders sans socks with just a squirt of Versace cologne.

"What'd you say?" Dean recited, making a Mafioso face. He pretended to smoke a cigar. "I'm gonna break ya face if ya don't tell me who killed Tiny B. He was like a fuckin' brotha." The face again. "Ya dead to me, Tone, ya hear me?"

With a snap, Dean was out of character and bowed before them.

"Bravo," the girls cheered.

Like Elvis, Dean said, "Thank you. Thank you very much," as he headed inside. "Any requests?"

"Chaka Khan," Harper said. "*Stompin' at the Savoy.*"

"Of course," Dean said. It was Harper's favorite and Dean knew it, always played it when she was visiting. Chaka's Eighties album with Rufus began shortly after.

"This is the best album she ever recorded," Harper said, turning her face to the sun, soaking up the vitamin D.

Finally alone, Grace looked intently at Harper, her sunglasses on the end of her nose. "Is that right?" she said, after kicking Harper's chair. That familiar flirtatious smile arrived on Grace's face, the one Harper had been trying to interpret for years.

Fishing an ice cube from her glass, Grace ran it across Harper's knee and down her shin. Cool drops of water dripped the length of her calf to her cracked heel.

With her tongue, Harper finagled out a sliver of ice and used it to make a heart on the teak wood table. "Mine," she said, pointing at Grace before leaning over for a kiss.

Grace looked quickly at the house and put a restraining finger on Harper's pursed lips.

"I heard Simons and Simons finally went public," Dean said as he descended down the stairs.

"That's what Mummy said." Grace swished the mint in her mojito.

This was Harper's cue to leave. She was reaching her breaking point; every time the word *Jamie* hit the open air it was like a spray of mace.

She wanted to get her camera anyway, as the light was nearly perfect. To cut the glare reflecting off the windows, Harper dug out a polarizing filter from her bag and screwed it on. It would be just what she needed.

From the upper deck, she began snapping photos of Dean and Grace chatting below.

Dean's voice carried in the muggy air. "They're grooming Jamie to take over after he graduates from Stanford?"

"I guess."

A line of sweat burned across her temple as Harper focused on the top of Grace's head. Standing above Grace and Dean, Harper caught several of them talking, their shadows long on the deck, stretching all the way to the box of herbs in the corner.

"Are you gonna see him while you're in town?" Dean asked.

Zooming in, Harper was focused on Boris chewing on a bone when she heard this question. She waited for the answer before closing the shutter.

"I don't know," Grace said, hushed.

Harper pulled the camera from her face.

"Left a message. I'm sure he's busy."

"Are you guys still, you know, doing...whatever it is you do?"

Grace fanned herself with Chet Baker's album cover.

"You called Jamie?" Harper asked.

Surprised, she and Dean both looked up.

"I just thought. I don't know. I should," Grace defended.

"When?" Harper demanded.

"Earlier."

"When?"

"You were in the shower."

Harper looked at Dean in protest. "But we're here to see Dean." She forced a smile. "And drink his vodka, and listen to his records."

"I'm sure word's gotten to him we're in town. Mummy has Jamie on speed dial."

With that, Harper turned and headed inside again. She'd had enough heat.

Grace found Harper in the bedroom, lying on her side facing the guest veranda. She was flipping through pictures on her digital camera.

"Bella," Grace said.

Harper continued clicking through the images—them leaning against the Alessi gates, them in the *bassetto* sprawled on the couch, Grace topless in the sun.

On the bed, Grace nestled in behind Harper.

Was she allowed to be mad at Grace for calling Jamie? Harper wondered. It was unclear how it all worked.

"I'm sorry," Grace finally said.

"I just don't get why you called him. Am I not enough for you?"

"Of course you are." Grace sighed. While Grace searched for a reason, they looked at the photos together.

"It's Mummy. I know she'd ask why I didn't and I wouldn't know what to say."

"Mummy? Really? Why do you still call her that anyway?"

While they talked, Harper continued scanning the pictures, the ones of their countryside picnic. With the camera propped up on the basket, the timer had taken shots of them at dusk. There were several like this, them toasting and kissing, Villa Mangiacane in the background like an impressionist painting—the light captured in ever-changing shades as it set against the archways.

"I wish we were back in that field," Harper said.

"Girls," Dean interrupted. "We need to get going." He sat next to them, saddled together on the bed. "What are you doing?"

"Reminiscing," Harper said, still clicking through the frames. Grace sat up.

"Let's go!" Grace said, suddenly enthusiastic. She stole the camera from Harper and turned it off.

Fortunately, Jamie didn't get back to Grace in time, so the three of them set out for dinner alone. They packed into Dean's shiny Avanti and hit Sunset Boulevard.

"That's where John Belushi died," Dean said, pointing out the Château Marmont. "And that sidewalk is where River Phoenix collapsed." Outside the Roxy, a line of grunge waited for a show.

Dean looked so cool driving his Avanti, with its glossy paint, its supercharged engine purring under the hood. As they drove along, the three of them sitting side-by-side, the wind batted Dean's salt-and-pepper hair, his thumb beat the steering wheel to the radio's song.

The bench seat in Dean's Avanti was covered in an Australian sheepskin, the kind you see in old ladies' cars. A scrap—a perfect triangle—was stashed into the side panel of the passenger door. Harper found it and held it up. "What's this?"

Grace grabbed the swatch and rubbed it on her face. "Mmmm. So soft."

The Avanti slowed at a red light. "It's my codpiece," Dean said, taking it from Grace. With a straight face, he placed it over his nether regions. "What do you think?"

This put the three of them into a laughing jag that would last all the way to the valet stand at Spago, the glamorous old-Hollywood establishment which had made Wolfgang Puck a household name.

Danny Devito was in the bar having martinis with friends and waved at Dean as they walked through the door. For years, Dean had bartended at Spago, even though, like all the Dunlops, he didn't need the money. The family trust was constantly expanding, with profits from its investments filling the pockets of the heirs daily.

"It's a great place to network," Dean would say when pressed by Cilla, who never understood. "I got to drive Marty Scorsese home. He told me to call him Marty. One night after too many limoncellos," he bragged. "He gave me a huge break the next week in *Cape Fear*."

After they were seated, at the perfect window table in the corner of the restaurant, Dean left to say hello to the staff of old cronies. They were in a huddle around a long tape of kitchen orders and greeted him with great affection.

Grace didn't waste any time; even before the appetizers arrived her hand was wandering under the table. Harper pinched Grace and whispered "Stop" like a ventriloquist, her lips not moving, as Dean ordered his entree.

This only made it worse.

While Dean told them about the temporary move he was planning to Mexico—a psychological sabbatical, he called it—Harper struggled for concentration as Grace's fingers worked their way across her thigh. Harper could see Grace in the reflection of Dean's wire-rimmed glasses, her blond widow's peak, her sharp-as-an-ax jawbone.

Harper saw Grace everywhere.

Throughout the night, Harper did her best to push away conversation, keeping the focus on Dean so she wouldn't have to talk, but the energy under the table was fierce. "Tell us more about San Miguel," she said, crossing her legs.

"It's a charming town right smack-dab in the middle of Mexico," Dean said. "It's old world. Colonial architecture. Lots of history. While I'm there, I'm gonna take some art classes. Learn about oils." He raised his eyebrows. "Maybe take a photography course."

"Really?" Harper asked, excited.

"I've got a brochure at home. I'll show you."

"Where are you staying?" Grace asked.

"I found this great little guest house in the historic district. Has an amazing view of the town. Was built in like 1710. And modeled after a famous Mexican homestead on the coast. It's really open and airy. And it has a very sweet housemaid. I think her name was Esmeralda," he added. "Her English was awful."

"Can we visit?"

"You better. I'm counting on both of you after graduation."

By this point, the tension under the table was becoming unbearable.

"Pardon me," Harper said, getting up and excusing herself to the restroom. She needed to splash water on her face. Take a moment to cool down.

"I have to go too," Grace said, leaving Dean with an attractive female server who'd stopped at the table. Harper didn't look back, but could feel Grace trailing close behind.

The unisex bathroom, a burgundy box with a toilet, was lit by a single votive candle. Jazz played through an overhead speaker.

As soon as Grace turned the lock, Harper pinned her to the door. The wave of desire splashing inside of her body was more frantic than anything Harper had ever felt. In an instant, Grace's hands were under Harper's top. Like the candle, their breaths flickered.

Hot fury between them, Grace shoved Harper to the sink. Harper momentarily wrapped her legs around Grace's waist, stabilizing them as they devoured each other, both unable to kiss deep enough. In the vase behind Harper, a Bird of Paradise snapped in half.

Grace held Harper's wrists together above her head and took each breast into her mouth, lapping up her nipples like a melting ice cream cone. Looking down, Harper was overcome by the sight of a frenzied Grace.

Finally, Harper twisted from Grace, and with both hands, pushed her against the wall, face first. It was her turn. Harper's knee, cut by a pencil boucle skirt, separated Grace's legs.

"Spread 'em," Harper said.

Grace immediately surrendered and obeyed. "Whatever you say, officer."

Grace's forehead against the wall, Harper began patting Grace like a policewoman. She started at the top and stroked her way down. "Do as I say," she said, lifting Grace's skirt, lined in leopard print, "and no one will get hurt."

She explored her stomach, her hips, her thighs. "Spread 'em further," Harper demanded. Grace widened her stance. "That's a good girl."

Suddenly, a firm knock at the door startled them.

"Damn it!" Grace said, pulling her skirt back down, fixing her hair.

Somehow, after three more knocks at the door, they peeled apart and returned to the table. Neither wanted Dean nor the people in line outside the door to wonder.

"Everything all right?" Dean asked, spinning his reading glasses on the tablecloth.

"Fine," Grace said, scooting into her chair. She reached for the sweets menu. "How about dessert?"

After a chocolate soufflé, they left Spago and hit Sunset again, motoring their way up Kings Road to Franklin Avenue, where Dean's house was situated right before the hillside bend. Its modern style wasn't unique to the street, but the large abstract sculpture in the front yard was; it had come with the house. Dean explained the muted cacophony of boxes was supposed to symbolize repression.

"Huh," Harper said. "Repression in Hollywood. Go figure."

Inside, everyone dispersed throughout the house, which was much cooler now. The high pressure system over Southern California had given in to the pervasive ocean stream, rolling through Santa Monica to the mountains.

Grace was in the bedroom, Dean on the deck with his phone and Harper in the kitchen pouring Courvoisier.

Meeting Grace outside the bathroom, Harper handed Grace her nightcap.

"Thanks officer," she said.

The strip search would resume shortly and they both knew it.

With leashes in hand, the dogs at his feet, Dean appeared at the door. "Do you have everything you need?" he asked. Chaka was still on the turntable, back at it again. "Ain't Nobody" this time.

Squatting on the floor, Harper was changing her camera battery. "We're good."

Grace, in a sort-of pose against the door hinges, was intensely sniffing her cognac.

"Smile," Harper said, taking a photo of Dean from the ground. He was still in his black high collar shirt and dark denim jeans, his bold John Hardy choker radiant against his neck.

"Goodnight," he told them, and left.

Standing halfway in the bathroom, Grace, provocatively, had one arm up and her eyes held the same expression as when they were in the Spago restroom. Two of Grace's sweater buttons popped open revealing her diamonded chest.

As soon as the front door latched shut, the show began.

Harper jumped onto the bed and rested against the red velvet accent wall, camera in hand. Slowly, to Chaka's beats, Grace's top came off. Her hips moved like she'd been peeling her whole life. The only thing missing was the stripper pole.

Grace improvised and slinked up and down the doorjamb instead, delicately unbuckling her skirt's cloth belt. The clasp clanked on the wood floor.

From there, in her G-string and sweater, which would shortly be in a heap in the corner, Grace danced to the song, working the furniture in the room like a professional.

It was all recorded on film, even when Grace leapt onto the mattress and stuck her finger in Harper's mouth as she slithered up and down the bedpost like a seasoned stripper.

Grace tweaked her own nipples, felt her own wetness and bent over for Harper, revealing everything. Harper's mouth was on Grace, who straddled Harper when "Sweet Thing" began. This was the point Harper put her camera down, as she needed both hands.

Grace knelt above her, moving her body with flawless rhythm. Almost channeling Chaka.

Where had this sexpot been hiding, Harper marveled.

Without control, Harper flashed on Jamie's face, jarring her for a very brief moment amidst their passion.

It was no wonder, Harper thought, they couldn't get rid of him.

"Secret Lovers"
Atlantic Starr

Getting back into the swing of school wasn't easy that fall. Especially with Grace's post at the sorority house. Presidency had its perks—your own room, the primo parking spot, the prestigious title—but definitely had its drawbacks. People were always pulling on Grace and congregating in her room. Harper and Grace had to be extra careful when they were at the sorority house.

They had some close calls; times when they let their guard down. During one of their formal chapter meetings, when everyone was dressed in Gamma's sacred robes, Grace and Harper took a crazy chance in the ritual closet, narrowly escaping the eyes of their advisor when they thought they were alone.

That night, while they studied into the wee hours at the Coffee Depot, they vowed to be more careful.

"We can't let that happen again," Grace warned, dipping biscotti into her latte.

"I know," Harper said. "But she didn't see anything."

"This time."

It had scared both of them, but especially Grace.

"It could destroy us."

Between chapters, Harper took a break from chemical

compounds to work on her summer photo album. She'd just finished developing the batch and found the perfect red book that would tell the visual story of her journey across Western Europe. Carefully, she peeled back each page and organized it chronologically, starting with when she first arrived in Germany and roomed with Barb at their hotel. From there, it recorded her weekend trips to Prague, Budapest, London, Zurich and Paris, and then, of course, their time spent in Amsterdam and Italy. The book had just enough pages to finish it off with LA.

"You're such a whore," Harper poked, getting Grace's attention. She held up a photo of Grace in only panties, her bra dangling from her finger.

"Give me that." Grace's eyes widened. "You're not putting these in your album?" Reluctantly, she handed it back to Harper, who was rifling through a stack of them, examining the best of the best of Grace's Hollywood striptease.

"Why not? It's just for me."

"Are you kidding?" Grace asked.

"No one else will see it."

"What if this gets in the wrong hands? Promise me you won't include ANY of these dirty ones."

"Fine. Promise," Harper said, sliding the incriminating photos into the back of the album to destroy later. "You worry too much," she said.

When she got back to the sorority house, Harper put the album on the top shelf of her closet to ensure its secrecy. She had to get a chair to reach the spot and covered it up with a bunch of old costumes that had been collecting dust. Until she had time to finish it and shred the bad photos, no one would find it there. She was certain.

Grace's first tennis match of the season was scheduled for Thursday afternoon that week. Harper left her photography lab early to make it. Grace was playing a girl from UC Davis she'd beaten the year before, pretty bad actually, but Harper made a point never to miss a serve.

The match—which was being played on center court outside the University Club House—was nearly over. Grace pulled back for an overhead, her finger scoping the ball, before hitting a ferocious shot. A winner. Then, suddenly, she dropped her racquet and fell to her knees, holding her shoulder. As Harper raced from the stands, she could hear Grace crying, wailing, on the court, doubled over on the asphalt. People immediately crowded around.

It had taken Grace three years to climb to the top of U of A's tennis ladder, but only seconds to tumble down. The whispers around Grace said she'd torn her rotator cuff, which everyone immediately knew put her collegiate career in jeopardy.

Even though she was surrounded by coaches and therapists, Harper was able to get her hand in through the swarm and squeeze Grace's calf amidst the chaos. "I'm right here, Gracie."

For Grace, tennis was all but part of the Dunlop pedigree, as ingrained in her daily routine as her Catholic guilt. She was barely out of diapers when she discovered her first ball, and for nearly a year, she didn't put it down, sleeping with it, carrying it wherever she went. On the Dunlop mantle, there was a picture of Grace sitting on Santa's lap; if you looked closely, you could see yellow fuzz sticking out of her small purse.

At the hospital later that day, Grace, doped up with a bag of ice taped to her shoulder, was, again, surrounded by people when Harper arrived with flowers. Red roses. From the hall, she could hear the radiologist going over the x-rays.

"There are tears in your supraspinatus and teres minor muscle."

Grace's tone was surprisingly strong and optimistic as they talked about options. "Ten weeks of therapy? I could be ready for the NCAA Championships."

Harper waited for most of the group to dissipate before entering. "Knock, knock," Harper said.

An older, heavyset nurse was taking Grace's blood pressure. Grace, who was staring out the window lost in thought, quickly snapped her head when she heard Harper's voice. A look of relief, or something equally calming, washed over her.

"Can you give us a minute?" Grace asked, her voice cracking.

"No problem," the nurse said.

Harper approached slowly. "Hey you."

All it took were these words for Grace to lose it. With her good arm, Grace reached out and pulled Harper onto the bed.

"What am I going to do?" Grace cried, burrowing into Harper.

A few days later, when she first saw Grace's shoulder out of the sling, Harper couldn't believe the discoloration. Already feeling weak, Harper had braced herself, but it was worse than she expected. Where her cuff had shredded, it was black and green. Gently, with her fingertips, Harper followed the jaundice streaking down Grace's arm.

"Jesus," she softly said.

Trying to be as thoughtful as she could, Harper waited for the right moment to talk to Grace about her surgery, about what the injury meant. It wasn't until a few days later, when they were lying around the sorority house—Grace's arm in a sling, still on ice—Harper knew the time had come.

"When do you go under the knife?" Harper asked, closing her notebook.

"They're talking about doing it next week."

Harper nodded. She was afraid of the answer, but asked anyway. "Did you hear it rip?"

"Not with my ears, but I heard it inside, you know," Grace said. She was peeling the label off her Gatorade bottle. She rolled it between her fingers. "I'd recently changed my workout and my muscles were more fatigued than usual. I felt it tear as I followed through. There was a crunch sound."

Grace talked matter-of-factly until the conversation turned to recovery.

"Coach Carter is livid. He's worried I won't be strong enough to compete in the championships. Even though I've given him three great years, I overheard him tell one of the therapists I was money wasted."

She didn't say it, but Harper could tell by the way Grace related his words she wasn't sure she'd recover either. "Athletes bounce back from injuries all the time," Harper said, doing her best.

"I know."

They were done talking. Harper reached for Grace's hand.

Later that afternoon, Harper gave Grace a ride to church.

"I want to ask Father Eric for a blessing," Grace said. She was unable to drive her stick shift.

For an hour, Harper ran errands and then returned to the parish. Groceries for the dinner she'd make Grace filled the backseat. In the car, she fiddled with the radio stations until finally deciding to go inside. She entered through the front, two tall red doors that met in the form of an arch leading into the sanctuary.

Inside, Grace was nowhere to be found. In fact, nobody was anywhere to be found. Harper stood alone near an altar surrounded by blue candles. One on the end was lit. She stopped near the parish hall to admire the organ's artful detail. She touched the dusty hardwood.

Suddenly, a man's cough. It came from the confessional. Beneath the drape, Grace's feet—two small Nike tennis shoes with a pink swoosh. Harper, startled, immediately felt intrusive.

She quickly bolted from the church and waited for Grace in the car.

God was nowhere to be found when the surgeons scrubbed up the morning Grace went under the knife. Everyone's worst fears did come true; the minute the anesthesiologist injected the juice into her IV, Grace's tennis career ended.

They ceremoniously burned Grace's tennis bag and all its contents on a drunken night at the Fiji house. It was a cleansing, what Grace needed to do, she said. The balls exploded like popcorn. The graphite melted like taffy. And they howled like wolves at the wonder and release.

In the days that followed, the girls spent much of their time at a secret apartment they rented off campus with Grace's leftover scholarship money. They furnished it sparingly and bought the essentials from IKEA. The low-lying Malm bed, a striped sofa and a small bistro table with chairs. And, of course, candles. Lots of them.

With the door locked and the blinds drawn, they disappeared for hours into each other, escaping the communal nosiness of the Gamma house. Occasionally on weekends, they even spent the night. It was their refuge, a place they could go and not worry.

Besides hunkering down in their sacred studio, sucking on each other's toes and fumbling into each other's panties, outside these walls, their life had become a covert mission: hiding their secret. It was a constant act, balancing what they wanted, what they needed to be happy, with what others expected of them. It wasn't easy considering how devoted they were to their pledge class.

For the first half of the fall semester, Harper and Grace dodged date parties and played the ellusive senior apathy card.

"We've got studying to do. We're tired of fraternity parties. We did happy hour last week."

But that only worked so long. Their sorority sisters started asking questions and taking it personal.

"What's your deal?" they asked. "Why are you avoiding us?"

And that was just the tip of the iceberg; they got chastised by everyone, and it only increased as people started gossiping about where they spent so much time. They found themselves wearing glasses and hats anytime they slipped into their love shack. They always checked the parking lot before leaving.

The fact they pulled away from everyone wasn't easy on them or their friends, yet it was all they could do, considering the circumstances.

Eventually, it became too much, and they tried to cram back into the sorority mold once again, which also wasn't easy. During their ruse that semester, whenever they could, they opted for the double date, a painful dance that usually left one of them crying. But still, it was better than being apart; better than checking their watches every five minutes wondering what the other was doing.

Aside from Jamie, who was always a menace in the background during their masquerade that year, there was another guy who proved to be trouble for Harper: Nicholas Zavros, known as Nico.

Despite Harper's objection, Nico's sophisticated air and good looks caught Grace's eye.

"He's a player," Harper said. "He's slept with more Gamma Lambdas than you can shake a stick at." She didn't know this for sure, but passed it off as gospel.

"I'm just doing it for us," Grace would say, her usual line, as she got dressed for their dates. "So we can be together."

Ultimately, Harper would agree—she knew what needed to be done—but she didn't like it. She didn't like Nico's green eyes; she didn't like the size of his pecs; she didn't like it when Grace said she recognized him from the gym when they first met at a mixer.

Born into a Greek shipping family, Nico was an heir to one of the biggest fortunes on the East Coast. But it wasn't his millions that concerned Harper. Grace didn't care about his money. She had plenty of her own, as her trust fund would keep her comfortable for life.

It was his handsome face, his generosity and class, the respectful way he treated her that kept Harper up at night. He turned out to be everything Harper complained he wasn't. A keeper.

On Halloween day, the front porch of their sorority house, a mansion on fraternity row, was loaded with jack-o-lanterns. An orange sign hung from the upstairs balcony that said *Halloween Party Saturday*. It was a party thrown with Beta Phi, another U of A sorority. Sloan Weasle was a Beta Phi and always tried to be chummy with Grace and Harper each fall when their sororities converged for the annual affair.

For the party, Grace had made her choices. Nico would be her date and they would dress in togas. Harper had procrastinated until the day before.

"I'm going stag," she decided.

"No you're not," Grace insisted, and proceeded to hook her up with one of Nico's friends, Brooks, another frat boy from the same stone. Harper had seen Nico and Brooks playing pickup football on the main lawn together, drinking massive steins of beer at Dirtbags Bar, dressed in starched white Polos on their way to Panhellenic Council. They were always together.

"We've got to do this," Grace said. "For us."

The afternoon of the party, a parade of girls came in and out of Harper's room, all wanting to gossip about the night ahead. One of them was Barb, Harper's roommate from Europe.

"I need help," Barb whined. "My cape ripped. Do either of you have a sewing kit?"

Harper looked at Grace, who was stationed out in her room, on the carpet stretching. In unison, they both said, "Sorry."

Towel in hand, Harper headed for the washroom. She wanted to beat the rush, the massive pilgrimage to the showers two hours before any event.

The set of showers, stalls separated by smoky glass, were empty. Harper started with her hair, wetting it sufficiently before lathering up the shampoo. Next, she loaded her loofah with soap and began scrubbing her body. She was bent over shaving her legs when someone entered the adjacent shower. She heard Grace's snigger and then the faucet turn, a familiar squeak all the old spouts made.

On the steamed glass, Grace drew a heart on the partition separating them. Harper put their initials in its center. After Harper rinsed the shampoo from her hair, she pressed her breasts against the glass and then her pelvis. On the other side, Grace did the same. Their tongues met on the glass as their fingers, hooked over the top of the stall, touched above.

It wasn't long before they were interrupted by the roar of girls suddenly looking for a shower.

Playtime was over.

In similar terrycloth robes, their wash buckets dripping on the worn carpet, Grace and Harper went their separate ways after their shower. They split up at the sleeping porch, headed to their respective rooms. The quarters for the president were on the far end of the north wing, and Harper's room was on the south end of the house near the staircase.

As Harper got to her room, she ran into Barb, who was wearing Harper's blond afro wig.

"Where did you…" Harper started to ask. She stopped when she noticed Barb was also laced into her roller-skates.

"I hope you don't mind," Barb said, wheeling by. "Grace said you wouldn't."

Harper stood motionless. Speechless.

Using the walls to stabilize her, retro Barb made her way down the hallway and disappeared around the corner.

Instantly, Harper feared the worst. Barb had rooted through her closet to find what she was wearing. The seven steps to her bedroom felt like seven miles. Her feet could have been made of lead, and everything around her faded into gray.

On her desk, amidst other costume pieces—a green St. Paddy's hat, bunny ears and handcuffs—her European photo album was wide open.

Slowly, a horrified Harper shut the door and sat down. Her hand shook. It was open to Paris, a shot Barb took of Harper on the phone. The damaging photos of Grace and Harper were sticking halfway out the back.

Harper closed her eyes and said a small prayer. Please God. Please.

Had Barb gone any further?

Had she seen anything else? Her face had revealed nothing.

If Barb had seen the sexy pics, Harper thought, wouldn't she have left it open where she stopped? Or put it back in the closet? Or maybe she didn't see anything?

These were questions to which there were no answers, so

she tried to have faith that their secret was still safe. Putting the album together, Harper thought, was an awful idea, and keeping it at the house even more dreadful.

Grace was right. It was too dangerous. I'm a fool, Harper thought. How could I have been so stupid? It wouldn't happen again.

Before heading out that night, wearing a full nun's habit with a fake baby bump underneath, Harper hid the album in her dirty clothes and swore she'd take it to the apartment the following day. That's where it belonged, Harper thought, along with anything else that could jeopardize their reputations, expose the mysterious force that had brought her and Grace together.

Held at the downtown Rotary Club, the venue for the Halloween party was decorated to the hilt. Inside, every lightbulb had been swapped with a black light and a hundred glow-in-the-dark bats hung from the ceiling on elastic bands. Smoke machines filled the room with an eerie fog and cobwebs covered every reachable fixture and doorway.

As the party got started, Barb showed up with Sloan, who was dressed up as a bloodsucking vampire. From the bar, with Grace beside her, Harper watched them arrive together, Barb rolling through the door on Sloan's arm.

Slowly, Harper felt the warmth drain from her face.

She was already on edge with Nico and Brooks in tow, but seeing Barb again, and with her enemy to boot, was almost more than Harper could take. She pulled a dripping beer from the trough of chilling bottles and ordered tequila to go with it.

"Did you let Barb get into my closet this afternoon?" Harper asked Grace, throwing back the shooter then biting the lime.

"Yes," Grace said. "She was desperate."

Feeling desperate herself, a grimacing Harper looked at Sloan and Barb again. They were standing near the coat check, still arm-in-arm, laughing hysterically.

"Why do you let Sloan get to you like that?" Grace asked. "Just ignore her."

"You don't understand," Harper sighed. She hadn't told Grace about the album and wouldn't.

"Let's go grab seats," Grace said. The room was filling and so were the tables for dinner.

"Save our spots," Grace said, ditching her purse before racing to the dance floor with Nico.

Harper turned away and set her things down too. Could she really rise above this tonight, she wondered. Having also just started her period, she was like an exposed nerve. Everything sensitive. On high alert.

She leaned Grace's and Nico's chairs against the table, indicating they were taken, and then slammed the rest of her beer.

"Come on," Brooks said when "Bust a Move" started. He grabbed her hand and led her beneath the disco ball.

Even though she was in a state, Harper forced herself to dance, trying to make the best of it. Purposefully, she kept her back to Grace and Nico, dancing a few feet away.

Finally, two songs later, the tequila made its way to her bloodstream and Harper let go. She closed her eyes on the dance floor and allowed the rhythm move her.

When dinner was announced, the DJ transitioned to something jazzy and Brooks and Harper headed to their table, where Grace was deep in conversation with Nico.

Harper was alarmed to see Barb and Sloan planted in their chairs.

"These are our seats," Harper protested.

"Sorry," Barb barked. "Not anymore." She pointed to another table. "There are seats over there."

Steam may've actually blown from Harper's eardrums and Brooks apparently could see it.

"Come on. Let's just—"

He was interrupted by Sloan. "Don't worry," she said, a line of dry blood dripping from her vampire mouth. "We'll keep an eye on Grace. Make sure she behaves."

At Sloan's condescension, Barb snorted.

Harper looked to Grace for backup, but she was still busy chatting with Nico, oblivious.

"Whatever," Harper snapped, flashing on the open photo album. "Let's go." She grabbed Brooks' hand, suddenly wanting affection as they headed to another table.

After dinner, Harper scanned the room for Grace, who was nowhere to be found. Their seats at the table were empty. Brooks busied himself with a group of fraternity brothers at the bar and she went in search of Grace.

She looked under each bathroom stall. She checked the foyer where partygoers bobbed for apples and were having their way with the popcorn cart.

Grace and Nico were nowhere to be found.

On her way back to Brooks, Harper noticed the patio door was ajar. Through the jade glass above the handles, she saw fire flames.

Her body followed her curiosity.

Outside, couples were gathered around a fireplace built into a worn brick façade on the edge of the courtyard. At first glance, there was still no sign of Grace. But then Harper suddenly spotted them—Grace and Nico roasting marshmallows on the far end of the patio.

With her hand on her faux pregnant belly, Harper watched them intently. Almost stalker-like. They were making s'mores. Pulling his marshmallow from the fire, Nico blew on it and then held it up for Grace. Carefully, she took a bite and he finished it. She then fed him a piece of graham cracker and gave herself one.

Harper's heart leapt from her chest.

This loaded exchange continued as Nico broke off a chocolate square and slid it into Grace's mouth. When Grace playfully bit Nico's roasting stick, Harper stepped back. Things around her started to fade. She took several more steps backward when Grace licked the chocolate off his index finger.

How could this be happening?

Emotion overwhelmed Harper like the swell of a tsunami, slow at first and then with irreversible devastation. As it consumed her, Harper wished it would carry her to the depths of the ocean and leave her there to drown.

With measured steps, Harper backed up until she reached the main doors.

Spinning, in shock and on the edge of drunk, she turned and rushed out of the party.

"Lady In Red"
Chris De Burgh

The Valley Debutante Ball fell on a blistery Saturday that year, just days before Christmas. In a champagne-colored, floor-length gown, Harper rode with her grandparents to the soiree at the Phoenician Resort. As post-debs, it was Harper and Grace's responsibility—or rather, obligation—to attend each year. It had been three years since they'd been presented.

The valet winked and offered his hand as Harper stepped out of the car. It made her feel sexy. Straight. She'd worn her hair down, soft and easy, and around her neck were the pearls her dad gave her for her debutante ball years before.

Inside the foyer of the grand ballroom, she turned quickly when she saw Sloan near the coat check. Even though she tried to dodge her, Sloan spotted Harper, waved and headed her way.

Like her mom, The Bitch, Sloan's stringy brown hair was pulled so taut it made her eyes slant awkwardly. The in-your-face diamonds were gaudy, Harper thought, and the lacy dress she wore with its rough edges matched her personality.

"Hello Sister Harper," Sloan said, giving her an air kiss and a fake hug, a very light tap on the back with no body contact.

"Where's Grace?" Sloan asked, looking behind Harper. "I've never seen you girls apart. It's weird."

"She's on her way."

"You two sure are connected at the hip these days," she said, spinning around her new Tiffany engagement ring.

Harper rolled her eyes and searched the grand foyer for Grace.

"Did you hear I got engaged? Mark finally popped the question."

"I did. Congrats," Harper said. "Are you pregnant or something?"

"Very funny."

Harper wasn't laughing.

Grace arrived. As if Harper had stuck cotton in her ears, everything was silenced when she saw Grace at the door. She moved through the room on Dean's arm like a celebrity. Watching her, Harper was weightless, hovering an inch off the carpet.

With her blond hair in a French twist, Grace was polished, her beauty crushing. Harper worked her way through the crowd of people. Between faces, she could see Grace's smooth curves, the fitted, red dress they'd found together at Saks.

From twenty feet away, Grace spotted Harper too. Grace's smile was measured and captivating. Across the high-ceilinged lobby, Grace's eyes revealed things they shouldn't have. In a room full of those conditioned to notice glances, intonations and long embraces, Grace obviously didn't care.

Grace looked Harper up and down as she approached. "Stunning," Grace said, touching her forearm. "Absolutely stunning."

The lights dimmed, signaling everyone to their seats. Extravagantly decorated, the ballroom was an ocean of white. Fish swam around in the flower vases, their colorful fins graceful in the water. Harper had learned the hard way that the fish—bettas—are vicious and must be kept in separate bowls. Like so many in the ballroom, they tear each other to shreds when given the opportunity.

Back to the wall, she sat by her grandparents, who greeted old friends nearby while she freshened her lipstick. From across the room, she caught Grace's eye as she lined her lips. She scooted over one setting so they, as always, had an uninhibited view.

During the debutante presentation, Harper flirted with Grace; she was a hundred feet away, but it felt like inches. They were the only two people in the room as they played their little game—Grace blew kisses while Harper licked the salty rim of her margarita.

The crowd roared and the debutantes, girls who'd known and gossiped about each other their whole lives, walked off the stage. Harper clapped and smiled at her grandfather, Papa, who'd cranked his neck to blow her a kiss. Nonna, leaning back in her chair with her camera, snapped a shot of Harper.

As the debutantes danced, Harper, in her mind, floated above the ball and disappeared into the crystal chandeliers, remembering Grace the night before at the sorority house. Everyone had left for winter break and they had had the whole Gamma mansion to themselves. After lighting mesquite in the old fireplace, they exchanged gifts.

Grace gave Harper a sixteenth century poesy ring from England, one engraved with the French words *autre vous et nul*—You and No Other. Harper, having struggled for months to find the right gift, chose a pair of gold earrings, Lee Brevard Maori Hearts.

"I give you my heart," she said in her card. "You're my everything."

Afterward, they each read Shakespeare's Sonnet Eighteen to one another before christening the chapter room—a daring move even though they were sure everyone was gone. They started on the couch and then moved to a pallet on the Burberry carpet.

Still lost in fantasy, Harper went further into the sky. Grace was calling her again, telling her to keep going, to take her where she'd never been before. A slow wash of pleasure moved over Harper, covering her heart.

Amidst her spell, a lustful trance she'd drifted into a hundred times, she let fear go—until, like a broken window in the night, Harper's fantasy was shattered when she caught eyes with Cilla. Harper hadn't noticed she was sitting beside Grace the whole time.

In Harper's mind, she came crashing down from the sparkling ceiling, knocking over wine, breaking gladiolas in half, and smashing the centerpiece into jagged shards. She and the betta flopped on the table, fighting for their lives.

Cilla's glare burned like acid against her skin. Harper quickly looked back to the dance floor, and then to the stage to gather her composure. She took a deep breath, pressed the coarse napkin to her lips and excused herself to the restroom.

Even walking to the door, she could feel Cilla's eyes boring a hole in the back of her head. The heat told Harper that everyone knew. That she was in serious trouble.

When she grabbed the brass knob, her fingers trembling, Harper stole one more look as she slid into the foyer.

Cilla stared her down until the door separated them.

"Private Eyes"
Daryl Hall & John Oates

In the minutes following the visual confrontation, Harper stepped outside to calm her nerves. Her hands shook; she was short of breath.

Shivering, she tried to convince herself that what had happened wasn't what had happened. Why would Cilla have looked at her with such disgust?

Something was wrong, but she was baffled at what it could be. Maybe Harper had misread her look? Was it really directed at her? Maybe Cilla was daydreaming?

No matter what Harper did, however, she couldn't smother the truth—Cilla was sending her a message, a nasty one she couldn't quite interpret, but one she knew was loaded with anger. And ownership.

As she negotiated her return to the ballroom, Harper promised herself she wouldn't look at Grace for the rest of the night. Not even once. This new strategy would smooth things over, make it all better. Harper was convinced.

Dean startled Harper when he pushed open the door.

"Little peanut," he said, digging in his pocket for a cigar. "What are you doing?"

"Getting some air."

"You've been out here for a long time."

Harper crossed her arms. Had he seen what happened? Had Grace? She moved her attention to the sky.

"It's bloody cold," he said, taking off his coat, putting it over her shoulders. "You must be freezing." Against his leg, Dean opened his Zippo then lit his cigar.

Standing next to him, Harper could feel his warmth, see her breath, proof she was still alive. Cilla's slingshot of animosity hadn't been fatal.

"Are you having fun?"

"A great time," she said, not hiding the sarcasm. "You?"

Together, they walked to the edge of the terrace. "It's just another winter ball," Dean said. "If you've been to one, you've been to them all."

"That's the truth."

Dean blew smoke into the dark outline of the mountain.

"How long are you going to be in town?" Harper asked.

"I'm staying through Christmas. My lease for that house in San Miguel starts Christmas Day, so I can go whenever."

"A psychological sabbatical." Harper sighed. "I could use one of those."

"I bet," Dean said, leaning against the railing. "You should come."

"We will. After graduation."

"Come sooner."

"I wish. If only."

There was a brief moment of silence as they watched the fountain in the distance bubble and splash.

"Do you and Gracie ever think about leaving this place?" Dean asked, blowing smoke rings, even bigger and smokier than Grace's.

"On a psychological sabbatical?"

Dean chuckled. "No, for good."

"For good?" It was a curious question.

"Is all this"—he waved his hand at the building—"ever too much?"

Harper looked at Dean; his question surprised her, as did his mood.

Before she answered, Harper saw Cilla's scowl, felt the sting of resentment for Sloan. She hated this town. In her mind, she saw fireflies and rolling hills of mustard.

Harper's bottom lip quivered when the truth came out.

"We think about leaving all the time."

And it was true. Harper and Grace had talked about it more than once, quite often during the prior semester when they'd had such trouble walking the tightrope. In years past, the practical side of Grace and Harper planned on buying a house in Tucson after graduation, something cozy in the hills until they both got into grad school, but, as things got more complicated, they often mused about running away in the night, escaping back to Italy. They still dreamt about unloading Grace's trust fund on a Tuscan villa and sending for their things.

Dean took his time with the next sentence, cautiously choosing his words.

"I've known you for a long time, right?"

Harper waited. "Right."

"And. You know I'm always here for you…"

She didn't like his tone, nor the direction he was headed.

"…if you ever need anything," Dean said, more serious than Harper had seen him.

Stepping back, Harper said, "I do. And I appreciate it. Now hurry up with that thing." She looked at the stars. "We're going to miss dinner."

He crushed his cigar in the rocks and then slowly turned back to Harper, somehow getting underneath her skin.

It was then, even before another word was spoken, that she realized he knew.

Dean whispered. "You can tell me anything."

Immediately, everything around him turned black.

Harper could hear dogs barking in the distance.

When Harper finally found words, they came out through a mouthful of gauze. "What are you talking about?" she asked.

Dean grabbed her hand. Gently. "You can trust me," he said.

Harper didn't feel the emotion coming, but there was something about his touch that made her collapse.

Neither Harper nor Dean spoke another word. In the cold night, as the fountain gushed water high into the sky and she cried in his arms, they didn't need to.

"My Boyfriend's Back"

The Angels

"Meet me at the car in fifteen minutes," Harper wrote on a wilted cocktail napkin, the letters bleeding. Through a waiter, she sent it to Grace when Cilla left the table after dinner.

They had to escape.

Grace was waiting in her black Mercedes when Harper got to the front drive. Before she got in the car, Harper decided not to mention her mother's razing glare. Christmas was two days away and she didn't want to spoil the holiday. Besides, by the time she ate her last bite of lobster and finished her wine, Harper convinced herself what happened with Cilla was nothing, a misunderstanding.

Her cryptic conversation with Dean was something else.

"Is Dean meeting us at Ernie's?" Harper asked, turning down the music.

"I didn't invite him. I just ducked out without saying goodbye to anyone."

"Did he say anything to you earlier?" Harper asked, still nervous, staring out the window.

"About what?"

It wasn't the right time, Harper decided, and she was sure she could trust him.

"About when he is leaving for Mexico."

"No," Grace said, turning into the parking lot. "I think he's staying through New Year's. Mummy's having a party."

That night at Ernie's could've been any other and it was just what Harper needed—anonymity and more alcohol. The jukebox was waiting for them in the corner, the usual patrons were in their places and the same cloudy haze hung near the ceiling stained with cancer and asbestos. The perfect place to disappear.

Harper picked the corner table, their usual spot, and ordered two beers while she watched Grace, with her long stride, make a beeline for the music.

The light from the jukebox illuminated Grace's face as she worked the controls, searching for the right songs. From their table, she could see Grace's voluptuous frame. With her hand on her hip, Grace tapped the glass in satisfaction—she'd found a good one.

When Olivia Newton-John's "Physical" came through the speakers, Harper could tell by the way Grace held her head that she was smiling. Over her shoulder, she looked back at Harper.

A sexy punch of adrenaline rushed through Harper's body before she sighed and lifted her beer. It had been a rough night and Cilla's scowl still troubled her. No matter how much she drank, she couldn't escape it.

The air changed when Grace approached and "Private Dancer" started.

"Good one." Harper flirted, remembering the boots Grace had worn two months prior when she'd given Harper an early birthday present—another striptease, this time to Tina Turner. Diamond earrings and high-heeled boots were all she wore as Harper's private dancer.

As Tina sang, Grace smiled and swung her hips. Harper could smell her perfume.

"I thought you'd remember."

"How could I forget?"

Closely, Harper watched Grace push quarters in the pool table and squat to gather the balls. Hanging on a gold chain, her Gamma pendant fell perfectly in her cleavage, flanked by each breast.

When Harper handed Grace the pool triangle, she told her she didn't want to stay until last call. There was no confusion when Grace grabbed it and stood. Captured.

"Me neither," Grace said, walking slowly in her direction, Grace's thick accent as familiar as the songs coming from the jukebox.

Harper pulled her in.

The taut line between them was cut when Harper looked over Grace's shoulder and saw the devil come through the door.

"Jamie just walked in," Harper said. She smirked and gave him and his buddies a slow, beauty pageant wave. "Why are they here? Of all places?"

"Mummy must've told him we still come here," Grace said. "She found a receipt in my pocket last time I was home. Said this was a dreadful place for us to hang out."

As Grace turned to the boys, Harper stared at the swoop of her dress—Dean's words and Cilla's eyes still smoothing themselves out in her mind. She lit a smoke before saying hello.

Jamie kissed Grace and introduced his clan from college, frat boys he'd brought home from Stanford.

"This is Grace," he said, yanking her in with one arm, spraying a circle around her.

Jamie was an Ivy Leaguer who had grown into a tall, tan, runner-type, who loved his pedicures and manicures as much as he enjoyed his immaculately tweezed eyebrows.

Harper rolled her eyes, reached for the pool stick and took a shot. Anything Jamie said made her curdle. She finished her cigarette from a few feet away while Grace told him about the ball. Over the music, Harper could hear the words *wanker*, *pretentious* and *drunk* fly out of her mouth.

While Harper smoked, she scanned the dingy room, envisioning the regulars dressed up for the debutante ball. The car salesman in the corner, Jimmy, sipping on mai tais with umbrellas, would choose a tux with tails. His shirt would be wrinkled. Betty, the token grandmother who could drink anyone under the table, would wear shiny taffeta. She'd bring her Betty Boop purse even though the clasp was broken, its lips opened like a wide-mouthed bass on the bar.

Harper smashed her cigarette into the ashtray as she watched Jamie and Grace interact. She cursed him for showing up, for being so handsome, for who he was in Grace's life.

Something had to be done to take him out.

When a large pack of girls marched in, Harper went to the jukebox with a five-dollar bill to monopolize the mood. She slid it in and began choosing some of their staples, looking for some new gems, ones neither of them had discovered. There weren't many of those. She played "Leave Him Out Of This" by Steve Wariner.

Through the glass' reflection, Harper watched Grace dig bobby pins from her hair. As she talked to Jamie, slowly, as if she knew Harper was peeking, Grace set them down one by one with a shitty grin.

Barbara Mandrell. "(If Loving You Is Wrong) I Don't Want To Be Right."

With her hands fixed on the edges of the jukebox, Harper tried to focus on the music, and what her next message would be. But it wasn't easy. As Grace's French twist came down, she looked less and less like the Grace she'd known years before when they used to ride bikes barefooted through the neighborhood as young girls.

The room heated as Grace's wavy hair fell to her shoulders, turning her into the woman Harper now knew in the darkness, the woman whose hot breath she craved more than her own. Harper closed her eyes and let Ernie's fill with music. Along with the cigarette smoke, she could smell innocence lost burning up and curling into the sky as her songs, dedicated to Grace, played.

The next song, one for Jamie, was loud and obnoxious, just like him. "I Hate Everything About You" by Ugly Kid Joe. The song, starting out like a ballad, dove quickly into its venomous lyrics.

Grace smiled at this one, glancing at Jamie, who was chatting with his buddies a few feet away, clueless.

Harper fed the jukebox every dollar and quarter she had, and like every other night, it was hungry. She heard the silver slide down its throat, felt the warmth it exuded, the fire against her fingertips, the inferno burning in its belly. As she flipped through the songbooks, Harper searched for heartache, for healing, for aphrodisia.

She tried to concentrate on the jukebox and the muted lights that lit its curvy trim instead of the force of Grace, pulling at her from behind. She'd stood there many times before, searching for a song to tell Grace that she was her cherry pie or, with a little help from Madonna, that Harper was crazy for her.

But this time was different. This time it really mattered.

With the push of two buttons, Jamie would disappear and Harper would be all she saw.

"Pressure"
Billy Joel

Jamie worked on getting closer to Grace all night. After each drink, he got better with his hands, with his charming quips. When she could, Harper moved between them like a chaperone, her teeth gritted.

After Harper scratched on the eight ball, she knew it was a good time to escape.

"Nice shot Harper." Jamie raised his glass and looked at the corner TV.

"Go to hell, Simons," Harper barked.

She smiled, but hated him. She'd beaten him plenty of times. Her mouth watered as she hung her stick—she wanted to spit on the ground, and onto his fancy leather shoes.

The lights hummed in the bathroom; orange paint and fluorescent lights didn't go well together, and grape Popsicles were never the same after management installed an automatic deodorizer above the sink, hoping to mask the grime living deep in the old tile.

Hurrying, Harper already had her gown partially pulled up as she closed the door. She had to get back before the next song started; her set was nearly over. As Harper squatted, she thought about the ball and how different the bathrooms were at the Phoenician—the attendants, the marble, the linen towels. She could sit on their seats.

Harper was just finishing when she heard the bathroom door swing open. *Swish, floump.* She listened, but didn't hear any footsteps. No one walked into the other stall, so she bent over and saw Grace's freshly-painted toenails, shiny and plum, in her strappy shoes by the sink.

Grace.

Harper unlocked the door and peeked out. There she was, leaning casually against the dryer with her hands behind her back.

"Hi." Grace's seductive draw ripped Harper at the seam.

"Hi."

With one hand on Harper's shoulder, Grace pushed her back in the stall and slammed the door with her foot. Her saliva sizzled when her lips met Harper's like an alcoholic to scotch, frantic and dangerous. Dependent. Addicted. Grace's warm hand moved to Harper's neck, pulling her inside.

As Grace's fingers slid under Harper's dress, the bathroom door swung open again. *Swish, floump.*

Harper flinched, and then smacked the toilet paper dispenser dotted with cigarette burns. The girls muffled nervous laughter and froze as a flash of green walked past their stall. Both were silent, just stood facing each other, Harper's breast in Grace's hand. They waited for the click of the lock before running for it.

Their steps were fast out of the bathroom and they split up at the dartboard—Grace veered to the jukebox and pulled out a handful of change. This time she moved through the music like she knew what she was looking for. Harper tried to act casual on her approach to the boys, walking slowly, counting the linoleum squares on the ground.

They'd never planned on taking it this far.

As she got closer, Jamie met Harper near the shuffleboard table. "My friends think you're hot," he said. "Especially Mitch."

"Really?"

The drink couldn't get into Harper's hands fast enough. As she walked past Jamie, he laughed, cackled really, and fiddled with his belt, which was holding up expensive Italian slacks. The pants, like his silk shirt, were perfectly tailored to his body.

Jamie stopped her again and put his arm along her shoulder. "So," he said, chewing on a straw, "talk to me about Grace."

In the past, he rarely pumped Harper for information. She didn't like answering him before, and this time it made her queasy enough that she had to lean into the chair for balance.

"What do you mean?"

"You know what I mean."

He was right and he had just enough alcohol in him to raise the subject.

"What do you want from her?" Harper asked.

Harper's head hurt, a slow building headache as she played an endless slideshow from the night—Cilla's eyes, the smell of Dean's cigar, the crowd clapping for the debutantes standing shoulder to shoulder on the stage.

"I don't know. For years, we've been doing the same thing, and I just don't know what she wants," he complained, watching ESPN highlights, adjusting his textured highlighted hair.

"She never talks about it," Harper said, reaching for a jar of sand above the shuffleboard.

"Riiiight," he chastised. "Like you don't talk about it. She's only been in love with me since...what, third grade?"

"Are you crazy?"

Jamie rolled his eyes and shot her an I-know-I'm-right look.

"Why are you always such a prick?" she spat, not believing the words made it to her lips.

"Excuse me?"

"You think every woman wants you," she added. "Grace isn't in love with you. Not by a long shot."

"You're just a resentful bitch who's always had this weird possessive thing for Grace. You're like her jealous girlfriend."

Jamie put his fingers up to insinuate quotes around the word *girlfriend.*

"Fuck off." Her palms sweaty, Harper began sanding for a new game.

Jamie, again, laughed obnoxiously. "Whoa," he chastised, "I hit a nerve."

"I'm just protecting her."

"From what?" He laughed harder now. "What a load of bullshit."

"You're a total womanizer. Just like your dad"—it felt good to hit below the belt—"and everyone knows it."

Jamie stopped, put his hands on his hips. "I'm glad you fell from the jungle gym. You've always been a cunt."

Completely shocked, Harper's rage paralyzed her as Grace approached carrying a tray of drinks. Her eyes narrowed. "What the hell's going on?"

"Nothing," Jamie lied. "We're just playing around."

Harper stared him down, her fists clenched.

As Harper continued covering the board with sand, her blood pressure off the charts, she saw the woman in the green dress return from the bathroom. Grace and Harper both watched her jump onto a barstool and whisper something to her friend.

When they looked over, Harper averted her eyes to the small Christmas tree in the corner, its body draped with lights too big for its branches. Like a cruel game, each limb was bent to its limit. Ready to snap.

Later that night, after three more rounds of drinks, the beer bottles lined up like a college frat party, quietly, Jamie approached Harper before she took her final shuffleboard shot.

"Okay," he said, trying to diffuse the bomb wired between them, "let's just forget about all this. Truce?" He stuck out his hand.

Harper took a deep breath, looked at his outstretched arm, then took her shot, knocking his puck off the table.

"Stay away from her."

Seeing the two of them together again, Grace hurried over. As she walked up, Jamie spun around and spanked Grace's ass.

Without hesitation, Harper slammed her bottle down onto the table, spraying beer everywhere, and stormed after Jamie. Grace was the one in shock now as Harper grabbed him by the shirt.

"Don't you ever slap her again you mother fucking piece of shit."

Getting between them, Grace broke it up before it went any further. "Harper. Stop."

"How can you let him treat you like that? Like a piece of meat."

Jamie was laughing again, his MO for the night. His buddies were gathered around too, trying to make sense of it all.

With serious effort, Grace dragged Harper toward the exit. "She's had too much to drink. I'm taking her home," Grace said, grabbing their purses.

"I have not!" Harper yelled, the straps of her ball gown off to her elbows.

Looking around the bar, Harper saw that the patrons were silent, watching the drama unfold at the shuffleboard table and now at the door.

The show continued in the parking lot as Grace tried to get Harper in the car.

"I'm not done with him!" Harper roared. Grace pushed her into the passenger seat.

Once she got the doors locked and the car started, Grace peeled out of the strip mall where Ernie's was the anchor tenant.

"What the hell was that?" Grace demanded.

"He fucking slapped your ass. You should've heard the things he was saying earlier."

"Harper. You can't go around acting like that," Grace said, heatedly. "It was embarrassing."

"Embarrassing?" Harper's breathing was labored. "I embarrass you?"

"That's not what I meant."

"Why do you like him? He's such an arrogant douche bag. What does he have that I don't?"

"Is that what this is about? You think I want to be with Jamie?"

Harper's anger dissolved into tears. "I don't want to lose you. And I fucking hate him."

"Sweetie, you have NOTHING to worry about. I love you. I

want to be with you. Not him. Remember, it's all about us."

With these words, Harper flashed on Grace and Nico by the fire at Halloween, the way she flirted, the way she fed him a cracker and licked his finger.

"Who'd want to be with someone like him anyway?" Grace asked. "Jamie's a prissy prima donna."

Harper put her head on Grace's shoulder.

"We've got to be careful," Grace whispered, kissing the top of Harper's forehead.

"I don't feel good," Harper mumbled.

As they drove through the golf course together, they watched the dashboard temperature gauge drop near the lake. The slippery haze emanating from the distance was as cool as the summer's first rain, giving the greens its nightly nourishment and the water an ominous breath of moisture.

Over the purring engine, Harper could hear the CDs shuffling in the trunk disc player; Grace was still searching for the right song.

Grace was soft in the headlight's reflection and, looking at her, Harper wondered how they'd ever fallen in love. Two girls. Two sorority sisters. They weren't supposed to be lovers.

Whatever were they going to do?

"How did this happen?" Harper asked. "How did we get here?"

Grace downshifted into second as she turned onto her street. "I don't know and—" she smiled, shook her head—"I don't care."

Harper reached for Grace's hand on the stick shift and raised it to her lips.

"I love you," Grace said, her Donna Karan perfume still strong. As Harper kissed where their fingers intertwined, Grace looked down with eyes Harper rarely got in the company of others.

"We'll die old maids, Bella, I promise," Grace said. "No one will ever know."

"The Carnival Is Over"
Dead Can Dance

Considering what happened with Cilla, combined with her bizarre conversation with Dean, she should've listened to her intuition and gone home. But she was drunk and Grace insisted she stay. Grace had an early morning riding lesson and she desperately wanted them to sleep in each other's arms.

Next to Grace in her twin bed, Harper woke from a nightmare in the middle of the night and then again about an hour later, sweaty and terrified. In her dreams, she was running from a Doberman, nearly escaping before it caught her. The first time in the driveway, the second time on the front steps. Each time Harper got closer to safety. Harper could see Nonna in the window while the dog pulled her toward the desert, where others were waiting, howling. Even after Harper woke up beside Grace, she could still feel the rocks against her back, the dog's coarse fur under her fingernails.

At some point when it was still dark, Harper got up to pee. In her tired stupor, she hadn't bothered to look at the clock. She'd purposefully set the alarm for five, planning to leave on Grace's bike before the house stirred. It was Christmas Eve.

From one nightmare to the next, Harper would never forget

Cilla's deep voice early that morning as she stood in the bathroom pulling up her underwear, half asleep.

"Wake up. You're late." Harper looked at the small clock glowing by the sink and saw that it was nearly seven.

Standing in the dark, just behind the door, feet away, Harper didn't move as Cilla shook Grace awake. There was urgency in her voice.

Harper held her breath as she watched the light come on in the adjacent room, able to see it all through an inch-wide crack at the doorjamb.

"What?" Grace said, disoriented. "Where did you get that key?" She looked around for Harper.

"Get up," Cilla said, making room on the bed. "We need to talk."

Harper had heard Cilla badger Grace before—skipping Mass, leaving dirty dishes in the sink, staying out too late—but immediately Harper feared the worst. This felt different.

"I found this card from Harper in your organizer," she said. "When I came in your room yesterday, it was sticking out."

The glare at the ball had been directed at her, Harper suddenly realized.

As Harper waited for more, she knew it was her Christmas card that Cilla found; the one she'd given Grace before they left Tucson with the sonnet folded inside. Harper saw Grace tuck it into her Daytimer the morning they pushed off.

"You know,"—Harper heard the envelope opening—"this is really disturbing." Cilla paused, for effect. "I think you should be leery of Harper. Some of the things she wrote here are not the sort of things friends with normal feelings write each other." She talked to Grace like she was still a child.

"How dare you go through my things!" Grace yelled.

When Grace broke her silence, Harper brought her hands to her face and covered her mouth.

Cilla ignored Grace's attack and continued with a sharper tone, a higher volume. "Giving you a love poem? Saying that you're everything? That she's never loved anything more? This is disgusting," she said. "And it isn't right."

"Mother!"

"She parties too much, and," Cilla paused again, "I hear she does drugs. She's a terrible influence and I don't want you hanging out with her anymore."

"What are you talking about?" Grace shouted even louder.

Shaking now, Harper wedged herself further behind the door.

"Besides all that, Sloan's mom recently told me some things that have made me question Harper...and then to find this letter? You need to stop spending time with her." The bed squeaked as she stood.

Stop spending time with me? Harper thought. A terrible influence? How could she say those things?

"I'm going to flush this down the toilet," Cilla said.

Grace jumped from her bed and stopped her mother as she touched the bathroom door. Harper braced herself.

"Don't you dare," Grace said slowly. Harper heard paper rip. "Get out of my room!"

Cilla conceded, and finally turned to leave. Her voice was still loud from the door when she added, "Grace listen. Mrs. Weasle told me there are rumors swirling around the university about you and Harper. Someone found photos or something. I know, it's absurd." Cilla dismissed the gossip immediately. "Quite frankly, though," she paused, "we're afraid Harper is a lesbian."

BOOM.

Everything exploded. Imploded. And Harper caved into herself.

"The feelings she has for you are not normal or healthy. Need I remind you what Granddaddy's will says?"

Harper immediately flashed on old, fat women she'd seen sitting at Ernie's bar, PE coaches from her past and scary dykes at truck stops she'd seen in the bathroom during family road trips.

And then she saw her second-grade teacher, Miss Jensen, her blond hair and tan legs, all the afternoons Harper stayed after school to help grade papers.

Harper suddenly pictured the first time she had sex with Rich. He had been gentle and afraid. They both were as they lost their virginity that summer night, when the temperature was high and they decided they were in love. To her, his dick was a like an animal Harper had never seen before—not an object of carnal desire, which she neither wanted nor despised. She wanted to put it in a box and study it, not have sex with it.

Harper continued to fade. Grace and Cilla were suddenly far away. Muffled now, a distant fight she could barely hear, Grace screamed at her mother. "What the hell are you talking about? That is ridiculous!" Grace yelled. "And I'm an adult, MOTHER. You can't tell me who to be friends with. Get out of my goddamn room."

Harper hadn't heard Grace swear at her mom before and she'd never seen her that angry. Behind the towels, Harper began crying. How could they be saying such horrible things?

In all the years, Harper had never put a word on what she felt. And hearing it this way made her sick.

After Cilla stormed out, Grace slammed the door and stuck the desk chair under its handle. She flipped on the TV and turned up the volume.

Harper's face was soaked in sweat when she dropped to her knees at the toilet. Grace held Harper's hair as she spit into the bowl, apologizing for what her mom said.

When Harper was done dry-heaving, she wiped her mouth and leaned into the wall between the vanity and the sink. Sitting across from her, only three feet away, Grace was distant and pale. As traumatized as Harper.

Ten minutes later, Harper cut through the laurel bushes along the Dunlop driveway, escaping through the neighbor's yard. Grace picked her up a block away in her riding outfit. Grace was tucking her breeches into her field boots when Harper jumped into the convertible.

"Tell me you destroyed those photos," Grace said, as pallid as the overcast sky.

"They're at the apartment," Harper said, even whiter than Grace.

"What could she have been talking about?"

"I don't know," Harper said

Grace let out a heavy sigh. "I'm sorry you had to hear those things," she said.

Harper was in a daze, lost in the morning horizon. Everything was coming unraveled. And fast.

"What are we gonna do?" Harper finally muttered.

"Don't worry," Grace promised. Firm. "I'll clear this up."

Grace grabbed Harper's hand as they pulled into her driveway. "Everything will be fine." She declared, "Of course you're not a lesbian."

"Fire"

The Pointer Sisters

Harper was on edge all day, even with the gaiety of the season upon them. She kept the landline cordless phone in her back pocket all day in case Grace called, and helped Ana and Nonna, who was wearing a bejeweled Christmas sweater, dress the tree with tinsel.

By four, there was still no word from Grace. She hoped they could talk before dinner; there was a chance they'd run into each other at the country club.

Every year from the time they had met, Grace had sneaked over on Christmas Eve and knocked on Harper's window right as the clock struck twelve. It had become a tradition of sorts, as much as anything for her—like stockings, the tree, even Santa.

Would Grace show up this time?

After dinner at the country club, where she saw Grace from a distance as they were leaving, Harper paced her bedroom in wait.

Would she come?

What would they do about Cilla?

Would she eventually get in touch with Harper's mom?

How far had the gossip spread?

The more Harper agonized and replayed the dreadful events of the morning, the more she panicked.

I'm not a dyke, Harper insisted. The rumor was absurd. Grace and I are just friends. Best friends. Things may've gone further than most friendships, but we certainly weren't gay.

Around eleven, Harper dug her European journal out of her hope chest and reorganized Grace's letters, Italian parchment bound with string. In her room, she lit a candle and slid into a chair next to her bay window overlooking the moonlit desert. Just having the journal, which was scratched to hell, in her hands stirred all kinds of emotions; longing mostly, but also a bit of melancholy. And now fear.

She started at the beginning. Carefully, she read each page, not missing a word, a scribble, a splash of coffee, a smudge of ash. She analyzed the marks, the scribbles, the drawings—what was my thought process, my sublimated message, she wondered. She struggled to make sense of it all, the layers underneath the entries.

She dog-eared the most evocative passages, intending to go back and reread them. How had things ended up this way? The two of them in love.

As Harper read, her mounting desperation was overwhelming. The swelling inside her chest made it hard to breathe. The room was getting smaller.

Lying there, she prayed the signs were wrong. She and Grace were in love, yeah, but it was a fluke, a cosmic accident. She definitely wasn't a lesbian.

With an Exacto blade, Harper sliced the marked pages out of her journal and wadded them into balls before tossing them to the floor. They littered the room like pages cast from a manuscript—a character, a plotline axed.

Even though her parents were asleep, she locked her door when she dug even deeper into her hope chest and pulled out her childhood diaries. Religiously, she'd written in them every night during her youth, even if just a few sentences. It had been mostly a log of sorts, a record of her daily activities. But as she got older, the pages began to pull her further in, unintentionally exploring emotion and motivation in telling ways.

Thumbing through diary after diary, Harper was shaken by Grace and her presence on the pages. She was everywhere.

After she was done scrutinizing her old diaries, Harper christened a new journal, its pages crisp like a stack of fresh dollar bills.

I'm lost, Harper scribbled. *Completely lost. I have no idea which way to go. Grace is everything.*

Harper chewed on the end of her pen, worrying about what it all meant, even about committing it to paper.

How could her mom say such horrible things? What if I lose Grace? What if she never wants to see me again?

As Harper wrote, the thought of being without Grace was so devastating, she could hardly write the words. She vowed, on the pages of her journal, to do anything she could to keep Grace close—even if it meant running away.

When she was done, Harper cut those new pages out, too, and with her shirt, scooped up the crumpled sheets and headed to the garage, where she found a can of lighter fluid under her dad's workbench.

In the powdered dust of starlight, just Harper and the universe, she dumped the papers into the fire pit near the tennis court. The frigid air smelled like the stars.

Will I regret this one day, Harper wondered.

Before she saturated her shame, Harper stood over it and gave herself a final chance. This is it. Once it's done, it's done. There's no turning back.

As Harper breathed, little steam clouds escaped from her mouth. Even in the darkness, she could see the Saltillo tile around the pit's edge, the same tile on the lip of the pool and the courtside gazebo. Carefully, she'd helped her dad lay each Mexican square; she'd watched the measured way he put them in order, the way he used his level, keeping everything straight.

It was finally time.

Harper emptied the can, pulled out a matchbook and stepped back.

Poof.

After an explosive plume, the papers caught ablaze like a firecracker's tail, angry and irreversible. Orange cinders dissolved into the desert sky.

She'd carved out the heart of the European journal, so she decided to burn the whole thing. When she dropped it into the pit, the leather squelched the flames and tried to kill the fire. It knew better than she did—the truth can never be destroyed, no matter how much lighter fluid you put on it. Harper squatted on the edge of the fire pit and watched the words *dying* and *soft* disappear into the red heat of the fire. *My bed is lonely without you.*

Crouching near the dying flames, Harper heard rustling in the shrubs. She looked at her watch; Grace was right on time. Midnight, straight up.

When Grace pushed through the bushes, Harper saw her blond hair shimmering in the firelight. She closed her eyes.

Her prayer had been answered.

In the kitchen, mulled cider had been brewing for hours. Harper rifled through the drawer for a ladle while Grace grabbed two cups. They'd hardly spoken after their long embrace. As Harper filled each mug, she wondered what Grace was thinking, where she was at.

They leaned into the center island and looked at each other. Grace's eyes told Harper what her lips yet hadn't—she was scared. Harper imagined Grace earlier that day on Sebastian, her thoroughbred, rerunning the morning's horror. Like Harper's own instrument of destruction, Cilla's words were an intricate razorblade trying to sever the connection between them, getting deep into the tissue, underneath the muscle of Grace and Harper's union. All day, Harper feared they'd succeeded. The fact Grace had shown up proved they hadn't.

Harper hadn't confessed what she was burning; when Grace asked, Harper told her it was wrapping paper.

Even without asking, Harper knew Grace's journal and

all the other letters she'd given her were at school, safe from her mother's eyes. Harper saw Grace pack them up when she was moving out of the President's suite. Along with the rest of her stuff, they were taped inside a box in the Gamma Kappa basement.

"How was church?" Harper asked.

"Okay. How was your night?"

"All right," Harper said, lying, warming her hands with the mug. "I saw you at the club."

"You did?"

"You were leaving with your parents." Out the window, the twinkling Christmas lights faded into the darkness, automatically shutting off for the night. "Where was Dean?"

"He left this morning, I guess," Grace said, reaching across the island, touching the poesy ring she'd given Harper for Christmas. "When I got back from my lesson, he was gone."

Harper slid off the band and put it on Grace's finger. "Where did he go?"

"Mexico."

"Already?"

Grace shrugged.

"There was a note on my bed saying he was sorry he left without saying goodbye. When I asked Mum why he split, she just rolled her eyes and made a snarky comment. I guess they had a fight or something."

It was at that moment that everything made sense. Dean had seen Cilla pull out her gun and take a shot at Harper at the ball. From a few feet away, he'd watched the whole thing go down. Maybe she'd even vented to Dean beforehand or after, ranting about Harper being a terrible influence, a lesbian. Even though he was Cilla's little brother, Harper was sure Dean defended her.

"Have you talked to your mom,"—Harper stood up straight—"you know, about everything?"

Grace sighed and handed Harper her ring. "A little bit. She tried to get into it in the car, but Dad cut her off. It was a screaming match."

Grace followed Harper into the living room, an intimate

space with ornate art from all over the world. Harper grabbed a pillow and sat near the fireplace, burning with pinion wood.

Out of the corner of her eye, she watched Grace kick off her shoes and jump on the couch next to Harper. Grace rolled onto her back before resting her head in Harper's lap. Looking down, she spread Grace's long hair out on her sweatpants.

There was so much they needed to discuss. Where to go from here. There was no next move, no escape route, no backup plan.

Grace turned onto her side and pulled a bison blanket over them as the movie started. It was the same film they'd watched every year: *A Christmas Story.*

For the next two hours, Harper tried to focus on Ralphie, once again pining for the Red Ryder BB gun, but all she could see was Cilla's glare across the ballroom, her scathing words penetrating her skin...*A lesbian.*

"Hold On"
Sarah McLachlan

Harper split town two days later. Nonna and Papa set sail on a cruise and her folks were headed to Bruges on the 27th—off on another assignment—so there was no reason to stick around Phoenix. Besides, she'd been banished from the Dunlop house and, so it seemed, from seeing Grace at all.

At the market, Harper was careful to get in and get out, terrified she'd see Cilla. And, her detestation for the Weasle family at a new high, she worried about seeing them too.

The day after Christmas, the most depressing day of the year, Grace had sneaked out again while Cilla was sleeping. By the lake in an old sand trap grown over by grass, they lay on their backs and watched for falling stars.

"Don't worry," Grace kept saying, each of them in a puffy winter coat. "Everything will be fine once we get back to school. It will all be back to normal."

At the last minute, Harper signed up for an elective during winter session, a concentrated art class—intermediate ceramics with a wheelthrowing lab—which met four days a week. It would be a good distraction, she thought, and help her pass the time until Grace returned.

Her professor, Ruthie, an old feminist with long gray hair, reminded Harper of her mother when Ruthie first walked into the room—her flowing beaded skirt, linen top rolled to the elbows and worn espadrilles. Ana was more conservative, in dress and in moral code, so it seemed, but they could've been friends, sisters even, she and Ruthie. Their spirits echoed their clothing, free and loose, and each was undeniably sexy.

Beyond Ruthie, the subject matter of the class also sparked Harper's interest. It was always something she'd wanted to learn, ever since sitting on Ana's lap as a youngster when she threw pots.

Grace and Harper planned on living together for their final semester because their posts at the sorority house were finally over. Under Grace, Harper had served as secretary. At the end of the fall semester, they'd picked out the perfect apartment, a Spanish Colonial building right off campus. They chose a two-bedroom, of course, as to not fuel any slow-burning fires, but they'd sleep in Harper's queen-size bed. Grace's twin would be there for show, a silly rigmarole to which they'd become accustomed. They'd mess it up each morning just in case anyone stopped by.

The whole fiasco with Cilla, however, had shifted plans dramatically. After Christmas, Cilla called the rental manager and arranged a separate apartment for Grace in a different building.

"We can be close," Grace had said, playfully mimicking her mother on the phone, "but not too close." As she unpacked boxes in her new apartment, Harper didn't see the humor. She knew she was only hearing half of what had really been said.

"I'll still be at your place every night," Grace promised, reassuring Harper. "Don't worry."

While Grace and Harper were apart, instead of obsessing about Cilla, Harper focused during the day on throwing the perfect pot and at night about what they'd do after graduation. They hadn't yet come up with a plan, so Harper wrote down the details.

They would run away after graduation, this she knew for sure, it was something they'd agreed upon in the grassy sand trap before Harper left. But where would they go? Would they join Dean in Mexico? That was Harper's top choice. Or would they go cross-country and put roots down on the East Coast? Somewhere no one knew them.

At dinner the first night Grace got back—a long overdue date—Harper shared her plan along with a timeline she'd fleshed out on several pieces of paper. Harper laid them on the table at the Moroccan restaurant.

"Boston?" Grace asked, leaning back in her chair sipping mint tea. "New York? Mexico? What are we going to do in Mexico? Get a flat on the beach and drink margaritas all day with Dean?"

"Yes!" Harper cheered. "Yes!"

"Apparently," Grace said, "great minds think alike." She pulled a small note pad from her purse. Her plan was written in a different format than Harper's, much like their disparate personalities, budding professionals that they were. The pre-law major, Grace's notes were written in succinct bullet points with pros and cons. Italy. Dublin. Vancouver. All international. With illustrations, Harper's were organized like the artist she'd always been, with excessive musings about what it would be like, their new life together.

"I don't care where we go, Bella," Grace said, feeding Harper a curried potato across the table, "as long as we're together."

Harper couldn't have agreed more. Despite all the outside pressure, the supposed gossip, everything was going to be fine and they'd make it through.

"Mummy's calmed a bit, too," Grace said, the candlelight flashing in her eyes.

"She has?"

"I think The Bitch made up the photo rumor thing," Grace said decisively. "It was just a coincidence. And then after my mom found the letter"—she chewed her bite—"she just went bonkers."

They spent the night in Grace's new apartment, even though it was disheveled and loaded with unopened boxes.

"Christening a new pad didn't require a bedframe," Grace said, lowering Harper to the mattress, planted firmly on the ground. It had almost been two weeks since they'd made love and they'd both cried about it over dinner, their tears having little to do with unsatisfied libidos.

That night was significant, Harper decided. If they could make it through Scottsdale rumors, they could make it through anything.

Anything, Harper thought.

"Gone Too Soon"

Babyface

Grace's scream woke Harper the next morning. It tore through the drywall like a bullet.

Seconds later, Harper found Grace nude in the kitchen surrounded by packing peanuts. Through the phone's receiver, Harper heard a panicked voice, a man saying Grace needed to come home.

Harper knelt next to her. "What happened?"

Grace didn't respond; it was like she didn't even know Harper was there.

Then suddenly, Grace smashed the handset against the tile, breaking it into pieces. Plastic flew across the room. A battery rolled under the fridge. Harper bit her lip. Whatever it was, it was bad.

As Grace wailed against the kitchen floor, Harper did what she could to console her. She put her hand on Grace's bare back, got her a glass of water, then tissue. Finally, Grace sat up.

"It's Dean," she gasped, hyperventilating. "He's dead."

"What!" Harper gasped.

In its own shock and panic, Harper's body lay down next to Grace. Somehow Harper kept breathing, her heart continued pumping. In the nude, they wept together until Grace was able to tell Harper more.

The Mexican authorities figured Dean was killed instantly in the head-on collision. Even without skid marks on the beaten road, they believed the driver crossed the centerline before smashing into his car. There wasn't much left of his Avanti, nor was there much left of him or the dogs. One of the first people on the scene stole his wallet so it had taken them several days to identify his body. Once they got the car cut open, they found papers in the buckled glove box.

Matthew Dean Dunlop. United States citizen. Los Angeles, California.

Harper held Grace's listless body until she said she had to go, and then helped Grace gather her things.

Harper took over packing after Grace, unable to find her rosary beads, threw a vase against the wall.

"Are you sure you don't want me to come? I could drive you and then turn around? Or I could stay at my parents so I'm close by if you need me?" Harper was desperate.

"I'm sure," Grace said. "I'll let you know the arrangements once they're made."

They both knew why Harper wasn't welcome.

Dean was dead. Dean was dead. Harper said it over and over, but couldn't believe it. She stayed on the same couch all day staring at the TV's black screen, teetering between disbelief and unmanageable distress. How could he be gone?

Much of the day lapsed before Harper tried Grace's cell phone. Even though it was agonizing to keep her distance, Harper knew Grace needed it. Around six, Harper made her first call. At seven, the second. Right before ten, the third.

Grace never answered.

Once she finally fell asleep, Harper dreamt of Dean that night. He was running on the beach, playing with Geisha and Boris in the foamy Mexican surf. His laughs were loud and stretched into the ocean. In her dream, they didn't speak—Dean just winked at Harper before diving into a breaking wave, splashing bright sparks of innocence into the air.

Hundreds of people jammed into Saint Augustine's for the funeral; they spilled into the entry room and out the propped doors. Guests fanned themselves with the program, which was filled with biblical verses and photos of Dean.

In a fog, Harper walked down the aisle toward the casket. It was hard to imagine Dean inside the mahogany box dressed in his favorite khakis and polo; her mind kept straying, imagining his bloody body, crushed and mangled in the wreckage. Harper wondered if Dean saw the truck coming, if he was more concerned about the dogs than himself. If he knew he was going to die.

She kept her eyes lowered and sat a few rows behind the Dunlops, just out of sight. From the back, she could see Grace's head, her blond curls still wet.

A friend sang "Ave Maria" as the family approached the pulpit. After communion, Grace stayed on her knees longer than anyone else in the church. Desperately, Harper wanted to run to Grace and wrap her arms around her shrinking body. The pain was so acute Harper hadn't eaten in days.

The priest called the morning a blessed event. "Dean is with us today, not in body, but in spirit," the Father said during Mass. "He's with us in the same way Jesus is. They're watching us from Heaven."

Sitting by herself, Harper studied the way the morning light scored the stained-glass, a soldered mosaic in the likeness of Mary, wondering if Dean was actually seeing it all unfold, the memorial of his life.

When Harper had wakened that morning, her closet door was ajar. She'd closed it before going to bed, as she always did, but something opened it in the night. She wondered now, sitting in the historic Catholic Church, if Dean had come through it as she slept, pushing it open with the air conditioning. In early daylight, in the stillness of Harper's bedroom, she imagined Dean in his tuxedo—his jacket unbuttoned and bowtie loosened—leaning against the dresser waiting for her to rise.

"Hurry up." Dean clapped. "It won't be complete without you there."

Harper was one of the first to arrive at the reception; caterers were lined up alongside the Dunlop house, in the same spot she used to park when she sneaked through Grace's window in the old days. Harper watched them carry scrambled eggs, fresh fruit and silver bullets of coffee through the garage.

Afraid to go inside, she waited for others to fill the house before paying her respects. Harper knew it would be awkward, so it would be a stealth mission, and she'd only stay a short time.

In the foyer, Harper stood against the wall with a cold Pellegrino as a man played Spanish guitar in the corner. Swirling through the voices in the room, freesia filled the air with a sugary scent, combined with fresh croissant and candle wax.

From that spot, she watched the Dunlop lawyer, Jack Stowe, and his wife come through the front door. As they both kissed Cilla on the cheek, Stowe's polished bolo tie reflected the sun coming through the skylight. Sharp blades of light and destruction sliced the room like a laser as he worked the room.

Harper moved deeper into the house. Grace was near the wet bar. She was talking to a neighbor and excused herself when Harper got close.

"I saw you at the cemetery," Grace said, withdrawing quickly from their embrace. When they caught eyes after the graveside prayer, Grace offered a small smile, one that was difficult to understand. Grace's features were dark and sunken. "I wanted to come over and say hi."

Standing before Grace, Harper missed her even more than she'd realized. "I've so looked forward to this moment," Harper whispered. She slid her hands into her pant pockets and they both looked around for Cilla. "How are you?" she asked, focusing again on Grace.

She shook her head. There were no words. Neither of them could believe Dean was gone.

"It's almost been three weeks," Grace said, running the edge of her sandal along the marble crease on the floor. Her toenail polish was chipped. "A very long three weeks." Because of legalities, it had taken forever to get Dean's body back to the states.

A big Irish woman interrupted; she lifted Grace off the ground when they hugged. Harper stepped aside and brought the bottle of water to her lips.

Through the crowd, Harper saw Cilla in the kitchen.

It was time to go.

After a quick, clumsy goodbye, Harper left through the back. It was quiet in the garden, only the distant sound of car doors shutting, Chopin's "Nocturne" coming from the living room. On her way out, Harper passed Duke's grave, partially hidden behind a row of bougainvilleas. It seemed like only yesterday when Harper and Grace found Duke, their family dog, floating in the pool. Even though it had been years, Harper could still smell and feel the golden retriever's wet fur against her lips from when she tried to give mouth to mouth. Harper and Dean had dug his grave, taking turns with the shovel for nearly an hour.

As Harper stood by the small tree they'd planted in Duke's honor—it was now twenty feet tall—she saw Mrs. Weasle leaning against the hot tub smoking a long Virginia Slims in her sober tweed suit. "How are things?" she hollered.

It was all Harper could do to be polite. "Things are fine," she said, heading in the opposite direction toward the car.

"What are you up to these days?" Mrs. Weasle tapped her cigarette ash into the planter.

Harper stopped, looked at her exit, a wood gate several yards away. "Not much," she said. "Just finishing school."

"That's great, dear. When are you done?" Propped up on her stomach roll, The Bitch's arm supported her smoking hand.

"May."

"Are you seeing anyone?"

Harper took another step. That fucking cunt. "Not really."

The Bitch looked at Harper before throwing her cigarette onto the sidewalk. "Well, don't worry," she said, grinding the butt with her mauve pump. "You'll find Mr. Right one day."

"I'm not worried," Harper said, walking toward the gate, her hand on the latch. "Take care."

It wasn't Harper's social graces that stopped her when The Bitch spoke again, louder and a few steps closer.

"Isn't it great Jamie's come home for Grace?" She watched Harper carefully.

Slowly, Harper's head turned toward the living room, her consciousness capturing every detail. She hadn't seen Jamie; she'd looked for him at the cemetery, and again as the house filled with people, but there was no sign of him.

But now, hovering between Mrs. Weasle and her worst nightmare, Harper finally saw Jamie through the sliding glass door. He was inside. Talking with Stowe. He held a plate of fruit with one hand and Grace with the other.

"Alone"
Heart

Grace was expected back to school midway through the second week of spring classes, so Harper unpacked her apartment. She wanted everything to be as easy as possible. In between gathering syllabi and buying books, Harper unloaded boxes until she got Grace's place in order. Things had to be perfect.

So much had happened since Grace's scream, since the immobilizing news of Dean's death, Harper didn't want there to be any reminders. No shattered glass from her outburst, no smashed phone. With a hanger, she finagled the receiver's battery from under the fridge, and she even put rugs down in the kitchen so Grace's bare feet wouldn't recall the way the tile felt against her legs that morning.

Hanging pictures and breaking down boxes was also therapeutic—anything to keep the image of Jamie's big hand in the middle of Grace's back out of Harper's mind, anything to push away The Bitch's outlandish allegations.

Although the timing was bad, Harper's art class had been a wonderful escape, as had her budding friendship with her teacher Ruthie. They were the only things that got Harper through January. Even though she had a full load her last semester, she signed up for advanced ceramics in the spring anyway.

On the day Grace was to return, a date circled with a yellow highlighter on Harper's calendar, Ruthie asked to see Harper after class.

Harper waited for the other students to leave before approaching Ruthie's desk. Over her spectacles, perched on the end of her nose, Ruthie watched Harper walk the aisle toward her.

"How are you?" Ruthie asked, pulling off her glasses. Two gem-laden cords kept them centered on her chest.

When Harper missed class after Dean died, she had shared with Ruthie the reason why; Harper told her how worried she was about her best friend Grace. Then, about a week later, after Ruthie caught her crying in the bathroom during a break, Harper admitted that she, too, was having a hard time keeping it together.

"All right," Harper said now, setting her books down.

As Ruthie hoisted her body up to sit atop her desk, her bracelets clanged against the wood. "How was the funeral?"

Harper envisioned the flowers on Dean's casket, blue hydrangea, and the fresh dirt piled next to his plot. "It was... sad," she said, tracing the rim of a fired pot on Ruthie's desk. "Very sad."

"How's your friend?"

"So-so, I guess. Haven't seen much of her. She's been busy with her family and stuff, you know."

With her hands, Ruthie reached back and let her aging hair free from the rubber band. Harper was surprised by how different she looked with her hair down; even more attractive. "When will Grace be back?"

"Any minute."

"Any minute?" she asked. "I won't keep you then." Ruthie jumped off the desk and reached into her bag. "Here," she said, jotting a number down. "Call if you need anything. If you need to miss class or," she smiled, "if you're having another meltdown."

Practically jogging, Harper moved as fast as she could

through the student union on her way home. What had only been weeks felt like years and Harper worried about the distance, about the things Grace's mother had said, about the damage that had been done.

Across the street from Grace's building, Harper stopped when she saw Grace through the kitchen window. With childish enthusiasm, she jumped up and down with her backpack.

"Graaaaacie!" she screamed.

Harper took a shortcut, hopped the small perimeter fence and ran through a bed of ivy to get to the door. All worked up, she tried to catch her breath, her cool, before knocking. Finally ready, Harper clenched a fist and lifted her hand, but Grace opened the door before she could knock.

Even though all Harper wanted to do was wrap her arms around Grace, she waited, again, when the door swung open and their eyes met.

"Hi," Harper said, still a little winded.

Grace held out her arms and Harper leapt into them.

Finally, Harper thought.

It was almost the hug she'd been waiting for.

Harper lit candles on the table while Grace warmed bread for dinner. Beyond unpacking her stuff, she had stocked the fridge with Grace's favorite things: persimmons, bangers, strawberry jam, scones, herbed goat cheese. She even made a special trip to the European market for clotted cream.

During dinner, as the girls sat across from each other, there was a cloudy void in Grace's eyes, one that chewed on Harper's insides as they ate.

"How are you doing?" she finally asked.

Grace tore off a hunk of bread. "I don't even know anymore," she said, dipping it in the soup. "Everything's numb." She pulled her arms into her sweater and shivered.

"Are you glad to be back?"

She watched the news over Harper's shoulder. "I'm not really glad about anything to be honest."

Sitting together, they were like old dorm buddies who hadn't seen each other in years, unsure where to pick up. Could she reach across the table and hold Grace's hand? She hadn't dared and hadn't expected the emptiness, the shell of a woman before her. Since they'd gotten together, she'd seen the hollowness before, the distance at unexpected moments, the mysterious tears which sometimes followed. She didn't always understand them, but the energy she was feeling this time was different. There was a dark, unsettling permanence about it now.

They went to bed early. Grace sat on the edge of the mattress for a few moments setting her alarm clock. Gently, Harper slid off her slippers, but kept her pajamas on, following Grace's lead even though they'd always slept in the nude.

After the lights were out, Harper inched her way over. There were so many things about Grace she missed—the sleepy noises she made and the smell of her damp skin under the covers. Harper stopped shy of touching her.

In the darkness, she waited, wanting to ask more of Grace, needing to know what the last month had been like, if it had been a slow burning hell for her too. Harper knew it had. Even though she'd been hurting, Grace's grief was much bigger than hers; it hardly fit in the small space between them.

And Harper needed answers about Jamie. They hadn't spoken about it; Harper told herself she wouldn't bring it up right away. She had to know if Jamie was moving back to Arizona. Or if he already had.

Once her eyes adjusted, Harper could see Grace facing the window, her back to Harper. Timidly, Harper touched her arm.

Grace grabbed her hand and kissed it as she pulled Harper closer.

"I've missed you," Grace whispered.

Holding back tears, Harper kissed Grace's shoulder and waited again. But just as quickly as she'd had reached for Harper's hand, Grace fell asleep.

Harper woke sometime in the night in an empty bed. Where Grace had been, the covers were pulled up to her pillow. If not for the fuzzy glow framing the bathroom door, Harper would've thought she dreamt Grace's return.

Harper got up and listened at the door. "Grace?"

When there was no answer, she spoke louder and tried the handle. "Are you okay?"

The stillness was even thicker near the light. "Grace," Harper warned, raising her voice, "I'm coming in."

With cautious steps, she opened the door and found Grace neck deep in the bathtub, curled on her side.

She stood over her coiled body, examining the naked scar on her shoulder, the bulbs of her vertebrae. Grace finally flipped over.

"What are you doing?" Harper asked, lowering the toilet seat, sitting down.

"Soaking." Grace studied the faucet, stuck her big toe in the dripping hole. "I just felt like a soak."

Harper watched Grace's lips move and then her breasts bob in the clear water, wondering who Grace wanted her to be. Her lover? Her best friend? She wasn't sure it was either. "Well," she whispered. "I guess I'll let you soak."

As she stood, Grace stopped her. "Wait," she said, reaching for Harper. "Stay."

Later that morning, as Harper sat across from Grace in the bathtub, her body pruning, she told Harper she was leaving school and had come to get her stuff.

"How will that make things better?" Harper first pleaded, anger before desperation. "Putting your life on hold for what? Dean wanted us to be together."

"What do you mean?" Grace asked, her forehead perspiring, the circles under the eyes even deeper when she narrowed them.

"I mean...Dean would want us...to be together."

"I need to be there for Mummy," Grace said.

Grace's dad had recently opened an office in Edinburgh and would be there through the summer, Grace explained. The anguish was too much for Cilla to bear alone, Grace said—Cilla had collapsed at the grocery store and had driven off the road twice, one time slamming into a cactus. The airbag had broken her nose.

Harper listened to everything Grace said, but only heard what she needed to hear: she was still the most important thing in Grace's life, despite her having to leave. It was contrary to every choice she was making, but Harper trusted what she said. She had no choice.

Crying, Grace told her it was the hardest decision she'd ever made, one she labored over for weeks. She loved Harper and she loved U of A, but it was what she needed to do. It was her duty.

When Grace had said all there was to say, Harper helped her dry off. In Harper's mind, she begged Grace not to go, told her that she couldn't make it without her and no matter what was better for her mom, Harper's needs were more important.

But the words never made it to her lips; she just took it all in, being the sympathetic friend Harper now knew she needed, not the enraged woman who was watching the love of her life slip away.

After Grace fell asleep, Harper put on grubby clothes and went to the dumpster to retrieve the boxes she'd unpacked. With one foot on the edge, she leveraged herself up. It reeked of soured milk and cat shit, but she went in anyway. She had to.

When her feet hit the pile of rubbish, it compacted and she sank. Harper tossed a broken desk lamp out of the way before launching the first box to the street. The paper bag between her and the next box ripped open and spilled brown bananas and dirty tampons on her clogs. This was disgusting, Harper thought, and useless. The boxes were unsalvageable.

Leaning against the filthy wall, Harper covered her face with her sleeve and gagged. She looked at the dawning blue sky and then at Grace's window, still dark. Asleep in a ball on the couch, Grace didn't know she had even left.

For the most part, she had kept herself together while they spoke in the bathroom, but now, alone in the garbage attempting to recover what was left, she was powerless. She was tired of being the strong one, the one who made all the sacrifices, the one always left behind.

Through her tears, it was the glitter that caught her eye, its twinkle amidst the waste. It was a card she'd sent to Grace from Germany.

For weeks, she had held onto it before mailing it. She'd not been sure it was appropriate, afraid it might seem presumptuous; depending on how you read it, it could be a love note, or, as Harper justified, a card for a friend you missed so much you'd stopped eating. The glitter was authentic, crushed glass made by a local artist. She'd purchased it at a flea market on the pier in Den Haag.

Harper fell to her knees, wiped the grime on her jeans and held the card with both hands before digging deeper. As she dug in the heaping pile of decay, there were others; the briefcase where Grace kept all of Harper's things had been emptied. She had thrown all of them out, hundreds of them. Grace had dumped everything.

In the putrid dumpster, Harper sorted through her words remembering each card, each reason behind them—their one month anniversary, Grace's birthday, just because, just because, just because. Under the cards, Harper found other mementos, too: the stocking Harper made her one Christmas with their names in a heart written in puffy paint, now dripped with egg yolk; a sombrero from their trip to Tijuana was smashed in; the dried flowers Grace had pressed from their hotel room in Amsterdam were nothing but broken stems in the dumpster now.

Harper gathered all the letters and brought them to her chest.

As she wept with reality, as she peeled back all the layers of denial that had been keeping her insulated, she was struck by the awful truth.

Grace's leaving wasn't about her mother.

It was about Harper.

"I Shall Believe"

Sheryl Crow

Nearly a month passed before Harper saw Grace again.

The call she'd been waiting for finally came a week after Valentine's Day, a night Harper had spent drunk at the bar by herself. She was in her PJs, her hair greasy and wound into a bun. Prior to her trip to the bar, she hadn't left the apartment in days.

"Mummy's going to London tomorrow and we can have the house all to ourselves," Grace said. "Can you come up this weekend?"

What a silly question it was. Harper would've dropped everything for Grace; in fact, she already had. Slowly, as the semester passed, Harper had skidded into a deep depression, the kind that sneaked up on you when you've unknowingly gone from feeling sorry for yourself to entirely shutting out the world.

Every time she spoke with Grace—in the mornings and once or twice at night—it only seemed to compound her condition, piling more weight on her shoulders. On the phone, she tried to sound upbeat each time:

"You shot an eighty-two on the course today? Wow!"

"I'm dying to see that play."

"I didn't know Madonna had a new album out."

Whatever made Grace happy made Harper happy. Well, almost.

By the time Grace invited her to visit, Harper had lost interest in school, a first in her four years at U of A. And she'd completely pulled away from Gamma Kappa; she couldn't hang out at the house or even walk by. The one time she'd stopped to pick up mail, she was sure she heard Grace's laugh coming from the kitchen. She sprang from the couch and rounded the corner, only to find a group of freshmen pledges.

Even though she avoided most classes where she'd have to interact with others, Harper did go to her photography lab because she would've been missed. It was her major and it was a small group, only four of them. The summit of her college career—everything she'd worked for culminated in senior studio.

But she had purposefully dodged Ruthie's class since the day she'd pulled her aside. She wasn't ready to see Ruthie; she wasn't strong enough yet.

Ready or not, Ruthie knocked on Harper's door the same day Grace called with her invitation.

Completely unprepared, when Harper saw Ruthie through the peephole that afternoon, she called out "Just a minute," ran to the bathroom and quickly tried to pull herself together. Aside from Harper's dirty hair, her eyebrows were unplucked, her legs unshaven, and her teeth had little sweaters on them.

"I apologize for just dropping by like this," Ruthie said, standing a safe distance from the door. She wore a long purple sundress and colorful bracelets stacked on one another.

"It's fine," Harper said, now wearing wrinkled jeans and a Wildcats baby doll tee, her teeth brushed.

"I'm sorry,"—Ruthie's eyes were lowered—"I don't want to impose."

"You're not imposing," Harper said. "I'm just surprised to see you. That's all."

"I wanted to make sure you're okay," Ruthie said. "I haven't seen you in class."

Harper invited Ruthie in. Holding a Post-it note with Harper's address, she tentatively stepped inside. "I've tried to call, but there was no answer," Ruthie said. "I was just…I was worried."

At the beginning of the semester, Harper had installed a caller ID box and hadn't been answering many calls, especially those coming from campus. She didn't want to talk to anyone.

Ruthie pulled out a chair at the kitchen table. "Sorry it's so dark in here," Harper said, cracking the blinds. Sun sprayed thin stripes of daylight across Ruthie's face and onto the living room wall.

Harper tried to justify her absence. "I'm sorry I've missed class. I haven't been feeling well."

Ruthie shook her head. "Missing class isn't a big deal. I'm just concerned about you. I know you've been going through a lot."

Sitting next to Ruthie, Harper actually felt some peace of mind. Ruthie had a soothing affect, one of those people that, just by their presence, made you feel that everything was okay, that things were less of a big deal. Harper's mom had that affect on her too, and being with Ruthie made Harper miss her more than usual.

Harper let her guard down. "How did you find me?"

"Well," Ruthie said. "I haven't mentioned it before now, but I was a Gamma Kappa here years ago. Probably lived in one of the same rooms as you in that old house."

"You were a Gamma Kappa?"

"Pledged in nineteen fifty-five."

Feeling even more vulnerable and gracious, Harper stuck out her hand and gave Ruthie the secret handshake.

"I saw the Gamma keychain on your backpack. Finding you was as easy as a phone call."

Dating herself, Ruthie didn't look a day over sixty. Harper imagined Ruthie had had an interesting life, one that would trump her own even if she lived to be over a hundred.

For much of the afternoon, Harper asked questions and Ruthie opened up about her years before teaching. They drank several pots of tea and ate a box of vanilla wafers. Ruthie told Harper about her youthful days of activism, protests she spearheaded, marches on Washington, political rallies she staged on campus, and about the night she spent in jail for refusing to let go of her friend's hand outside the Capitol. In awe, Harper listened as Ruthie shared with passionate energy her calling for social justice.

Harper was fascinated and intrigued by Ruthie's colorful life, as she had never stood up for anything she could remember, only passively lived in the shadow of her parents, of Grace.

After she ran out of questions, Ruthie got up to fill her glass. "Can I tell you one last story?" Ruthie asked, standing at the water cooler.

"Of course. I love your stories. You can go on all night."

Ruthie was pleased by this. "In the summer of nineteen fifty-eight…it was a long time ago, I know…a fellow Gamma and I joined this radical animal rights group on campus." Ruthie pulled her chair closer to Harper. "I'm not sure how it is now, but back then, the house looked down on stuff like that."

"It's still kind of that way."

"This group caused all kinds of ruckus at the medical school. They were notorious for breaking into the labs and letting the testing animals out of their cages. They called the mission Noah's Ark and pulled a renovated paddy wagon up to the back doors to load the animals. This was way before it was cool to be a vegetarian. And way before they had sophisticated alarm systems."

Listening intently, Harper tucked her leg under her seat, engrossed in Ruthie's world, in her hazel eyes.

"On this particular night, it was late, way past midnight, when Cheryl and I met the others near the football field," Ruthie explained. "We were dressed in black. We were going to hit the campus big time. Rescue more than twenty animals. Everybody was given their orders, and because we were rookies, Cheryl and I were given the easiest task, one that would, unbeknownst to me then, change my life forever."

"What was it?" Harper was intrigued.

"We were to hang a canvas sign from the top of the Science Building. It was huge. I remember when we unrolled it, it hung down three stories."

"What did it say?"

Ruthie paused before she told Harper. "Arizona = Animal Auschwitz. It was a full moon, so it was easy to climb to the roof. I remember how campus looked from up there. The blue glaze on the buildings. The palm trees like ice. I'd never seen it so bright. The luminescence was magnificent. Everything was silent and still. After we nailed the banner into place, we sat on the fire escape and shared a joint Cheryl pulled from her bra."

Harper smiled, remembering the one Grace had pulled from her bra in front of the Royal Palace in Amsterdam.

"She was wearing a black silk scarf around her head," Ruthie said, getting lost in memory for a moment. "With our feet swinging beneath us, we passed it back and forth and talked about our childhood dreams. She told me she wanted to be a ballerina."

Ruthie set her tea bag on the saucer. "I'll never forget how she looked that night." Again, briefly, she drifted off somewhere else. "I didn't even see it coming," she said, playing with the fringe on her dress.

"See what coming?" Harper asked, imagining police surrounding the building or the fire escape breaking.

"Out of nowhere," Ruthie said, looking toward the window, "Cheryl kissed me."

Wham!

"And...and just like that, everything changed. The lens I saw the world through, the way my heart beat. Everything. Changed."

Harper squeezed the pillow she was holding and blushed.

Ruthie looked at her. "Am I making you uncomfortable?"

Harper felt her skin stretching. "No. No. Please. Go on."

It was at that moment Harper began to fully understand the passion she had for Grace, the tiny tugs she'd always felt toward women through the years, those that got stronger as she began to mature, her breasts beginning to fill out. They all started to push from the inside out.

"That night was a turning point," Ruthie said, looking at Harper intently now.

"How do you mean?"

The soul-searching philosopher in Ruthie answered: "I

guess, sweetie...looking back, my growth as a woman is best measured by stepping stones. Most have been small and flush with the river. I've moved quickly across those. However, some of the rocks have been monumental. Strong and enormous. That night, Cheryl, the kiss we shared, that was a big one. It was for both of us."

In her mind, Harper saw Grace in the snaps of light in their Amsterdam suite. She heard the thunder, smelled the incense, and felt the river's current change as Harper held on for dear life.

"It could have been anyone, really," Ruthie continued. "Cheryl was just a springboard to the next stone. One I'm really thankful for. Even though, for a while, I'd worked it all out in my mind. Negotiating, justifying really, that it was simply her, that our friendship had just reached an uncommon, intimate level."

Ruthie shook her head. "Deep in my soul, I knew I was a lesbian. And had been my whole life. Funny now, I can see it so clearly. My sexuality chasing me around the playground as a child. It's been woven into every friendship I've ever had."

Harper sat back. "Are you guys still together?"

"No. After graduation, we moved to Berkeley for graduate school," Ruthie said. "Not long into the program, she fell in love with one of our professors. He was a judge. As far as I know, they're still together. I've got a great partner now. Her name is Frieda. We've been together for thirteen years."

Harper stood and went to the sliding glass door. From her patio window, she watched the cars in line at Taco Bell as the room ran out of air and she processed the possibilities—what if Grace actually fell in love with Jamie and they never saw each other again? Up until that point, she'd been so sure of Grace's devotion, so certain of her unwavering love. She'd never considered such a thing. At least not consciously. Was there a chance they wouldn't be together? That they'd drift apart?

Harper was faint, and Ruthie helped her back to the couch, where they sat as Harper uttered words she'd been running from her whole life.

That afternoon, Harper told Ruthie everything. Every little detail.

Ruthie confessed that from the moment she saw Harper's tears in the bathroom she'd known that she and Grace were more than friends. "I could see it in your eyes when you said her name," Ruthie admitted.

As the sun set, Ruthie flipped on a light and brought Harper a box of tissues as she came to the most recent events, Grace telling Harper she was leaving.

"I don't know what to do without her. I can hardly function."

"I know," Ruthie said. "I was heartbroken when Cheryl left. I understand."

"It's different though." Harper blew her nose. "You guys were like a gay couple."

"How's that different?"

"I don't know. I mean, Grace and I are best friends. We're not gay really."

Ruthie smiled.

Had Ruthie caught her on a different day, say another week later, her wounds might have healed just enough that she'd have been able to hide the raw anguish from Ruthie, deny herself and deflect the pain like she always had. But Ruthie's intuition was sharp, and she trusted her gut—just like Ruthie told Harper she should—and taken a big risk that day. Together, they'd both jumped to a new stone.

Besides the details of their scandalous love, Harper confessed to Ruthie about what she'd found in the dumpster.

"She threw away everything I'd ever given her," Harper cried. "After my cards and letters, I found pictures, even the best friend charm we got when we were kids."

"I'm so sorry you had to find that stuff," Ruthie said, still holding Harper's hand on the couch. "Were you able to salvage any of it?"

"I kept the best friend charm and a few other things."

Harper saw Grace's journal, pictured it in the drawer by the side of her bed. Its stained brown leather, the bent oil-spotted pages. "I found her journal from when we were living in Europe last summer. I haven't opened it. I'm too afraid of what it says. What if it says she loves Jamie?"

"Where is it?" Ruthie asked.

"In the bedroom."

"Can I see it?"

For fifteen minutes, Harper lay next to Ruthie while she thumbed through the pages. Wrapped in a fleece blanket, she watched Ruthie's facial expressions, trying to gauge what she was discovering.

Finally, Ruthie set the journal down. "You've got to go home tomorrow and fight like hell for her," Ruthie said. "In those months leading up to your first kiss, her feelings were just as strong as yours. She was falling in love with you while she was in Spain. There's no mention of Jamie. On this page"—Ruthie flipped to it—"she even called you '*Mi Amor*,' which means *my love*."

Harper sat up. "What else does it say?"

Ruthie read some passages:

"I can't remember her face, mi amor. Is it round, like the Spanish women I see on the streets? No, I remember now. She's beautiful. I hope she calls soon and that she's good and high tonight. She's so sweet and unguarded."

"I'm on the train headed to Amsterdam where my sweet Harper waits for me. As I race past the countryside, I wonder if she's missed me like I've missed her. I never expected it to be so intense. This wanting. I wonder if she, too, feels this strange fire."

Sitting in the soft light of Harper's apartment, with only a small green lamp lighting the room, Ruthie and Harper came up with a plan. The next day, Harper would pack a bag, drive to Paradise Valley and show Grace what they had was worth saving. She'd do whatever it took to prove to Grace they were meant to be together, and no matter what the pressures were, Harper wouldn't let Grace slip away like Ruthie had Cheryl.

Harper wouldn't allow Grace to become a faded moonlit memory.

"Hangin' By A Thread"
Jann Arden

Harper broke the speed limit all the way to Phoenix. She held the pedal down and focused on what she'd say to Grace, rehearsing her monologue.

She'd win her back, Harper vowed, as she drove through Casa Grande, halfway to Phoenix, listening to a beat-up mixed tape Grace had made her, one anonymously left in Harper's school mailbox months before. It smelled like Dolce & Gabbana and was loaded with sexy songs lifted from the jukebox, tunes that were a salient ingredient in cementing their souls together.

When Harper arrived at the Dunlop house, it was clear they hadn't left for the airport; the garage door was open, as was their Bentley's backend. On her second drive by, when she saw Cilla on the phone in the office, Harper kept driving. She was way too early.

Even though the sun was setting, Harper drove to Camelback Mountain, only a stone's throw from Grace's house. She wasn't sure what drew her to the trailhead that night—it was where she often went for hikes during the day when home—but it was pulling her in like a magnet, like her attraction to Grace, a force she had no control over.

Harper parked outside the gates, already locked for the

evening, and took her journal along with a flashlight she found jammed in the emergency kit under the spare tire. Also in the kit was a small candle and a book of matches.

With each step on the trail, Harper looked for rattlesnakes in the twilight, listening for their cobbed rattlers. They always came out with the moon. As she was headed up, late afternoon hikers were laboring down the dusty rocks. They looked at Harper, and then at her sundress and sandals when they passed, saying "Good evening" and "Careful."

As darkness covered the Valley, Harper arrived at the cave. The abandoned Indian ruin was off the beaten path, tucked around a rock face that appeared to go nowhere. Carefully, she held onto the small finger holds worn into the rock as she scooted along the tight, nondescript trail.

As Harper stepped inside the ruin, she ran her fingertips along the rough rock. The organic room looked like a hollowed-out potato with puttied walls straight out of a Native American museum. She'd always wondered what lucky Pima family lived there back in history. Before they were run out by settlers, rich white people with guns, whiskey and whores—not a far cry from modern-day Scottsdale.

Harper sat down where she always did and let her feet dangle above the barbed labyrinth of cactus. On the edge of the cave, she pushed the votive into the soft soil and lit the wick.

From her seat, she could see the six-bedroom Frank Lloyd Wright-inspired home where she'd been raised. It was surrounded by a wall of mesquite; three illuminated palm trees sprouted from the backyard. She wondered what her parents were doing inside. They were home that month.

Around the bend, Harper saw the Dunlop's Tudor estate encircled by towering eucalyptus trees and Malibu lights. A few blocks from the Dunlop's was the country club's golf course. Her eyes followed the jet-black maze that wove through glowing multimillion dollar homes. In the blue distance, perched high on a nearby hill, just beyond the groomed links, was Nonna and Papa's house. Their kitchen light was on.

As she sat in the red dirt looking out over the Valley, Harper's chest hurt—not the acute pain of a heart attack, but a bulging discomfort that pushed on her organs. Something inside her wanted out, tearing at her ribcage.

Harper crossed her legs and opened her journal.

Ruthie had given her an assignment the evening before, a personal one that had nothing to do with ceramics. She was to write two letters. The first was to the young Harper. "Write a letter to yourself," Ruthie said, "to the seven-year-old you." The second letter, the more important of the two, was to be written to the grown-up Harper from the seven-year-old's point of view.

It seemed like an impossible task. Harper wondered where she'd start, what she'd say. She stared at the blank page and clenched the sweaty ballpoint, hearing Ruthie's words: "Keep the pen moving," she said. "No matter what comes out, don't stop."

As she started her letter to the young Harper, no divine inspiration came—no lightning bolt split a nearby Joshua tree, no shooting star burned across the sky.

It was much more subtle than that. Her truth crept into the cave slowly.

Dear Harper,

I have no idea what to say. You're so far away. It's almost like I've blocked you out entirely.

There are many things I still don't understand even though I'm much older. I know you feel alone, like no one ever stays for long, but just trust that one day you'll find someone who will always be there, who you'll always be able to love.

Once Harper got the first few sentences out, it made way for a weak voice which had, before this night, been completely stifled.

I've betrayed you.

I had a little secret, huh? I danced with the boys even though I didn't want to. I met them in the baseball dugout even though I'd rather have helped Miss Jensen in her room after school. I'd rather have scrubbed Miss Jensen's floors with a toothbrush, but I went to kiss the boys anyway. It was just like I planned.

I lied about the first time I touched myself. Remember how it smelled like sour candy? The church said I'd go to hell if I liked how it felt, so I shut that part of myself down too. I made sure the lights were off before I stuck my hand under the covers, denying it even happened.

The thick skin pulled over us makes it hard to breathe sometimes. I'm sorry. I wish I had more to offer you, some hope even, but I don't have much to spare. It seems I've lost my way.

Where should we go from here?

Harper

She stopped writing and bit her lip, gripping the corners of her journal as her nose started to run. She wiped it with her bare shoulder.

Her fingers were firm around the pen and her chest wide open as the young Harper Alessi finally got her chance.

Dear Harper,

On the playground, I hate the names the boys call me. Tomboy. Lezzie. I try to fight back under the jungle gym, but I don't have the words to make them cry. My fists are sore from punching their stupid arms.

I like to sit on top of the slide and watch everyone play. It feels better up there. It feels better when I'm alone. I'm not like other girls. I wear different clothes and bring different things in my lunchbox. Mom and Dad are never around.

I hate my skin. I always have. With the brush in Mom's shower, I scrub as hard as I can, but I get in trouble when school sees the scabs. Mom and Dad get called in for a conference. Questions are asked. Questions that never have answers.

Even though I smile, and try and hold my head high like Daddy says, everyone knows I'm not like the others.

Friendships with girls are my toughest battles. Sometimes when Sloan teases me about having a crush on Miss Jensen, I tell her that people call her fat behind her back. My words do just as much damage and they aren't even true.

Life would be more fun if I just could be myself. If we could just face the truth.

Harper put the pen down and closed her journal.

Pushing into the cave with eerie timing, a desert wind blew the candle out.

She sat in the moonlit darkness processing the message which had been delivered. She swallowed hard, hoping to re-ingest the secret. The knowing.

Her nose was really running now and she used her dress to wipe her face.

How could I have known, Harper thought amidst her anguish, but not known I was gay all these years?

She grabbed the matches again. Striking one twice, it caught fire at the same time she noticed the dark streaks on her arm. As the wick captured the flame, Harper looked at her clothes, and at her fingers and hands. All covered in blood.

Her nose wasn't running, it was bleeding, dripping like paint on a fresh canvas.

Harper had tasted the truth, but not the blood as her body purged the old Harper.

As another gust killed the candle again, she scrambled for the flashlight just beyond her purse. Tendrils of blood dripped down her face and neck.

Harper heard rustling in the bushes. She needed to get down the mountain.

Grace was waiting for her at home, and she'd never needed her more. Not in the same way she'd needed her hours earlier—when Harper's heart was an open sore, maligned by their imperfect love—but in a way Harper had never needed her before.

Harper needed the old Grace; the one she knew before they were lovers, before it got complicated.

Frightened and dismantled, Harper needed her best friend back.

"Love Bites"
Def Leppard

The front of Harper's dress was still wet when she pulled into the Dunlop's driveway. With napkins from the glove box, she slowed the bleeding and cleaned her face with wet wipes.

Harper had stood at the towering front door hundreds of times, but it seemed bigger, twice her size now, as she rang the bell.

The light came on first, and when the door swung open, Grace gasped at the blood. "Oh my God! What happened?"

Harper wasn't crying until she saw Grace's reaction.

"Are you hurt?"

As Harper shook her head, a line of blood jumped over her lip and hit the marble floor. "I can't stop it," she said, holding a wadded napkin against her nose.

Grace led Harper into the kitchen and helped take off her dress. In her bra and panties, Harper used a clothespin and a bag of peas to clot the bleeding while Grace wiped her down with a damp cloth.

"Where did it come from?" Grace asked, rinsing out the blood-soaked rag.

"I don't know."

Grace brought Harper clean clothes and warm slippers. "All

better?" she asked, coming from the laundry room.

Harper drew a long breath. "Not really."

"What do you mean?" Grace hoisted herself onto the counter and pulled Harper between her legs. "What's going on with you?"

Harper lay her head on Grace's chest and closed her eyes. In Grace's arms, a memory she'd buried under layers of shame floated to the surface:

It was the first time Harper felt an attraction for Grace. Since her admission on the mountain, all sorts of memories and bits of understanding were working their way to the surface. Harper and Grace had been twelve, maybe thirteen, and had tiptoed outside to the pool house to watch the cable channel Cinemax in the middle of the night. When it warned viewers of sex and nudity, Grace turned down the volume before double-checking that her parents were asleep. On the couch together, as they watched a dirty movie, their legs touched and they were both sweaty. Like so many things, Harper had never admitted it before, to herself or to Grace.

"Whatever it is," Grace whispered, "just tell me. It'll be all right."

Harper wasn't sure. She was so afraid of the words. "I just hiked to the cave on the mountain and…" In earnest, she tried to explain.

"Mountain?"

"Camelback."

"You just came from Camelback?" Grace leaned back and looked at the oven's clock. "What were you doing up there?"

"Killing time. I got to town early."

"You hiked to the cave in that outfit? In those shoes?" Grace eyeballed the bloody mess in a heap on the tile. "It's been dark for hours."

"I went at sunset. I had a flashlight."

Grace looked at Harper crookedly. "Okay," she said slowly. "What happened in the cave?"

"I took my journal and did a lot of writing," Harper said, easing into it. "And…a lot of thinking."

Grace paid careful attention.

"That's where my bloody nose started. You know how I get

those?" Harper stalled.

"Right."

Harper took another breath. The room, again, was running out of oxygen. "And I came to this realization."

With that, Harper began crying. "I'm sorry," she said.

"Bella, what's wrong?" Grace was really concerned now as Harper fought to gain self-control.

"I'm sorry. It's just that this awareness"—she grabbed her mouth and whimpered—"is something that's really scary."

As if unsure if she wanted to know, Grace asked her next question more slowly. Suddenly, the conversation was like a record from the jukebox playing at the wrong speed. "What was it?" she finally asked.

Harper's knees weakened, and she leaned into Grace. "I've realized..." She paused, her last chance to abort. "That it's not just you," Harper said, holding on tighter as Grace let go. "It's not just us."

Grace waited for more.

"I think I'm a lesbian. And have been my whole life."

"What?"

Harper held her breath.

"That's it?"

Harper didn't look up, unable to believe she'd actually said the words.

"Sweetie," Grace said, kissing Harper on the forehead. "Look at me." She tucked a strand of loose hair behind Harper's ear. "Everything's going to be fine. I thought you were gonna say something awful happened to you up there. Don't worry."

Standing before Grace, stripped down to the core, Harper wanted to believe what she said. She pulled on Grace's shirt, bringing them together. Relieved by her reassurance. The support.

"You've just worked yourself into a fit. Once you calm down you'll realize you're being silly."

Being silly?

Harper pulled back. "I'm not being silly."

"Harper, give me a break. You're not gay. All this carrying on is crazy."

Harper stepped back even farther. "No," she said, "I'm

serious. It's taken me a long time to finally admit it, but I'm sure."

Grace shook her head and jumped off the island. "This is ridiculous."

Harper watched Grace, dumbfounded. "It's not ridiculous," she cried.

"It is too." Even more emotion swelled with Harper's defenses, and she slithered down the fridge to the floor, pulling in her knees.

"You're not gay," Grace said, hovering above her.

Harper pressed her teeth into the cotton pants. "Yes." She lowered her head again, trying to be strong, hoping to hide the tears. "I am."

"Listen to me," Grace said. "You're not gay."

The more Harper cried, the angrier Grace got, and the harder it was to speak. Grace squatted before Harper and gripped her arms.

"This was just something I was doing with you. I'm not gay. And you aren't either. WE are not gay," Grace yelled. "Now get off the floor."

Harper reached up. "Gracie. Please." Crawling closer, Harper wrapped herself around Grace's leg.

"What is wrong with you? You're being so"—Grace looked down at her with disgust—"foolish. Irrational."

"I know it's true," Harper whispered.

"God damn it! You're not a FUCKING dyke!"

When Grace raised her voice, it startled Harper; it was a side she'd never seen, not even when she'd yelled at her mother.

Lying on the floor, Harper thought admitting she craved other women might hurt Grace's feelings. But the anger, Grace's inflexible insistence that Harper wasn't gay, those were things she wasn't ready for. She'd had no idea she was going to have to fight for it.

As they went back and forth, Grace's eyes narrowed. She ripped her leg from Harper's grasp. "Why did you even bother coming up if you were going to act like this?"

"What? You invited me. I didn't know..."

"I invited you for a nice, relaxing weekend, not some bloody pity party."

Kneeling beneath Grace, Harper couldn't understand the shift; Grace had never turned on her before. Never. Sure, as her secret lover, Harper half expected the betrayal with Jamie, a knife or two in her back—Grace was, like her, just trying to survive—but she never anticipated this unmeasured rage. Where had their friendship gone? And how could they get it back? Was there no line to recross? Had the sex muddied the boundary between the two?

Apparently, it had.

"Get out of this house," Grace said.

"What?"

"Get out of this God damn house." Grace pointed to the door.

"I'm sorry. I didn't mean to..."

"We're done talking," Grace said, storming away. "Get out."

"Grace PLEASE!"

The alarm beeped, the front door opened. Harper stayed put, waiting in the kitchen for Grace to come back.

She did, a few seconds later.

"Didn't you hear me? Get the fuck out."

"Grace?"

Grabbing her arm, Grace reached for Harper's purse and pulled her along the slick stone as Harper pleaded. "Why are you doing this? Please, I'm begging you. I NEED YOU!"

With one final thrust, Grace pushed Harper out and slammed the door.

Harper's nose began bleeding again as she said her name one last time.

Grace.

Sitting on the doormat, Harper pinched her nose and waited for Grace to come to her senses, for that moment of clarity Harper knew was imminent.

But only a few seconds passed before the lights went off.

And they stayed off for twelve years.

Part Two

"Somewhere In My Broken Heart"
Billy Dean

2005
Portland
Oregon

"A bottle of Veuve," Alex said. "Yellow label."

In a faux fur coat, Harper stood next to Alex holding a shopping bag in each hand. They were saying goodbye to their friends, Sabrina and Juliet, who'd be coming over to make gingerbread houses the next night.

"And don't forget to bring powdered sugar," Alex added, adjusting her winter cap. Snowflakes were caught in her blond pixie hair and on her eyelashes. The snow was a foot deep in some places between the groups of people waiting for the lightrail.

"*Au revoir*," Sabrina said, blowing a kiss into the air. Juliet did the same as the train doors closed. They barely squeezed on.

It was Christmastime and they'd just watched the mayor illuminate the lights for the city's tree, a bushy seventy-five foot fir at the center of town. Harper had been late meeting the group that night; she'd been stuck at her gallery framing one of her prints for a rush order. When she arrived, Santa was dragging a sack of gifts toward a chorus of boys singing Christmas carols. A giant menorah glowed behind them. When the jolly old man started the countdown, amidst the crowd, she could feel the building enthusiasm as he got close to zero. Until suddenly, an explosion of light. Screams. Whistles. Flashbulbs. "O Holy Night" a cappella.

On the edge of the town square, Harper and Alex, standing arm-in-arm, waited for the train to pass so they could begin their snowy trek home. Around them, thousands of holiday revelers dispersed into the night, scattering like ants in every direction. It only snowed but once or twice a year and locals made the most of it. A group of teenage boys were in a serious snowball fight and a little girl was doing snow angels by a cart selling roasted chestnuts.

Alex pulled in Harper. "Brrrr."

"I know," Harper said, fastening her top button.

In front of them, the train rang its bell and lunged forward.

Despite the foggy glass, and despite the clumps of falling snow, Harper saw on the train a face she'd never forgotten. It was Grace.

Without thought, she ripped from Alex's arm and took off running.

Over a decade had passed since they'd seen each other, Harper and Grace—nearly a third of her life—but she ran anyway. It was instinctual, flight or fright adrenaline, her sprint along the snowy sidewalk. A mad dash.

Determined, she darted in and out of clusters of people. The buildings she burned past were old, glazed and wintry, a seeming backdrop to a Christmas Day movie, shot on some sunny Hollywood lot. Icicles—long threatening daggers—gripped the eaves above her. Her snow boots made for horrible runners and her shopping bags, one of which had split down the side, didn't help either.

All combined, it was too much. She didn't make it.

By the time Harper got to the next stop, some three blocks away, the doors were closing and she was left standing with the few who'd stepped off at the stadium. None of whom were Grace.

She was gone again.

Just like that.

She'd had so many dreams where Grace slipped away, it was hard to know whether it was real or imagined.

Walking back to her girlfriend whom she'd left standing on the corner, Harper wondered if Grace had really been there—she was seriously questioning it now—or if she was slowly losing her mind. It wasn't the first time it had happened, Harper doing something rash because she thought she'd seen Grace. She'd run after her once before in Los Angeles when she thought she saw her driving a convertible on Melrose. Harper talked her way out of it that time, but she wondered what she'd say to Alex now as she hurried back.

"What the hell was that?" Alex's hands were on her hips.

"Sorry," Harper said, breathing heavily. "I just realized I still had Sabrina's gloves."

"What?"

Harper set the bags down and pulled off her hat, covered in heavy snow. Her dark, wavy hair fell to her shoulders as she shook it clean.

Alex spoke softly. "You ran after the train to give Sabrina her gloves back?"

"Yeah," Harper said, sliding the wool cap back over her ears. She looked defiantly at Alex. "What?"

In silence, Harper and Alex made a trail, two girls wide, on their way home. The streets had thinned out, quiet and deserted, and the snow was plowed in a steep pile against Alex's building in the Pearl District.

When they opened the heavy, industrial door to her loft, Alex's cats, snuggled together on the couch, barely moved. Inside, all of Alex's guitars were lined up along the wall, including the one Harper had given her as an early Christmas present. Hanging from the exposed brick was a wreath packed with apples, pinecones and acorns. With an extension ladder, Harper had helped her thread white lights through the rusty pipes on the ceiling, remnants of yesteryear when it was an old warehouse.

Alex started dinner and opened a bottle of pinot noir while Harper changed into sweatpants and a long-sleeved Rolling Stones shirt, Alex's favorite, which she found on a hook in her bathroom.

Before joining Alex in the kitchen, Harper let herself cry, silently, in the bedroom. She covered her mouth as she caught her breath. The incident, seeing Grace or whoever it was, had hit her hard.

In the living room, a fire blazed and wood popped as Harper turned on the TV. A line of white candles glowed on the mantel.

"So," Alex said, pouring wine. "You took off running just to give Sabrina her gloves back?"

"What's the big deal?" Harper said.

"The big deal is that it's bizarre. We see them like every day."

"Every day?"

"Every couple days," Alex snapped. "What's your problem?"

"She was nice enough to lend them to me, and I wanted to return them. Simple as that."

It was a weak alibi, and Harper knew it, but there was no turning back.

Alex sighed and leaned into the island. Her jeans were stylish, purposefully tattered at the knees. "You absolutely don't make sense sometimes."

"What do you mean?"

"There is just so much about you I don't get. You're always so secretive." Alex pulled out silverware. "It's hard to explain. I've tried a hundred times."

Alex slammed the drawer with her hip. Her petite body could be tough when it wanted to be. Harper closed her eyes. She hated when Alex slammed things.

"You always have a barrier up."

"No I don't."

"You do. Even now."

Harper surfed the cable channels looking for the weather. "Me explaining why I ran after the train isn't a barrier."

"Will you mute that?" Alex dumped a bag of frozen beans into the wok. It sizzled. "What about us not living together?"

"That's not fair. I just don't want to be one of those ridiculous couples who move in after their first date."

"Harper," Alex sighed. "We've been together for two years. You sleep here every night."

"Every night?"

"God. Stop it!"

"I'm just not ready," Harper said. "You know what they say: no wine until it's time." She turned up the TV's volume.

"No wine until it's time." Alex threw her wooden spoon onto the counter. "Give me a fucking break," she said before disappearing into the bedroom.

Snow was still falling when they went to bed. The weather person said it would last all night, turning into an ice storm by morning, locking down the city. Things were going to get worse before they got better. Opposite one another in bed, they were gentler now.

"I just want to start our life together," Alex said. "I love you. And I'm ready. And I can't understand how you're not."

"I know. I'm sorry," Harper said. "I just need more time." The words saddened her as much as they did Alex, for she didn't fully understand her resistance either.

"More time for what?"

Harper had no answer.

"What were you running after tonight?" Alex asked.

Harper pulled the covers over her head.

"And right now, what are you running away from?"

Silence.

"Goodnight," Harper finally whispered, and drifted off to sleep.

In the deep end of the pool, Harper is holding on with everything she has.

She is dangling from the diving board, both arms above her head, waiting for Grace.

Abrupt desert gusts roll across the yard, singeing the bougainvillea blooming along the wide perimeter fence. It is half past midnight, maybe later.

From the house, Grace saunters down the hand-cut lawn which starts at the back door and rolls like a green carpet to the pool's edge.

Harper watches carefully.

There are no words. Only fierce eye contact as Grace moves closer.

Through the outdoor speakers, hidden deep within the wild lilac, Lakme's "Flower Duet" *plays like a serenade.*

As Grace steps into the water, Harper readjusts her grip.

Like a python, Grace glides through the water with ease until suddenly, slick and ellusive, she takes a breath and disappears.

Harper searches the water around her, but the darkness and the pool's pebbled bottom make it difficult to see.

A bubble, a few feet away, breaks as Grace resurfaces.

"Come here," Grace says, her skin sparkling blue in the evening light, her blond curls suspended like reeds in a lake. Water splashes as Grace approaches, slowly snaking her arms around Harper's midsection; she stops just inches from her face.

"Kiss me," she says.

Heaven is in this moment, Harper thinks, as Grace brings their bodies together.

The moon, full and crisp above, sinks behind Camelback Mountain as Harper's fingers give way, plunging them as one into the water.

It is unstoppable, the force between them.

As Grace pulls Harper to the pool's edge, the scene is captured in frames in her mind.

Harper braces herself as Grace pins her to the wall.

With her eyes closed, Harper can feel Grace's hot breath against her cheek before their lips come together.

A deep, wet kiss follows.

Harper trembles—they both do—as Grace gently, then forcefully, shoves her knee between Harper's legs.

Harper shot up into a sitting position. She was out of breath, sweaty, her heart too big for the space between her ribs and spine.

"God," she whispered, before falling down next to Alex in bed.

In their quiet darkness, Harper tried to will herself back

into the moonlight, back into Grace's arms, back into the dream she'd had before, always ending when Grace gets her to shallow water.

Outside, snowflakes were still falling. The wall of Alex's bedroom, painted in gold light by an outdoor lamppost, was a movie screen of winter bliss. Shadowed snow flurries floated down the high ceilings into her closet and onto her dresser.

With a sigh, Harper lifted her arm and inspected her new tattoo, a small Cornicello horn on the inside of her wrist, her third since leaving home. It was a nod to her Italian heritage and supposed to ward off evil. Of them all, this ink was the most visible to the world; the others were covered, hidden, like so many other things. As she examined it, Harper could hear Nonna rolling over in her grave.

In a sleepy daze, Harper went to the kitchen and fired up the teapot. She twisted her thick hair into a bun and fumbled for her glasses, square, designer frames folded near the phone. Standing in her robe with her arms crossed, she waited for the whistle while she looked around Alex's kitchen, illuminated by a dull light coming from the refrigerator's ice maker. She rubbed her eyes and thought about her bottle of Valium in Alex's medicine cabinet, untouched for over a year. A fresh tea bag was already on the stove, so was a clean mug. Considering the night's events, she'd anticipated this late-night intermission. Serenity, the tea was called, a blend of herbs to help with insomnia. She'd try the tea first, and then the drugs.

It was that kind of night.

With her favorite chipped coffee cup, Harper stood at the floor to ceiling sash windows and sipped her tea. The storm had worked up into a near blizzard, the wind blowing sideways. Snow, like pieces of sand, tinked against the glass as if they were living in a violently shaken snow globe.

Had it really been Grace? Harper wondered with a heavy exhale of breath.

Could she really be in Oregon?

"Missing You"

John Waite

2007

Tucked into a refurbished industrial building in downtown Portland, Bluehour was a trendy spot where people went to be seen. It was also a restaurant and lounge where locals flocked to celebrate a promotion at work, a birthday, an anniversary, anything really.

On this particular night, Harper and Alex, along with Sabrina and Juliet, were toasting for two reasons. First, the recent purchase of their new home, a 1917 bungalow in the Hawthorne neighborhood. Harper had bought it—she had some cash she needed to invest for tax reasons—but Alex would help with the upkeep and live there as if it were hers too. Second, Alex's new album and the kick off of her twenty-city tour, part of which Harper would join on the road.

"To Alex," Juliet said, "may you sell out every show."

"Salud!" Sabrina said.

The four of them, sitting at an intimate, candlelit table near the kitchen, tapped their glasses.

"And to us," Alex said. "To Harper and I moving into together. Finally! We unpacked our last box yesterday."

"Hear, hear!" the table roared.

While Alex's tour was a big deal, the new house was really something to celebrate. After keeping separate places for so long, Harper had decided she was finally ready to move in with Alex. They'd been together for almost four years—almost four years and almost together—and she'd finally conceded.

Even though the house Harper bought for them had great curb appeal, the old craftsman needed work. Before they moved in, they'd added a bathroom and renovated the basement into a darkroom for Harper.

By this time, Harper had been living in the Pacific Northwest for over a decade. After graduating from U of A—about eight months after Grace threw her out—Harper had decided a change would do her good. She had her sights on the University of Washington's MFA program, which she was accepted into the following year.

There were many torturous nights when she was single, and days which seemed to go on forever. Like the loneliness, the abandoned phone calls came in bursts, dialing Grace's number without hitting *send*. On one particularly dark Sunday night, when there was nothing on TV, one call had gotten through. Harper set herself back, her therapist said, after she heard Grace's voice on her voice mail greeting.

Even suffering souls can push on, Harper's counselor said. So, somehow, with the passage of time, a new puppy and thousands of dollars spent, Harper managed to move on.

And then came Alex. They met in Seattle right before Harper's thirtieth birthday when they were both living in Capitol Hill; Harper, closing in on her master's degree and Alex, performing at local bars, working on her singing career.

They got together before Alex was a big star, before she signed with ChaCha Girl and sold over 100,000 albums. She was no one back then, back when they first saw each other across the bar on a rainy Seattle night. Alex was getting a bottle of water before her show and Harper was buried in the *New York Times*, smoking a French cigarette.

When they first made eye contact, Harper looked away. Butch women weren't her thing; she was a femme on a femme diet. Then something brought her back. A scent, an energy, an aching loneliness. Some said Alex looked like Annie Lennox, others Sharon Stone. Harper thought she was an amalgam of strength, beauty and gentleness with a voice that puts girls in a trance.

She was a lover like no other, Harper thought.

Except one.

Their relationship had had more downs than ups. Many of the ups: trips they took together each year, especially those to Australia. For weeks, they'd hop from one small beach town to the next, where no one knew them, where there was no connection to home.

During their courtship, on a whim, they'd taken off to the Gold Coast to spend their very first Christmas together, a bold move to travel internationally after only knowing each other two months. It could've been a disaster. It was anything but. The risk was, Harper thought, perhaps the reason it worked out.

It was in Byron Bay in Queensland where Alex and Harper first slept together. Harper cried right before she climaxed, so did Alex, but they were crying for different reasons. They'd waited awhile because Harper hadn't been ready.

Not long into their relationship, together, they moved to Portland. Alex wanted to be closer to her friends Juliet and Sabrina, and Harper wanted to be closer to her parents, semi-retired on the Oregon coast. So much of Harper's life had been spent too far away from them. That, too, she'd been working out in therapy.

As Alex's career blossomed, she spent more and more time on the road. Her being away so much made it hard to keep their romantic roller coaster on the incline. They both complained to their couples counselor of feeling disconnected, but neither was willing to let go.

"I can't stand the lonely nights," Harper cried.

"I can't stand knowing you're alone," Alex said, but Harper knew it was more than that. She'd seen girls' names and numbers wadded up in Alex's jeans, and when she was on the road for extended periods of time, it was almost more than Harper could handle. But still, they pushed on and right around their second anniversary, they'd decided to open up their relationship.

The rules were clear: One-night stands only, no romance, no emotions, only sex. They knew better, but it was all they could do at the time. "It's impossible for lesbians not to get emotionally involved," their friends warned. "We're nesters. We're romance whores. We're programmed that way," they claimed.

They were all correct, and both women knew it, but they gave it a go anyway.

In the end, after even more tumult, they recommitted to each other. They were done screwing around, ready to settle down, and Harper, despite having a successful photography business, decided to join Alex on the road more often. It was a sacrifice she was willing to make.

For them. For their future.

On this particular night at Bluehour, Alex and Harper were in a good, solid place. It was one of the ups. So were Juliet and Sabrina, so it seemed, holding hands at the table as they discussed their impending commitment ceremony.

"We're having trouble with the seating chart," Juliet complained. "We can't figure out who to sit Sue Stevens next to. She is such a chatterbox."

"That reminds me. You'll never believe who I ran into at the market yesterday," Alex said, reaching for the cheese knife.

"Jane Sipperly," Juliet guessed. Alex laughed. This was a joke, apparently, one Sabrina and Harper didn't get. They smiled at each other awkwardly.

"Even better," Alex said. "Jody Stone."

"You're kidding," Juliet gasped.

This name didn't mean anything to Harper either, though Sabrina was in on this one. Harper looked at the entrée menu, still with an ear in the conversation.

"She cut all her hair off," Alex continued. "It looked like she did it herself."

"Shut up."

"And, get this. What was left was bright pink."

"What?"

"Pink." Alex shook her head. "I can't believe I dated her."

"Me neither," Juliet said, eating the last prosciutto-wrapped scallop.

Harper was suddenly focused on what they were saying. Just the summer before, Harper had her stylist put some color in her own hair. Two ribbons of blue on either side of her face. She wondered now, hearing what they had to say about this hapless dyke getting groceries, what they'd all said behind her own back.

"Speaking of blasts from the past," Alex said. "Did I tell you I saw Brooke in LA last time I played House of Blues?"

"Ohhhhh God."

The three of them, again, all knew this name.

"Sometimes I wonder what kind of crack we were smoking back then."

"Seriously," Sabrina said, "I dated Brooke too. At UCLA."

"Really?" Alex asked, shocked. "Then we've all slept with Brooke?"

They got a huge kick out of this and laughed wildly.

"Lesbians," Alex said.

During a lull in conversation, Harper studied Juliet's and Sabrina's engagement rings, which were almost identical, the same princess cut stone and gleaming tapered baguettes. The two of them, who were slowly morphing into one another, were also dressed similarly. Simple black tank tops, denim bottom half—Juliet in a skirt, Sabrina in peg-leg pants. "This is what happens to lesbians," Alex had once said. "It's called enmeshment."

Juliet pulled Harper into the conversation, asking her a question it seemed she'd pondered before this night.

"Harp, tell us about some of your exes. Surely you have a freak show lurking in the shadows. A Jody Stone? A stalking story or two?"

Harper paused. She'd faced this question from others and once before from Alex when they first started dating.

"You know"—Harper thought for a moment—"most of them were just forgettable women in college." She stopped again. "Nothing freaky. No stalkers."

"Was there anyone serious?" Juliet asked. Alex shot Juliet a look, probably kicked her under the table. "I know you dated that professor of yours for a while, right?"

"No! Ruthie and I have never been more than friends."

"Well surely you've been in love before Alex."

The three of them stared at Harper as she swirled the wine in her glass.

"Not really."

"Again"
Janet Jackson

Mid-tour, Alex came home for a few nights before one final West Coast stop in Seattle. After Seattle, she'd have two weeks off before hitting the road again for almost a month, touring the Midwest and the Eastern seaboard.

The morning of her show, Harper awoke to Alex tossing a jar of Carmex into the air while humming her hit single. Even at home, Alex never slept well before a big concert. Nerves always got the best of her. Over her song, Harper could hear rain smacking the window and the recycling truck picking up the neighbor's bottles.

"How are you feeling?" Harper asked.

"All right." Alex opened the yellow tin and covered her lips. "The Paramount is such a big venue. I can't believe it sold out."

Harper rolled over and rested her head on Alex's stomach. "You're going to be great."

"I hope so."

"What time is the bus leaving?"

"Ten."

"What time are you heading out?" Alex asked. "You'll be there by the time I go on?"

"Of course," Harper said. "I've got some work to do on

the montage, so I'll be on the road by three or four." Harper was putting together a photo montage for Sabrina and Juliet's reception.

Alex frowned. "I'm still really sorry about the other night. I didn't mean to be so pushy."

"You don't have to apologize," Harper said. "Even though I was playing, I shouldn't have been such a smart-ass."

The two had gotten into a heated argument on the phone several nights before about their own commitment ceremony. Or lack thereof. It was something Alex had been hinting at for months and something Harper, no surprise, wasn't ready for.

After Alex asked about it for the twentieth time, Harper joked on the phone: "You just finally convinced me to move in with you. Now you want to get married?"

Alex didn't think it was funny.

Harper spent the morning in the darkroom. Shortly after they'd moved to Portland, Harper opened a small gallery in Old Town where she sold her own prints, along with much of her parents' *National Geographic* work.

Picture by picture, Harper sorted through negatives in the basement for Juliet and Sabrina's long-awaited walk down the aisle. They'd been together for fifteen years. An eternity, Harper thought.

As she waited for the first photograph to develop, a sharp sliver of light cut through the old windowpane sealed shut with black paint. Examining the leak of daylight, the swirls of dust where its blade sliced the darkness—the things she unknowingly ingested—Harper's eyes burned; she'd been in the dark too long.

The negatives were old, some over twenty years—Juliet and Alex had been lovers in college—but Harper tried to steal moments from them anyway.

Bolted to the beams above her head, a dull, tangerine light glowed from the ceiling, casting her fuzzy outline into the vinegary developer. Harper closed her eyes and inhaled—the smells, the process took her back to childhood.

With her weight on one leg, Harper watched the image come to life. And although it was overexposed, she could make it out. They were in Paris—Alex was perched on a barstool and Juliet was holding Sabrina in her arms. Harper had taken it with a Royer IV, an old French folding camera from the Fifties she'd found at a shop in Saint Germain-en-Laye.

As Harper lifted the picture from the chemicals, she remembered the moment Alex first declared her love; they were on top of the Eiffel Tower and had just come from a relaxing eight-course dinner in Versailles. Although Harper hesitated in reciprocating, she really did love Alex, even then, and appreciated their life together.

Rummaging through the strips of film, Harper found a batch of negatives from their week in Maui and chose her favorite. Strapped into their parasailing gear, Alex, with much longer hair, had her thumbs up as Juliet and Sabrina were being sucked off the boat by the Hawaiian wind. In the next frame, they were tiny flies in the sky.

Along with the happy memories, darker ones surfaced as Harper poked the paper with tongs. She remembered their fight the evening before their parasailing adventure, the one no one else heard, the one where Alex complained of Harper's apathy. It was right before they ended their open relationship. Neither of them could connect knowing there were other women in their bedroom.

"I know," Alex had said, throwing her empty rum bottle into Lahaina Bay, "I know there is more inside you than this. Fucking let me in."

As Harper scattered negatives on the light table, she saw a shadowy figure walk past the sealed window, eclipsing the slice of sunlight. She looked up, remembered their busted doorbell and untied her apron. Slipping from the darkroom door, she crept to the window above the washer and dryer, a rickety porthole with webbed corners.

Harper didn't see anyone in the driveway, so she jumped down and went to the window facing the backyard. On her tiptoes, Harper scanned the brick patio and the bushy wall of azaleas, but there was nothing. No one. It was her imagination.

When Harper finished the photos, she spent the early afternoon in the garden. Their rose bushes needed trimming—they'd exploded with buds and taken over the hydrangea—and she'd picked up some perennials at the nursery the day before.

In the yard, she was wearing an old sundress that had gone from hanging in the closet to a wad in her drawer to her gardening bag. It was loose and tattered around the edges, and its buttercups were fading into the powder blue background. Her hair was twisted sloppily into a straw hat. On her knees in the dirt, Harper worked in the side yard for most of the afternoon as the sun, whose intensity grew as it moved across the sky, scorched her back.

Alex hadn't phoned and Harper was worried. She was hours overdue and she'd tried her cell phone several times.

Harper was popping the last peony out of its can when someone called her name.

"Harper."

She stopped and waited, staying close to the ground. An earthworm wiggled in the damp dirt as Harper told herself she was crazy. Still imagining things. Running after the train years earlier had been foolish enough; she wouldn't fall for it this time, or ever again.

Then the voice once more.

"Hi Bella."

Harper's Jack Russell terrier, Quincy, jumped from the portico and barked.

Sitting up, Harper stabbed the shovel into the mulch. "Who's there?"

She couldn't look.

She'd given up so long ago.

Harper heard shoes against the brick pathway.

"It's me."

Twelve years.

This moment, not even a full second, suspended itself in time. Harper felt the wood grain of the Dunlop's front door against her fingertips, the doormat crushed under her knees, the taste of blood in her mouth.

"Grace."

Although she wasn't ready, with wet soil stuck to her shins, Harper took off her gloves, stood up and slowly turned around.

Grace was less than ten feet away, and even more stunning than Harper remembered. Grace's hair, still an even honey blond mix, was layered now. She wore black dress pants and a sheer top with delicate beading, a nude tank underneath. Covering her eyes was a newer version of her signature Gucci sunglasses, which she slid off as she walked toward Harper.

"Jesus Christ," Harper said, wiping sweat from her forehead.

"Nope," Grace said softly. "Just me."

Face-to-face, they looked into each other's eyes and beyond their initial words, said nothing.

It was a flash Harper had visualized in her dreams.

There was no exchange of affection. Grace was waiting for a hug, Harper could tell, but the phone rang, interrupting the moment. Harper let her gaze go from Grace to the cordless phone, set on the kitchen stoop along with a glass of lemonade. Her body followed.

When Harper picked it up, she immediately turned back to Grace, who was walking around the yard inspecting their English garden.

"We're here," Alex said. "Finally. We broke down and I couldn't get a signal."

Harper's hand holding the receiver shook.

"When are you leaving?" Alex asked.

"Soon."

"Okay. I'll see you at the show," Alex said. "I love you."

As Harper said goodbye, Grace turned around and from twenty feet away, nearly knocked Harper over. It wasn't intentional. It was just the way she had.

Harper hung up, leaned back, and, as quietly as she could, set the phone on the table. Grace got closer again and sat on the step in front of Harper. Eddies of perfume and Aveda swirled in the air.

"What are you doing here?"

Beneath Harper, Grace's eyes were open, expansive pallets

of blue. "That's a good question," she said, tracing the edge of the sandpaper guard on the wood stair.

Harper waited, but Grace had no answer, only another question. "Do you have any idea how hard you were to find?"

"No," Harper said, lifting the shaking glass before putting it down quickly, "I don't."

"Well you are."

Harper wondered how long Grace had been looking, and what in God's earth she wanted now. After all this time. Harper could see the oil painting in her therapist's office, an empty boat at dawn.

"You didn't want to be found, did you?"

"What makes you say that?"

"Let's see, an unlisted number, no forwarding address. No one I know has talked to you since you left."

Everything Grace said was true. Maybe she didn't want to be found. Or maybe she just wanted Grace to have to find her.

"I was on your trail a couple years ago," Grace shared, "and actually found you in Seattle. But by the time I got up there, you'd already moved from that yellow triplex. There was even a piece of junk mail with your name on it still in the mailbox. After that, I lost track. Well, until..." Grace stopped and stared at her hands.

Harper finished her sentence: "Until I ran into your mom."

A deeply pained look flushed Grace's face. "I was really, really sorry to hear about your parents," Grace said, looking Harper straight in the eyes. "I'm sorry I couldn't have been there. I wish you'd have called."

"Called?"

A car alarm beeped in front of the house. Then there were footsteps coming up the driveway before Juliet surfaced with a Pyrex dish.

In her green scrubs, Juliet shouted, "*Bonsoir*!" She and Sabrina were both nurses at OHSU, a teaching hospital in the hills overlooking Portland.

Grace and Harper stood.

"Just returning this," Juliet said, playfully licking her lips. "Yuh-hum. We finished it this morning." She spoke to Grace.

"Harper made this amazing casserole. Was it called Death By Eggs?"

Harper shook her head.

"Anyway, it *was* to die for."

Juliet smiled at Grace then looked at Harper. Grace stuck her hand out.

"This is Grace, an old friend of mine. In town for…work?"

"I just moved here actually."

"What," Harper gasped.

"I'm starting law school in a couple weeks down the road. Lewis & Clark College."

Juliet set the dish on the Adirondack chair. "What kind of law?"

"You never went to law school?" Harper asked.

"Environmental," Grace said, keeping her attention on Juliet.

"You picked the right city."

"That's what I've heard."

Juliet sighed, a long day behind her.

"When are you leaving?" Juliet asked Harper.

"Soon."

Juliet looked at her watch. "I figured you'd be on the road by now."

"What time is it?"

"Four."

"Fuck."

"She goes on at eight?"

"Yeah."

"You better get movin'," Juliet said. "Alex'll have a fit if you're not there when the show starts."

Out of the corner of her eye, Harper saw Grace look twice when she said Alex's name.

"Will you be joining us at the beach Friday?" Juliet asked Grace.

"Joining you?" Grace questioned.

"What are you up to this weekend?" Juliet asked.

"Nothing, I guess."

"You're new to town. You should join us at the coast this weekend, right Harps?" Juliet suggested.

"Oh. I don't..." Grace started to say.

To Harper, Juliet asked, "Is that okay? I guess I should let you invite her. She's your friend."

Harper was at a loss. "Ah, of course it's okay."

"Have you been to the Oregon Coast?" Juliet asked.

"No," Grace admitted.

"You're coming then. There's plenty of room at Harper's."

"I..."—Grace looked at Harper, who was staring blankly at Juliet—"am not sure that'll work."

"Why not?" Juliet asked. "We won't take no for an answer. The more the merrier." Juliet turned to leave. "Now get going. Chop Chop."

After Juliet drove off, Grace and Harper made plans to see each other once she returned from Seattle. Coffee at noon on Wednesday. Before Grace left, she pulled a Montblanc pen from her purse and jotted her cell number on the back of a receipt. Harper flipped it over. It was from Bluehour.

Her heart rate quickened.

How dare Grace come to Portland, she thought. And still be so beautiful.

Life was going to get complicated.

"Thinkin' About You"
Trisha Yearwood

On her way up to Seattle, Harper listened to the Dixie Chicks, contemplating, replaying the resurrection of Grace in her mind. Hearing her name. Seeing Grace's face. The way Grace touched Harper's arm when they parted.

Harper was to blame for the Juliet debacle. Even though Juliet was overbearing at times, pushy even, she should've been honest with everyone about her past, especially with Alex.

Harper arrived at the Paramount Theater with few a minutes to spare. As she hurried to her seat, there was a buzz in the auditorium, similar to the one in her head. An elevated energy. Anticipation. One that everyone could feel. Alex, Harper knew, was feeling it in her room too, where she prepared for her show, meditating and eating licorice, lights low and lavender candles burning.

Above the crowd, the Paramount Theater's expansive vestibule was filled with the smell of popcorn and history. The theater, built in the Twenties, had seen some of the best performers of the twenty-first century. Their presence was tucked into the bronze pockets of the magnificent ceiling—Madonna's bravado from her first world tour, the psychedelic cadences of Jerry Garcia and the old money of Sinatra and his entourage.

When Alex walked on stage, the women went wild. As she took the microphone, her eyes moved along the front row until she found Harper, sitting on the end with her camera. Alex winked and blew her a kiss before welcoming the crowd.

Alex's popularity had grown since her last tour, and considerably so. She'd gone from selling out bars and small venues to the big time: huge summer festivals, opening for well-known headliners, filling a theater like the Paramount.

Harper was proud of her; if anyone deserved the sweet taste of success, it was Alex. Many nights Harper had woken up at two or three, and found Alex in the living room strumming the guitar with her spiral notebook open, scribbled lyrics and titles in the margins amidst musical notes. She was a true artist.

In the bright lights, Harper snapped several shots of Alex performing. One with just her and the microphone, the spotlight illuminating her body as she sang a capella with the guitar slung around her back.

During intermission, Harper got a beer and leaned against the pewter railing above the mob of dykes. Before her first sip, Harper dug into her bag to make sure the Valium was still there. The prescription had expired, but she'd thrown it in the small zipper pocket of her purse anyway. Just in case. Doctor's orders after she'd ended up in the emergency room for sleep deprivation years before. Harper could feel the swallowing fear of panic coming back. Suffocation. Claustrophobia.

As Harper nursed her lager, she replayed her conversation with Grace for the fifteenth time since they parted, focused now on the tail end of their conversation, the piece that occurred at Grace's car door.

It *had* been Grace that snowy night in December. She'd been in town visiting Lewis & Clark's law school and to see if she could find Harper. Harper didn't tell Grace that she'd gotten close, nor did she tell Grace that she'd run after the train in a humiliating tear down the sidewalk. These details were Harper's. And hers alone. Grace didn't deserve to know.

After Grace found Harper's empty apartment in Seattle, she

explained, she'd all but given up until Harper bumped into Cilla when she was home settling her parents' estate.

"She told me you were in Portland," Grace said, propped against the car with her glasses back on.

By the time Grace found Harper, her parents had been dead for almost two years.

Traveling from Chile to Buenos Aires, Ana and Blue's small, twin-engine plane had gone down in the Patagonian Andes. Harper had traveled to Santiago with Alvaro to retrieve their bodies.

The photos from their last trip were framed in sequence in Harper and Alex's hallway; the halogen lights really brought out the sparkle in Ana's eyes. Harper's favorite shot of her mom was the last one her dad took before he died. She was sprawled on a rock on the edge of Rio Picacho, her boots off and her feet crossed in front of her. Ana had that look; the one Harper's father fell in love with in Kenya, the one he mused about when he drank wine.

It was a miracle the film survived. If only they had.

Before Harper left Arizona with their ashes, mixed together according to the instructions in their will, she stopped by the cemetery to see Dean. It had been years since Harper visited, so she took a boxed lunch for herself, a pot of pansies for Dean and had planned on staying the afternoon.

Except for a graveyard truck and an old man on the other side of the pond, Harper was alone that day. It was quiet, only a fading lawnmower in the distance. The grass had grown over, but Dean's grave was just where Harper remembered, past the mausoleum under a willow tree. After she threw out the blanket and kicked off her sandals, a pair of Canadian geese waddled along the water's edge.

Harper worked on lunch, a half sandwich, egg salad and two cookies, both peanut butter. Halfway through, a piece of mayonnaisey yolk fell from her spoon and landed on the slate headstone beneath her. Harper was startled—she hadn't noticed she was lying on someone. Ethel Ramsey. She lived to be ninety-one. Harper apologized to Ethel as she cleaned her mess and scooted over.

A car door closing, a jarring discord of metal, woke Harper from her nap.

Lifting her head, Harper could've picked out Cilla's black convertible anywhere; even though it was a newer model, she'd ridden in her Bentleys hundreds of times. They all looked the same, just upgraded year after year.

When she first saw Cilla, she was pulling geraniums from the trunk. Harper gathered her trash, blown and scattered about, and braced herself as Cilla approached.

Harper saw the hesitation when Cilla realized it was Harper at Dean's grave, a short pause before continuing her way.

"Harper," she said, setting the flowers down.

"Hi Mrs. Dunlop."

"What a surprise."

"I was just leaving."

She stood over Harper in a wide hat, her tangerine linen dress whipping in the wind. "You don't have to go on my account," Cilla said. "How are you? It's been ages."

"I'm all right."

She started to walk away and stopped. "It's so nice that you're here...visiting Dean. Seems no one comes to visit anymore. Only me."

In the shade of the tall trees, Cilla was dappled with white flecks of flickering light. Harper studied her as she gracefully strolled back to the car. Once Cilla had come back and was sitting on her own blanket a few feet away, she spoke to Harper again. "Do you come here often?" she asked, rubbing her temples and looking longingly at Dean's headstone.

"This is my first time, actually, in many years. If I still lived here, I'd come more often."

"What do you mean?"

"I live in Oregon now."

"You do?"

"I moved away a long time ago," Harper said, embarrassed she didn't know. "I've been gone since 'ninety-five. I went to grad school in Seattle then moved down to Portland last year."

"You're kidding?" Cilla said, taking off her sunglasses. "I wonder why Grace never mentioned it."

Harper knew why, maybe they both did.

There was a cavernous depression in Cilla's eyes. Up close, without the speckled sunlight and the dark lenses, she looked thirty years older. Almost like an old lady. "I just thought you and Grace grew apart."

Harper unfolded her legs and rolled her pen up and down the cover of her journal. "That happened too," she said.

As these words came out, Harper went back in time, wondering if Cilla even knew that one Christmas, some time ago, she'd destroyed Harper's life.

After this exchange, Cilla concentrated on Dean's headstone. Harper, too, got lost in the words—*brother, son, uncle, beloved, home*—the deep etch of the stone, the grass grown up against it.

"I can't believe it's been twelve years," Cilla said, still mourning. "Everything changes, you know, when someone dies."

Harper leaned back onto her hands and said, "This, I know," with a deep pained, empathetic sigh.

Together, they sat with this for a long time.

After Cilla cracked the spine of her hardback, Harper pretended to scribble in her journal for a spell. Even though she was curious, she didn't ask Cilla that day how Grace was or what she was up to. Part of her didn't want to know, as it was the stuff of Harper's nightmares. Instead, she asked Cilla if she was hungry.

"I have an extra cookie," Harper said, opening the paper bag.

Cilla set her book down. "What kind?"

"Peanut butter."

She smiled and reached out. "Peanut butter's my favorite."

Before Harper left that day, Cilla asked her why she'd come home. Like so many things, she hadn't heard.

Harper opened up about her parents passing, even wept in Cilla's arms at one point, something she'd never have imagined she'd do again.

It wasn't the first time; it had happened once before when Harper was a little girl and had woken up in the middle of the night with a fever at one of Grace's slumber parties. Cilla had wrapped Harper in a blanket and held her on the couch until nanny Mariana arrived.

"Reunited"

Peaches & Herb

Grace's handlebars glistened in the sun as she rode up on her bike Wednesday. It was similar to the one she had in college, a wide-handlebar cruiser they'd ridden together Laverne & Shirley-style through U of A's campus. A head-turner, Grace didn't realize the effect she had on passersby—her golden hair blowing in the breeze outside Starbucks at Pioneer Square commanded everyone's attention.

Sitting outside waiting, Harper watched Grace lock up her bike. Around her, in sharp contrast to Grace's beauty, Portland's "concrete living room" was oozing local color; students kicking Hacky Sacks, artists scribbling in their sketch books, the homeless panhandling with signs and holding pit bulls on rope leashes. On an Indian summer day, it was a far different place than the snowy night in which Harper had run after the train. Peppered amongst the bustling diversity were pinstriped suits, briefcases and cell phones. The square had it all, even Grace, on the far corner fussing with her lock.

Harper and Grace sat outside on a patio above a group of hippies passing a pipe around a drum circle. Their tribal rhythms were hushed by the fountains, but nothing shrouded the pungent ganga floating over the bricks like mist rolling in on a lake. The scent took Harper back to the letters she wrote in Europe, the confused journal entries she'd burned months later.

"I love this town," Grace said, crossing her legs.

"Me too. I've been here for three years and the novelty still hasn't worn off."

"You haven't told me why you left Seattle."

Harper used her straw to maneuver a dollop of whipped cream into her mouth. "Just needed a change. Portland felt right."

For a moment, while Grace and Harper sat enjoying the downtown energy—the live music below and the impromptu guitar accompaniment from across the street—it seemed no time had passed. But it certainly had.

Grace pushed a suede satchel across the table.

"What's that?" Harper asked.

"Open it."

Slowly, as if Harper were reaching into a bag of spiders, she stuck her hand inside the cinched sack. Wrapped in a swatch of velvet were two artifacts from their sordid past: Harper's polished Yurman bracelet, the one Rich had given her years before, and the poesy ring Grace had slid on her finger when she pledged forever.

"My God," Harper said.

As Grace told Harper where their housekeeper, Ophelia, had found them—on top of the kitchen TV, where Harper left them the night Grace threw her out—Harper remembered how it had happened, seeing herself take the jewelry off before Grace finished wiping her with a bloody washcloth. Before Harper shared her secret, before their connection was violently severed.

"I completely forgot about these," Harper said, putting them back on. "I didn't forget at the time, but there was no way I was coming back to get them," she said. "Wow, it's amazing. The mind. How there are some things we can so easily forget and others...well, that aren't so easy."

She looked up at Grace quickly, and then her eyes switched back to the ring, the words engraved on its side. *Autre vous et nul.*

"Is this why you've been looking for me," Harper asked, looking up once more.

"Yeah," Grace said as she stood. Somewhat sarcastic; it wasn't clear whether she meant it. "Do you want anything from inside?"

Her curvy hips rocked back and forth under her capris as she walked away. She still had a helluva figure. Minutes later, she returned with a muffin and water.

"So," Grace asked, sticking a chunk of blueberry in her mouth, "who's Alex?"

A moment of truth. Harper took the straw from her empty cup and wound it in a tight loop. "My girlfriend."

"Your girlfriend?"

Harper held it up, and with her long finger, Grace popped it in one flick.

"My girlfriend," Harper said, grabbing Grace's muffin, tearing off a piece.

"I thought you weren't hungry."

"I'm not."

"How long have you guys been together?"

"Four years."

"Four years?"

"Yep."

Someone was vibrating in Harper's purse. The gallery, she thought. Harper had left her cell number on a sign in the window.

It was Alex; Harper hit *ignore* and set the phone down.

Only a few breaths were taken before it buzzed on the table again.

"What about you?" Harper focused on the tanless halo on Grace's finger. "Did you marry him?"

Before Grace could respond, Alex called a third time.

"I'm sorry," Harper said, suddenly concerned. "I have to take it. She never calls like this."

Alex was frantic. "I'm on my way to the emergency room."

Harper looked at Grace. "What's wrong?"

"Sabrina's been in an accident on her scooter."

"Is she all right?"

"I don't know."
"Where is she?"
"OHSU."
"I'm on my way."
Harper quickly gathered her things. "I'm sorry, I have to go."
"Is everything okay?"
"I'm not sure. Sorry. Call me tomorrow. Maybe we can try this again or have lunch," Harper said, leaving her card on the table and Grace alone.

When Harper arrived at the hospital, Sabrina was in ER 8, a barren space separated by a cloth drape on an oblong track. A few feet away, a woman Harper couldn't see moaned and called out the name Beulah.

The cuts on Sabrina's face had already been sutured, as had the gouge on her thigh, seven stitches long. They were waiting to set her ankle. Sabrina's brown hair was down around her face and she still had on her golf clothes.

"What in the world, Sabrina?" Harper said.

"I know, I know."

"What are we going to do with you?"

Alex and Juliet were sitting on either edge of the bed. Juliet, who was still in her scrubs and had rushed to the ER from her post in the pediatric unit, was holding one hand and Harper reached for the other.

"Are you all right?"

"I'm fine. Just some cuts and bruises."

Juliet rolled her eyes. "She means stitches and broken bones. You're lucky you didn't kill yourself."

"Seriously," Alex interjected. "How many times have we begged you to get rid of that thing?"

"Come on guys," Harper said. "Accidents happen." She knew how much Sabrina loved her scooter.

"I'm sorry you had to leave work," Sabrina said, shifting the ice pack taped to her foot. "It wasn't necessary for you and Alex to come. But I appreciate it."

"Don't be silly. We wanted to be here," Harper said.

A nurse both of them knew approached and loaded Sabrina into a wheelchair.

"Don't think for a second we're not going to the beach this weekend," Sabrina said, swinging her leg onto the outstretched gurney. "I won't let this stupid little spill ruin the fun."

"We'll see about that," Juliet snapped. "Stupid little spill. Can you believe her? She gets run off the road, flips upside-down in a ditch and calls it a stupid little spill?"

"You're not my mother," Sabrina playfully shouted as the nurse wheeled her away.

Juliet blew Sabrina a kiss and then rolled her eyes. In lesbian years, they were an old married couple.

"Is your friend still planning on coming?" Juliet asked.

"Friend?" Alex asked, confused.

Juliet looked at Harper.

"I forgot to tell you," Harper said. "An old friend of mine—someone from a long time ago—stopped by the other day. She just moved here."

"I invited her," Juliet added. "I met her when I was dropping off your casserole dish."

"I've been meaning to tell you."

"Who is it?"

"It's no one you know. We grew up together."

"That reminds me, we're going to have to meet you at Seasmoke on Friday," Juliet said, picking up a magazine. "Somehow I got the late shift. We'll be there in time for dinner."

"What's her name?" Alex asked, focused on Harper, still interested in this mystery friend.

"Grace."

"She was adorable," Juliet said, flipping through a tattered, outdated issue of *Good Housekeeping.* "Maybe we can hook her up with Janice."

Alarms went off in the room next door. Feet scrambled. Voices were raised. Someone yelled, "Clear."

"She's straight," Harper said. "Let's go wait in the reception area."

"Why"

Annie Lennox

The next day, Harper was at Whole Foods getting ready for First Thursday, a monthly art walk downtown, when her gallery assistant, Mona, called. Five months pregnant, Mona had been throwing up all morning and needed to go home. Standing in the frozen foods, Harper dug out the Bluehour receipt and called Grace's number. There'd been a text message from her with a time and place for lunch.

She called and left a message for Grace as she threw a wheel of brie and some chévre in her basket. "Listen, I'm super sorry. Again. But my assistant who usually manages my gallery events has gone home sick, so, I have to postpone lunch today. We're having an open house tonight and I need to get things ready."

Harper grabbed a box of mini quiches and paused, making her decision. "You're still more than welcome to come to the beach with us this weekend." The freezer door bumped Harper's elbow. "It would be good for you to see the Oregon coast."

Over a hundred people were expected that September night,

the high-season for art in Portland. At four thirty, customers started winding through her three-room gallery with exposed brick.

While people discussed photography, balancing plates of food and glasses of wine, a stout man in a fedora played the piano. The yellow doors, propped open with tall baskets of black-and-white panoramics, spilled Rachmaninoff into the street through hanging wild flowers.

The gallery drew a surge of people right before six, when a group of tourists was headed down into the historic Shanghai Tunnel. One of the access points into the dark, dank and certainly haunted underground tunnels wasn't far from the gallery's front door. People were always chatty before the tour, as they descended with flashlights into the 1870s, and somber when they came out, preoccupied with images never to be forgotten. Trap doors, tight holding cells and piles of dusty shoes left behind from unsuspecting Portlanders who were drugged, gagged and taken to boats headed to Shanghai.

Alex showed up around seven, stopping in before a session at the recording studio. She brought Harper dinner, tofu tacos with guacamole. Standing on the top step of the ladder, Harper asked for help hanging a frame.

"A little to the left," Alex said.

"How's Sabrina?" Harper asked, moving it slightly.

"A little more. Perfect. She's fine. Getting around pretty good with just a cane." Alex held the ladder while Harper descended each step. "She, of course, is refusing crutches, which Juliet is insistent on."

"Those two."

As Alex folded up the ladder, the pianist began the prelude to *Lakme*.

Harper leaned into the counter, one hand on the roll of brown paper used to wrap prints. The memories from the song knocked Harper out—lightning reflecting off the Amstel River and Grace's eyes, the incense, the sweet surprise of a woman's tongue in her mouth.

"Harper!"

"What?"

"Where'd you go? I've asked you the same question three times."

"Sorry. It's been a long day."

"Do you want me to put out more food?"

"Sure."

Totally immobilized, Harper stayed in the same place until the *Flower Duet* came to its thunderous close. Others with a similar affinity clapped and put dollars in the performer's tip jar.

Harper collected the empty bottles of syrah as Alex came out with another tray of spanakopita. With a spatula, she was dishing them onto the table when Grace walked through the door. Panicked, Harper turned and rushed into the backroom.

At the recycle bins, Harper waited, negotiating her next move. "God damn it," she whispered. She should've known Grace would show.

"Should we put out more turnovers?" Alex asked, startling her.

Harper set down the bottles. "Don't worry about it. I'll take care of it. You can go," Harper said, sitting at her desk for a moment, digging for nothing in particular in the drawer.

"I've got five minutes. I'll put in another batch."

When Harper walked back to the gallery door, Grace was standing near the window looking at one of Blue's books.

"I set the timer for ten minutes." Alex kissed Harper's cheek. "Don't wait up. I'll be late."

Harper cleaned all the dishes and reapplied lipstick before returning to the gallery again. As she came out with a hot tray of turnovers, Grace was standing in front of Harper's nature collection, transfixed on a purple poppy. Harper walked to the food table with confident, hurried strides.

Tim, the Arts editor at *The Oregonian*, called Harper's name. She'd received a message from him the day before; he was doing a piece on a project for which Harper had recently done pro-bono work—a series of shots of the Columbia Gorge in sepia tones. While he scribbled notes and Harper described the commission, Grace walked past. She made two more passes before they finished the interview.

"Nice place," Grace said, approaching slowly as Tim excused himself. Her timing had always been seamless.

"Thanks. It's a work in progress." Harper motioned to the construction equipment stacked in the corner.

"Your body of work is amazing," Grace said.

"They're not all mine."

"I know. I recognize those lions and tigers," Grace said. Harper watched her lips move. "I did, after all, grow up in the G Wing."

In Harper's youth, an entire section of their home—playfully known as the G Wing, or Gallery Wing—was dedicated to her parents' photography and her mother's remarkable yet overshadowed clay sculptures. Harper's bedroom had been at the end of the hall.

"Your stuff is very impressive. You've got a great eye," Grace added. "You got it honestly."

When they ascended to the rooftop deck during the ten-cent tour, a light breeze blew through the trees, a row of maples lining the street below. They stood at the railing, both watching the Shanghai Tunnel tour exit.

"Look," Grace said, turning to Harper, "I know you're busy, but I just needed to see you. I need to tell you something before we go to the beach…if that's still okay," she added. "It was something I didn't get a chance to say yesterday."

"Okay."

"I need you to know how sorry I am. I was a horrible shit and you had every right to never want to see me again. I'm sorry for all the tears, and for the blood, and for abandoning you, and for slamming the door. I just"—she shook her head, ashamed—"couldn't open it back up."

Harper watched Grace speak words her soul had needed to hear for over a decade. In the spirit of the moment, Harper decided to make a confession of her own:

"You know, I found everything you threw away when you left school."

Grace was puzzled.

"The cards, your journals, everything. Even your half of the best friend charm."

It was clear by her facial expression Grace suddenly remembered.

"I'd gone to the dumpster the morning I found you in the bathtub. I was trying to dig out your moving boxes."

"I'm sorry you had to find those things," Grace said softly. "I'd give anything to get them back."

An older woman, dressed in a colorful sari, appeared at the top of the stairs. "Excuse me," she said. "Do you know where I can find the manager?"

"I'm the owner."

"Sorry to interrupt. I'm interested in a zebra print."

Harper looked at Grace, who hadn't taken her eyes off Harper since her apology. "Wait here," she said. "I'll be back."

Downstairs, in front of the striped horses, Harper answered several questions about the expedition her parents had been on before wrapping the print up for the woman, a bohemian from the East Coast. She wanted it shipped overnight to a Manhattan address.

After she left, it was customer after customer—one wanted Harper to get a picture down, another was interested in showing Harper's work in her Vancouver gallery, a man with a bushy beard bought the biggest purchase of the night: a forty-inch by thirty-two-inch framed portrait of a young aboriginal boy washing his sister's feet riverside.

Grace finally gave up and came downstairs. From a few feet away, as she was changing the credit card machine tape, Harper told Grace she was sorry. "I didn't mean to leave you hanging."

Grace disappeared into the backroom, surfacing with a piece of paper. "What time are we leaving tomorrow?" she asked, handing Harper a folded note.

"Noon."

"All right." Grace raised her eyebrows. "I'll be at your house at eleven forty-five?"

"Great. See ya then."

Harper watched Grace leave through the open door while

she continued fixing the tape. When she was out of sight, she stopped and read the message. It was simple, only three words.

Please forgive me.

"You Still Move Me"

Dan Seals

The next day, Harper was packing items into a red cooler when Grace arrived. Standing with a brick of cheese in her hand, she heard Grace say a muffled hello to Alex, who was in the driveway loading their Land Rover.

At full tilt, Harper burned from the kitchen to the dining room window where she'd have a full view of the driveway. Ever so gently, Harper pulled back the side of the curtain and spied.

"You must be Alex," Grace said. A deep breath followed. Just like she had at their tennis first match, Grace stuck out her hand.

"Hi," Alex said. "It's nice to meet you." She fumbled a bit as they shook hands. "Harper told me you guys grew up near each other in Arizona. You used to play tennis against each other?"

"Yeah," Grace said, a smile pushing through. "And we went to college together, were sorority sisters and kinda roommates for a while."

"Sorority girls? Roommates?" Alex paused. "Huh. She never mentioned that."

Peeping in on their conversation, Harper cringed.

"Here, let me help," Grace said.

"I've got it." Alex loaded a suitcase into the backend. "Thanks."

"It's gonna be a fun weekend. You already met Juliet?"

"Yeah, the other day."

"She and Sabrina will be joining us later tonight."

"Awesome," Grace said. "Thanks for the invite."

An awkward moment passed as they smiled at each other.

"Harper's inside. We're just about ready."

"Okay," Grace said, turning toward the house.

When she headed up the stairs, Alex looked twice at Grace—a lingering double take—before reaching for the next bag.

Rushing again, Harper ran back to the kitchen and pretended to be busy when Grace rang the doorbell. "One minute," she said, taking a fast look at the microwave's reflection. She tousled her hair.

"Hey."

"Good morning," Harper said, opening the screen door. "You're right on time."

In her Mercedes Coupe, Grace followed Harper and Alex to the coast.

The beach house Harper's parents had left her was a luxury she didn't take for granted. They'd lovingly named it Seasmoke—an homage to the movie *Stealing Home*—and had its name painted on a piece of driftwood at the front door. Situated on the sand in an exclusive coastal community, Cannon Beach, the cottage was loaded with charm. The clapboard had been partially replaced and the electricity brought up to code, but Harper had refused to sanitize it any further with upgrades.

After a lazy afternoon on the beach, right before sunset, Harper headed inside to start dinner. It was her night to cook. From where Harper was standing in the kitchen, she could see Alex and Grace chatting outside by the fire. As she minced scallions, she wondered what they were discussing. She couldn't imagine they had much in common. Alex had grown up on a farm.

As Harper moved to the stove, she caught Grace watching

her through the window. It was a look she'd seen before—a look, in fact, that had many times brought Harper to her knees.

This time was no different.

Grace wasn't casually watching Harper make dinner through the glass—instead, she was a melting candle too close to a fire, suddenly bending into Harper without even realizing it.

"Can I help?" Alex startled Harper when she came up from behind.

Harper scooped a bite of paella. "Does it need anything?" she asked, blowing on it before sliding it into her mouth.

She stole one more look at Grace as Alex chewed. "Um. A little more saffron. And some garlic salt."

Alex's breath was balmy when she whispered, "I like your friend." Her breast pressed against Harper's arm. "Why haven't you mentioned her before?"

Harper let her gaze go back to the fire where Grace was sitting in a worn Adirondack chair. Illuminated, her face had an amber glow as she continued watching them inside. In the firelight, she was even more beautiful than Harper remembered.

It was a good question. An important one.

"We lost touch for a while," Harper said as she sprinkled saffron threads into the sauté pan.

Some time passed before Alex set the table and fiddled with the stereo. Harper watched Grace talk to Sabrina and Juliet, who'd just arrived from the city and let themselves in through the back gate.

Grace's accent was subtler than it used to be, Harper thought as she mixed the corn bread. But she knew, like she knew her own alcohol limit—one she was getting close to drinking through—that with each sip of wine, the Brit in Grace would eventually overpower the watered-down American drawl.

Still healthy and firm, the physique you get from the right genes and two decades of training, Grace was still in impeccable shape. She was taller than she was in Harper's fantasies, but her embrace had been the same as she enveloped her body days earlier, an impossible moment she'd imagined a thousand times.

Alex grabbed two glasses and the pitcher of sangria before heading for the door.

"Wait," Harper said. "Come here."

In a robin-egg blue yoga suit and flip-flops, Alex walked to where Harper was standing at the chopping block.

"I love you," Harper said, reaffirming for herself. She stepped closer for a kiss.

"I love you, too."

Watching her walk out of the kitchen, Harper let out a private sigh as she put the bread into the oven.

Grace was mid-story when Harper finally stepped into the summer night. An ocean wind flirted with the flames, and even though the sun was down, the gulls floating over the crashing surf could still be heard in the darkness. Sabrina and Juliet had gone inside to change.

"After they separated us," Grace said, "Harper started a food fight." Her laughter was effusive, bigger than the ocean, the soundtrack of Harper's childhood.

Alex looked at Harper as she sat down. "How come you never told me you were a debutante?"

"What?"

With an impish grin, Grace shrugged.

"I never told you?"

"No."

"It was years ago."

Curiosity was still on Alex's face. "I'm sure learning a lot about you today."

"It was just a small blip on my radar screen," Harper said. "I didn't realize I hadn't told you." She looked at Grace. "And it was *you* that started the food fight that day."

They all had their secrets.

Alex pulled a strawberry from her sangria. "So," she said, "how long have you guys known each other then?"

Grace did the math. "Twenty-five years."

"Twenty-six," Harper corrected. She knew the answer, had never lost count. "You moved to Arizona right before third grade."

"I'm surprised I haven't met you before," Alex said, dropping the sliced berry into her mouth. "Where have you been?"

Grace looked at the flames and then to Harper, regret burning along with the fire's reflection in her eyes. Somehow, thinking about the past, they were both able to smile.

"It's complicated," Harper said, "I mean, I don't even know where you've been for the last—how long has it been?"

Grace looked at her glass. "Twelve," she said, pausing, "years." Harper knew that number too.

Just then, the timer buzzed in the kitchen. Harper stood to check on the bread. "She's here now. That's all that matters."

But that wasn't the truth. Other things mattered.

After pulling out the corn bread, Harper spent the next ten minutes in the bathroom sitting on the edge of the tub. With her elbows on her knees, her drink centered between her sandy clogs, she gave herself a pep talk.

"Don't you dare do this," she whispered. "We made a pact. And worked hard to get here."

She drew a long breath then lowered her head. Inviting Grace for the weekend had been a bad idea. She wasn't ready to spend this much time with her.

In the mirror, even in her turtleneck, Harper could see her skin was blotchy—wine always did that to her—and her eyes bloodshot behind her glasses. There hadn't been a restful night since Grace surfaced.

Why had she come back? Why, of all places, had she ended up in Harper's backyard? Literally. That day, when Grace had called her name, Harper almost couldn't turn around, knowing, forever knowing that voice.

Grace was still so striking, Harper thought. She'd fooled all her critics who'd predicted she'd lose her looks—the jealous girls growing up who wished for her slender torso, her button nose and dollish curls.

Earlier that afternoon, as she and Grace were rinsing off the boogie boards, Harper noticed she was curvier, her hips fuller than she'd remembered—the natural way a woman's body settles onto its bones with time—and her chest had more freckles than it once did. Sun spots. Her wetsuit was unzipped halfway revealing her red bikini, her voluptuous cleavage. Eyes hidden by her sunglasses, Harper tried not to look, but couldn't help herself.

Sabrina, back outside in flannel pajamas, was sitting on Juliet's lap with her broken ankle propped up on the fence. She and Grace were engaged in conversation when Harper finally rejoined them. They were talking about the cabin she and Juliet had bought at Mount Hood, a small A-frame near Lost Lake.

"Remember all those summers we spent at the cabin?" Grace asked. With Harper's parents, the two of them had spent innumerable weeks in the woods of northern Arizona at the Alessi's getaway.

"Of course."

"And that fort we built."

Harper sat in between Grace and Alex. "*Casa de madera*," she said, her Spanish still within reach.

"We made it out of old logs," Grace said. "Nailing pieces together with rusty nails we found in the garage. We worked on it for days and even made a chimney out of rocks. I bet some of those logs are still nailed together"—with her smoky eyes, Grace looked directly at Harper—"probably fused into one by now."

What Grace hadn't mentioned was what happened years later in the ruins of their fortress. At her beach house along the Oregon coast, Harper could still see the woman's face, the neighbor who caught them naked in the snow that winter night. It was years after they built their secret log castle in the woods. They'd just made love on the bear rug and the drift was to their knees. After a snowball fight, Grace had pinned Harper down. Neither of them realized she was watching until it was too late.

"Our cabin is pretty rustic," Sabrina said, bringing Harper back to the beach. The stitches on her face were covered by a butterfly bandage. "But it'll be fun in the winter. You should come up sometime."

"Thanks," Grace said.

Harper refilled her glass and headed back to the kitchen.

Dinner was served on a distressed round table in the dining room, and as they ate, consuming endless pitchers of sangria, Grace and Harper continued reminiscing about the old days, telling childhood stories all the way through dessert, a flaming, chocolate something-or-other Alex, the pastry chef, created. Beyond her sultry singing voice, Alex had serious skills in the kitchen—something she could always fall back on, she said.

Afterward, the women played board games well into the night. During several heated rounds of Pictionary, the marine wind howled as they scribbled unintelligible stick figures.

"You're funny," Grace blurted to Harper midway through. "You're still really funny."

Through the laughter, each time the salty breeze blew into the house it carried Grace's perfume through the room, tearing through Harper's armored shell.

"Against All Odds"
Phil Collins

It was late when Harper dug deep in the kitchen drawer for the stashed cigarettes. She waited until everyone had gone to bed.

When she sneaked outside, the fire was barely smoldering and the tide was high, crashing against the mossy boulders. She scratched the matchstick against the stone fence and lit the cigarette, drawing the stale tobacco into her lungs. She didn't smoke anymore—had kicked the habit years ago—but kept them hidden for nights like these. Emergencies.

Sitting on the fence, she pulled her coat in tight, buttoning it up all the way, cinching the hood over her head so the down feathers muted the rest of the world. In the muffled distance, she could still hear the waves crashing, the wind whistling, but everything else was lost in the feathered static, the padding between her and her chaotic life.

Barefooted, her feet dangled in the sand as she, again, for the hundredth time, contemplated Grace's return. She didn't hear Grace come out, didn't sense Grace standing behind her. She didn't know until Grace reached over and took the cigarette, her pinky grazing Harper's thumb.

"God. You scared me," Harper said, pulling off her hood.

"Sorry." Grace's English accent was extra thick. Pulling the red quilted coat around her, she took a drag before passing it back.

"You still smoke," Harper said.

"More than I should."

We all had our vices, Harper thought. Her own was chocolate. And the pinot noir grape. And the occasional joint.

She wondered what other vices Grace still had: eating candy for breakfast, drinking lots of coffee and stout, masturbating in the shower.

Behind them, except for the nightlight in the kitchen, the house was engulfed by dark silence.

"I love Alex's new album," Grace said, putting her foot on the short fence. They'd listened to it over dinner. Harper looked at the house and then back to Grace as she spoke. "I get what you see in her."

With no light from the fire, only the fuzzy moonlight through the passing clouds, Grace looked twelve years younger, Harper thought, just like the last time they'd seen each other at the Dunlop's front door. Since then, not a day had gone by when Harper hadn't thought of her, about the life they could've had if only—if only things had been different.

"Do you love her?" Grace asked.

"Do I love her?"

"Yeah," she said, softer now, watching Harper carefully. "Are you in love?"

Harper pulled hard on the nicotine. "Yes." She blew out the smoke. "I am."

In bed the night before, Harper had felt compelled to lay her book down and touch Alex's face while she slept. Her gentle breaths, the way her square mouth was partially open, filled her with guilt. She was lucky to have Alex, Harper thought, crying a little—for her own reasons—as she rolled over and kissed her temple.

"Why do you ask?"

Grace turned toward the ocean. "No reason."

There was always a reason.

A breeze blew in and they both adjusted their coats. With the wind, Harper felt a surge of audacity.

"What inspired you to waltz back into my life after all these years anyway?" she asked. "You know. After slamming the door? Shutting me out? I mean, what made you think I'd even speak to you?"

"All I had was hope," Grace said.

Silence filled the space between them before Harper, her rage passing, asked another question, one she'd wondered for well over a decade.

"So tell me," Harper said, handing the smoke back to Grace, "like Alex said, where *have* you been for the last twelve years?"

Staring at the burning cherry glow, Grace didn't answer right away and that was fine by Harper, as a big part of her didn't want to know. Waiting, she looked at the full moon now peeking from the clouds and then at the minuscule light floating on the ocean's horizon, a hint brighter than the stars above.

"Getting over you," Grace said.

Harper kept her focus on the white surf just beyond the beach grass, the breaking waves that stopped, frozen when she felt the weight of Grace's eyes upon her.

"It took twelve years, huh?" Harper's flip words barely came out as her chest caved in.

Grace still had that way. After all the years.

"We'll see," Grace said, throwing the cigarette into the fire and taking a step closer. "When I get there, I'll let you know."

Harper sensed the energy building, saw it coming in slow motion even though she wasn't looking—Grace's knees bending as she sat down, her hand coming to Harper's neck, her face getting closer.

When their lips came together, mixed with cigarette smoke, Grace tasted pure and soft, unlike anything she'd known before or since their first kiss in Amsterdam. Just like old times. Primal, organic, earth fucking shattering.

For the moment, nothing else mattered—not even Alex—and Harper let herself go, imagining they were drifting in a coral sea, just her and Grace. The sun was warm as they worked their way against the side of the boat, the wall of the fire pit. Harper wanted to peel off Grace's skin and wrap it around her naked body.

As Harper worked her hands into Grace's coat, the heat gave

her chills; they covered her skin. Grace's topography, shoulders and arms and face as familiar as her own.

Grabbing her, Harper pulled Grace in forcefully as she straddled her on the fence.

Grace.

My Grace, Harper thought.

A secret I'd kept from Alex.

The only one.

Her tongue was so familiar, its strokes and texture. Harper had imagined it so many times, dreamt of it when she made love to other women.

With the rising moon, Harper dissolved into a meditation of Grace—her knowing fingertips, the velvet skin behind her ear, the way her tongue fit into Harper's belly button.

As the water moved farther from the house, Harper could feel her integrity slipping out with the tide. She was aware. It was the price she was willing to pay.

Time passed—unclear how much—before Harper pushed Grace away.

"I can't do this," Harper said, suddenly mortified, overcome with a sobering strike of reason. She wiped her mouth. "This can't happen."

But it was too late.

It had.

And as she stepped back and took in the full scene, she saw Alex standing in the kitchen window, her outline revealed by the dim light above the stove.

She was in her black robe. The one Harper gave her for Valentine's Day.

Seeing Alex too, Grace let go of Harper's hand and took off for the ocean. Harper watched her sprint down the sandy steps until she was out of sight.

And then fearfully, Harper looked back at the house.

Alex was gone.

Standing on the deck, adultery on her fingers, Harper had an enormous decision to make. Should she run after Grace and take her again into her arms? It was, after all, what she'd wanted all along.

Or did she face the wrath of her girlfriend, whose semblance of love and trust she'd just destroyed?

She went after Alex.

She was too late. By the time she got inside, their car keys were gone, so was their Land Rover. Harper rushed out front, but only saw taillights in the misty distance.

The house was quiet when Harper came back in, the monotonous rhythm of the peaceful waves crashing through the French doors, an acute juxtaposition. She sat down with the phone and held it tight against her chest. What had she done?

Harper tried Alex's cell before taking the beach car, a vintage VW van covered by a tarp in the garage, to try and find her. It had been her mom's and she barely got it started.

Slowly, the engine puttering, Harper drove around looking in dark parking lots and at the public beach. She stopped at the corner convenience store, the bars that were still open. The police station even, but there was no sign of Alex, or of Grace.

When Harper got home, Grace's car was still parked in the driveway and the house was still quiet, nothing touched. Juliet and Sabrina were asleep, unaware of the demolition outside their door. They'd know soon enough.

Drunk and exhausted, Harper tried to stay awake on the couch until one of them, if not both, came back.

Neither of them did.

"Guilty"

Barbra Streisand & Barry Gibb

The next morning, Harper's pounding head rivaled the scathing memories. Her pain only worsened when she opened her eyes. The smashed pack of cigarettes on the coffee table next to the phone. The nearly empty bottle of scotch. The wadded tissues.

Her terrible hangover was compounded by how she woke—Juliet, fully dressed, shook her with spitting accusation.

"What happened last night?" she demanded.

"What?" Harper asked, blurry-eyed.

"How could you do that to Alex?" Juliet held her car keys. Sabrina was behind her. "Get up." They'd already gathered their things. "We need to go."

The throbbing blood pressure started in Harper's forehead, and then moved to her arms. She even felt the beat in her toes.

Inside Harper, everything hurt. Most poignantly her heart, the control center—the current command post. One which bitterly betrayed her the night before.

"Alex is moving out," Juliet said.

Grace had taken off sometime in the night; her convertible was gone when Juliet—with Sabrina and Harper in tow—backed out of the driveway.

Confined in the car as they were, tension was thick.

"How could this happen?" Juliet questioned, as if Harper wasn't deep enough in her own anguish.

She did her best to pull together a response. "There's just so much," she bemoaned, "you don't know."

Silently, staring at the farms burning past the window, Harper wondered what she'd say to Alex. She wasn't ready to lose her. They'd finally built a life together of which Harper was proud. Beyond the echoes of regret, Harper couldn't help but wonder about Grace and where she was at, both physically and emotionally.

Was she sorry?

Did she regret what she'd said?

What they'd done?

When Juliet pulled up to the house, Alex's moving truck was already half-full.

Harper dreaded going inside.

After letting Quincy into the backyard, Harper entered through the side door. In the office, Alex's guitars were packed up next to her music books, which were in three cascading piles. The Chihuly vase Harper gave her for their anniversary was on the desk with her matchbook collection loaded inside, ready to go. She'd been packing all night.

Standing in the hallway, Harper listened carefully for Alex's movement in the old house, the cracks of the wood floor, squeaking closet doors. She paid close attention, but there was nothing. Not a creak. Harper climbed the stairs to their bedroom, each step louder than the next. Harper didn't call Alex's name. She knew she'd find her, and as Harper got closer to the top, she knew where it would be.

In the attic, Alex was kneeling in front of Harper's antique hope chest surrounded by pictures of Grace, letters and random things Harper kept through the years, things from their past Harper had locked up for her own good, and, so she thought, for Alex's, too.

The homemade Christmas stocking Harper had found in the dumpster, as well as that ratty piece of a piñata and the flowerless stems were scattered amongst Harper's journals, the hundreds of pages that helped Harper get through her last few months at U of A. In the strewn items was Harper's bloody journal from the mountain, the brown drops on the cover almost indiscernible.

As Harper stepped closer, she saw a picture of her and Grace sticking out from a stack of warped 45s. They were at Ernie's and Harper was holding a pool stick, a make-believe microphone, with her arm around Grace—they stood in front of the jukebox, its glowing edges behind them, bright and curvaceous. The lens captured more than the moment, but also the stale smoke, the blue pool chalk, the music blaring through the speakers. Grace's lips brushing Harper's neck.

Another picture, halfway covered by a broken ukulele, was of Grace and Harper in Europe standing in the middle of Dam Square, stoned out of their minds. Both twenty, they were like children wrapped around each other. Cast under a spell. Past the point of return.

With her back to Harper, Alex spoke first.

"I saw her at the gallery," she said, inspecting a photo of Grace and Dean on his LA balcony, a ring of sweat at his armpit.

Harper's knees locked.

"I wondered who she was. When I came back to get my wallet I'd left behind, I saw you talking on the roof deck."

In the picture, Grace was wearing a haltered sundress, her hair feathered.

"Now I know," Alex said, almost too quiet for Harper to hear.

Feeling weak, Harper sat down on a box of sporting equipment near the door.

"I'm such a fool," Alex said.

"I'm the fool," Harper corrected.

"How could I have been so blind?" Alex asked.

"Alex."

She set the photos down and covered her face. "I had no idea."

"Alex," Harper said, touching her shoulder.

"DON'T."

"I'm sorry," Harper said, getting weepy. "I never wanted to hurt you."

"Well, you did...you fucking did. I mean, how could you hide her from me? Look at this." Alex waved her hand over the things she'd unloaded. "I never even knew you."

"I thought if I ignored her memory, it would go away."

Alex shook her head.

"I love you," Harper said, reaching for Alex again.

"How can you keep lying?"

"I'm not lying. I love you."

"Stop!"

"I'm sorry."

"You're sorry?" she asked. "For what part? For kissing her? Is that it? You're sorry for kissing her?"

Alex picked up a mini Phoenix Suns basketball and threw it against the wall.

"Or maybe you've already fucked her. And you're sorry for that?"

Silently, Harper watched the ball bounce off the lath and plaster in steady measure.

"Have you?"

"Of course not."

"Maybe you're just sorry for allowing me to fall in love with you then? Or you're sorry for being such a coward?"

Harper dropped her head.

"Which part, Harper? I wanna know."

"All of it."

Alex grabbed the edge of the chest and pulled her body up. "At least it makes sense now." She looked at Harper, her eyes swollen, inflamed. "I finally know it's not me that's the problem."

"Whatever I can do to make this right, I'll do it," Harper cried. "I'm begging you."

"You've already done enough."

"I don't want to be with Grace. What happened between us

was a long time ago. Last night was a terrible mistake. We were drunk."

"Do you really believe that?" Alex asked, getting right in Harper's face. "If you do, you're a bigger fool than I thought."

Standing in the attic, Harper kept her head down, at a loss. They both knew Alex was right.

"What a waste. I should've left you a long time ago," Alex said, walking out of the room.

Harper helped her load the big pieces of furniture, those which Alex had brought into the relationship and some they'd purchased together. She also taped up many of the boxes and did what she could to help.

Her attempts to convince either of them she was over Grace had been futile.

By late afternoon, after an awkwardly cold goodbye at the curb, Alex left Harper standing on the sidewalk in a daze.

"I Just Fall In Love Again"

Anne Murray

It was a mean night alone for Harper. As the evening crawled along, the ramifications of her choices became more of a reality. Before dawn, she got up and walked the house, surveying the scene. Except for dust bunnies, a single striped chair and a leather ottoman were all that was left in the living room. A box of tablecloths on the dining room table.

It was a disaster.

Their home.

Her life.

Harper returned to Seasmoke the next day, and as usual, the beach house wasn't locked; it never was. She had accidentally left the back door wide open when she'd hurried out with Juliet and Sabrina. Sand had blown inside and a small crab had taken residence in one of her clogs.

Bringing along some canvases and tempura paints, Harper planned on burying herself in art, as it always calmed her. She'd also packed an Andrew Wyeth book from which to draw inspiration.

She lit a fire and then set up her easel, which had been Ana's, by the window. A clear view of Haystack Rock was in the distance.

Harper covered three canvases before she washed her brushes. Her fingers grew tired quickly; it had been some time since she'd painted. A bath followed.

While she filled the tub, an evening routine she'd also let slide after coupling with Alex, she dug Grace's phone number out of her purse. She opened it, stared at the numbers, and then put it back.

She couldn't.

She'd promised herself.

Deep in the bubbles, Harper tried to relax, but the memories were rousing eruptions in her mind. The kiss. The look in Alex's eyes. Grace running down the stairs. She was an idiot, driven by madness. Her mournful loneliness was well-deserved, she thought. But still, despite her internal badgering, she wanted to see Grace again more than anything else in the world.

Leaning back in the tub, Harper closed her eyes. She didn't know when or if she'd ever see Grace again. She didn't know how long it would take for Grace to get in touch, or if she would.

And she wondered if Alex really was gone for good. They'd hit rough patches before. But this damage seemed permanent.

It was.

She was certain.

Harper painted another scene the following morning. Pulling on her emotions, she used various shades of blue to capture a storm overcoming a small town. She tried throwing in the perspective of changing seasons: fall leaves barely hanging on; piles of snow along the dirt road and a snowman in front of a dilapidated barn.

When she finished, she grabbed her car keys and headed out. Not bothering to call, Harper drove the short distance to where, coincidentally, Ruthie and her partner, Frieda, were living, a town about ten miles south on Highway 101. Ruthie said she was always welcome and she knew they'd both be home; they hardly left the house anymore.

Frieda answered wearing her standard cottons. Always in the same or a similar outfit, she must've had twenty different sets, some pants, some shorts. Frieda, too, had been painting; a smudge of orange was smeared across her forearm. That day, her white hair was as wild as ever, Einstein-ish. Of German descent, she was a bulky woman of seventy-five with hands that amazed Harper by their girth and brawn.

Their cats, Tom and Jerry, greeted Harper at the front door, doing figure eights around her legs as she chatted with Frieda.

"Oh my goodness, Ruth's going to be so excited," Frieda said, looking behind her.

Harper could hear Ruthie approaching, the rubber end of her cane squeaking against the floor. "Who is it, Frie," she yelled.

When Ruthie finally got to the door, she let out a small yelp. "Baby girl! I've been thinking about you," she said, joyfully, and then suddenly stern. "Where have you been? It's been months."

"I'm sorry. Just busy."

"Yeah yeah. Get in here." Ruthie said, lifting her chin and putting her arm around Harper.

The same year Harper's parents bought their home on the coast, Ruthie and her long-time partner had also retired to the beach at Manzanita, another quaint beach town. She and Frieda had been together for twenty-five years even though the intimacy had long since dried up. No longer lovers, Ruthie explained, they still cared for each other and enjoyed the companionship. "We're all we have," Ruthie once said.

A woman of few words, Frieda joined them for lunch—a mix of cheeses, salami and fruit—but left Harper and Ruthie alone afterward.

"Something's going on," Ruthie said. "What's up?"

"Let's talk about your hip first," Harper said. "It hasn't gotten any better?"

"Certain days are worse than others. Doc wants to replace this one too,"—she slapped her leg—"Can you believe it? It took me almost a year to bounce back from the other one... Ah well."

"That's what running twenty miles a week your whole life will get you—bad hips. I'll be right behind you in line for new knees," Harper reasoned.

"You sound just like Frie…I don't want to talk about me. We could go on forever about what aches. What I want to know is what's wrong with you."

"How do you know me so well?" Harper asked.

"We're soul mates, you and me. And, you only come around when you need to talk."

"That's not true."

Ruthie flashed a smile. They both knew it was.

"I'll try and be better."

"Good. Now what's going on?"

"God, I don't even know where to start."

"Oh dear. Is it Alex?"

"Yes." Pausing, Harper envisioned the moving truck pulling away. "And,"—she took a big breath—"it's Grace. She's back."

"Grace?" Ruthie paused. "Grace, Grace?"

"Grace Grace."

"Jesus."

"Yep. That's pretty much what I said."

"How did she find you?"

"Remember when I ran into her mom?"

"At the cemetery?"

"She's been looking for me ever since," Harper said. "And remember that snowy night I freaked out and ran after the train in Portland?"

Ruthie's mouth was wide open. "Yes."

"It *was* her."

"No way. I said you were going crazy." Ruthie laughed, rocked backward.

"I know." Harper laughed along with her. "I thought I was too."

"So you've obviously seen her."

"Oh I've seen her." Harper looked out on the sea, rain clouds thundering in like the ones she'd painted, her tear ducts filling.

"Tell me everything. What was it like?"

"We kissed the other night."

"What?"

"And Alex." Harper stopped. "Saw the whole thing."

"No." Ruthie was suddenly stern again. "Harper."

"I know." She closed her eyes, shook her head.

"How did it happen?"

Harper's heart raced as she told the story.

"I don't know what to do," she concluded. "Tell me what to do."

Reaching over, Ruthie put her hand on top of Harper's.

Frieda delivered a tray of steaming drinks and patted Harper on the head.

"Are you still in love with Grace?" Ruthie asked.

Harper looked up from stirring cream into her coffee. "I wish I could say it was the alcohol. Certainly the slip of judgment was, but"—Harper sighed—"I still think about her every fucking day."

Ruthie sat with this admission as she sipped her cappuccino. "So," she said, "what happened once you went inside? I mean, what did Alex do?"

"She took off running. Drove straight home and started packing the house," Harper said. "And then she left."

"You're kidding. She didn't give you a chance to explain? Time to try and make it right?"

"Nope. I tried to explain, but I guess I didn't need to. She found a bunch of stuff I'd been hiding in the attic. All of Grace's things."

"You'd been hiding?" Her tone was incredulous.

"I never told Alex about Grace," she admitted. "I never got around to it. You know? I never thought it was important and I'd moved on so long ago. Remember when my therapist told me I'd turned a corner? I mean, you agreed. It was right before we bought the house."

Shaking her head, Ruthie said, "Why did Alex think you were in therapy all those years?"

"For my other issues," Harper said with a laugh.

"Right." Ruthie bit her lip.

"Where is Grace now?"

"I haven't seen her since we kissed. When she saw Alex in the window watching, she ran away, too. In the opposite direction."

"You haven't called her?"

"I promised myself I wouldn't." Harper played with the tassel on the tablecloth. "She said she'd never gotten over me."

Five minutes went by as they both watched the surf.

"Believe it or not," Ruthie finally said, "I don't know what to tell ya. I know this is a first."

"I'm a fucking fool. That's what you should tell me." Harper's eyes welled again. "I just needed to vent, I guess. And see you. You always make me feel better."

"Don't be so hard on yourself," Ruthie said, reaching for Harper's hand again across the table. "We all make mistakes. None of us are infallible. Alex's had her share of slips, too. Don't forget that."

"I know, but things are different now. Or they were. We were doing so well. This was all so unexpected."

"Well life's that way. And you mustn't hold a grudge. Not forgiving yourself will only give you cancer. You've got to let it go and move forward as soon as possible."

Ruthie glanced around to see where Frieda had gone. "Look at Frie," she whispered. "Not going home for her mom's funeral has eaten her alive for twenty years. She's never been able to forgive herself, no matter how contentious their relationship was. I know that's why she can't get rid of the cancer." Ruthie let go of Harper's hand. "It's come back three times."

A long run on the beach was just what Harper needed in the afternoon. The adrenaline, rushing through her veins, helped clear out some of the anxiety she was feeling. Finally. Release.

By late afternoon, the Oregon coast was covered with a blanket of fog. Socked in, the weatherperson said. The beach cottages were a medley of sporadic lights, fuzzy and golden through the mist as Harper's feet pounded the damp sand. One foot in front of the other for an hour.

About a mile from home, Harper took off her shoes and walked in the water. She picked up and skipped sand dollars, the flat skeletons coasting like Frisbees on top of the bubbling surf. Getting lost in the ominous waves, Harper thought about the decisions she'd made—right and wrong—the path she was on, and now off. And she reconsidered what Ruthie said, the weight of her sage words.

As she got closer to Seasmoke, someone, a cloudy figure, was walking in the hazy distance.

It was Grace. In Harper's yellow raincoat. Harper would know Grace's mannerisms anywhere. The measure of her steps. The way she carried herself.

Grace was smiling under the hood, a shy gesture revealing much—her desires, her trepidations. Embarrassment.

"I followed your footprints," Grace said. "I hope you don't mind."

"Of course I don't mind."

Grace was beautiful. And Harper's attraction was bigger than ever, even bigger than days before when she'd pulled Grace frantically against her in those careless moments outside.

"It's good to see you."

Grace put her arm through Harper's as they walked up the berm toward Seasmoke. "You okay?" she asked.

Harper paused, unsure. "I think so."

And it was true. Despite the pain and destruction she'd caused, part of her was relieved. Especially after spending time with Ruthie. For so long she'd denied what she wanted, what her soul really needed. It was refreshing not to be running any longer.

"I'm sorry," Grace said. "I never intended to cause such trouble."

"I know," Harper said, pushing the door open with her arm, backing into the house. She smiled. "But you did."

"What happened"—Grace stepped inside—"after I left?"

Throwing her running jacket on the couch, Harper stopped in the middle of the room. "She left," she said, turning to Grace. "I tried to convince her that what had happened was nothing…a drunken mistake."

"Was it?"

They stood face-to-face, the coffee table between them.

"I don't know," Harper said, hesitant. "I need a shower."

Harper turned the water as hot as she could stand it before getting into the clawfoot tub. Steam billowed as she stepped in, puffing from the shower curtain like a smokestack. In the old bathroom, as Harper stood in the piercing jet, she thought about their kiss, a trespass against someone she loved. A trespass against herself.

But the kiss. The cigarette smoke, her breath.

With her arms up on the wall, Harper let water massage her scalp.

Her hands. Her tongue. The burning.

Beneath the showerhead, in the soft lamplight, Harper showered until the water ran cold. She was falling again. And there wasn't a damn thing she could do about it.

Grace was leaning against the counter eating raspberries when Harper came out. She was wearing jeans and a shrug sweater over a wide-neck top, her hair down. Candles were lit. There were two champagne glasses and a chilled bottle waiting to be opened.

"Are we celebrating something?" Harper asked.

"I don't know. Are we?" Grace said as she popped the cork.

Standing with a towel wrapped around her body, Harper took a glass and stood across from Grace.

"Seems crazy to celebrate the last forty-eight hours, no matter how much I enjoyed kissing you."

"OK. Not celebrating," Grace said. "Honoring." She stepped closer.

"Honoring works." Harper held up her glass.

They tapped and drank, their eyes intensely connected, just like old times at Ernie's, when it was all they could do to escape the caged moment, the nosy bystanders, and quench the thirst intensified by the jukebox.

But this time there were no prying eyes. No walls. Nothing between them now.

There might have well been a jukebox in the corner, for Grace hit one button on the remote control and, just like that, they were transported back to the Nineties. Chaka Khan's familiar beats pulled the moment further into the past as they headed back through the fire.

Harper took Grace's hand and they danced as angry squalls pounded the beach outside. They were both barefoot. Both nervous.

Before the song ended, Harper took Grace's face into her hands. Slowly, their bodies came even closer together. Their foreheads and noses touching.

"I never stopped loving you," Grace whispered, closing her eyes.

With everything she had, Harper kissed Grace, completely and wholly this time. No fear. Sober. Their insatiable fever, the one constant in their relationship, was a different temperature than it had been twelve years prior, even a few nights before. In the past, it was crazy hot and they were ravenous, overwhelmed by their desire, unable to get close enough, tearing at each other's skin. But now, standing as grown women with nothing to lose but each other, it was even bigger than before.

This time, they both knew what was at stake. Harper led Grace down the hall and up the steep staircase to the bedroom, where the ocean wind licked the wainscoted walls and the high-beamed ceiling. At the balcony door, Grace undid Harper's towel, and let it fall to the ground.

Harper kissed Grace again when she went for her clothes, more forceful and impassioned as Harper undid her blouse one button at a time. She was in control.

Lowering Grace's body to the bed, Harper let her eyes move down Grace's torso, examining what she'd missed since they last made love, the naked body so telling. At one time, she'd had a belly button ring; now above her innie was a small scar the size of a sesame seed. She'd never stopped working out. While there wasn't a six pack anymore, her pubic muscle was still cut below her waistline. Perfection, Harper thought.

Harper started at the top, kissing Grace's face before moving to her neck, her pulse beating against Harper's lips. She licked the skin around Grace's breasts and bit at her nipples, remembering she liked it hard.

Tracing Grace's ribcage with her hands, she counted each bone as she moved farther down. Grace's legs tensed, and then relaxed as Harper gently spread them open.

The closer Harper got, the more Grace arched her back until she was finally in Harper's mouth.

Crack boom.

There was an explosion. A big one.

The entire evening, as the moon moved from east to west behind a layer of marine clouds, they took turns with each other, one orgasm after another. Sometimes together.

Finally, after they collapsed in exhaustion, Harper purposefully took her time dissolving into another world. In the sea of white linen, she relished the evening—the tears, the whispers, the trembling honesty—as Grace slept on her chest.

There was calmness. Still an easy silence about them.

The doors leading to the balcony were wide open and the wind, blowing in from the sea, caught the wisteria blooms and carried their sweetness into the bedroom, where Grace's scent lingered on the sheets. From the bed, Harper could still see the tip of Haystack Rock poking over the vines which had grown the full length of the house. Through the northern windows, the purple, low rolling mountain range seemed to crash into the coast like the waves beating its rugged shore, like Harper had crashed into Grace once again.

Was this really happening? Harper wondered.

She almost couldn't believe it.

"We're All Alone"
Crystal Gayle

There were rose petals from the bedroom, trailing all the way down the carpeted staircase to the kitchen, where Grace was making pancakes the next morning.

Grace's hair was tied back with a red headband and she wore a black apron. "*Buon giorno, Bella,*" she said.

From behind, Harper put her arms around Grace's waist.

"I haven't slept that well in years," Grace said.

"Me neither."

With her cup of coffee, Harper sat at the island on a tall barstool and watched Grace cook breakfast. She was in Harper's slippers.

Grace had brought home a whale watching brochure from the market and Harper reached for it, just beyond her mug. Grace, the perpetual early riser, had already gone shopping and returned by the time Harper woke.

"In all the years," Harper said, "I've never been on one of these."

"Really?"

"We've gone whale watching before. But I've never been on a guided tour. Dad used to take us all the time. We'd go to his favorite spot, right near Heceta Head lighthouse, and we'd just drift with the ocean current all afternoon."

Grace wiped a dollop of butter on the steaming stack of pancakes. Harper said, "Sometimes Dad would drop a fishing pole in the water. I caught a marlin once. A baby. It broke my heart, that poor fish when it came onboard flailing about." Harper looked through the brochure. "Mom would pack the greatest picnic baskets."

After a leisurely breakfast, they put on their tennis shoes and walked down the beach to the pier where they met the boat for their afternoon whale adventure. It was Grace's idea. And she'd made the arrangements.

The forty-nine foot excursion boat was already packed with people, mostly college students from an oceanography class. It was a breezy day and the clouds were puffy cotton balls overhead, the artful blue and white a stark contrast to the dark sea, which extended out into a rounded oblivion. For the ocean, it was relatively calm. The boat rocked back and forth—slow and measured, like a baby's cradle—and the engine purred as everyone waited for something to happen a mile offshore.

As they watched for movement, they picked up where they left off at breakfast, Grace now revealing the details of her failed marriage.

"A year after you left," Grace said, "I married Jamie." She looked off into space, hypnotized by the horizon's subtle curve. Beneath them, a wave from a passing boat slapped against the weathered wood of the *Discovery*.

"He was so persistent," she said. "Saying yes was the only way to get him to shut up. He and Mummy. She was the worst."

"I remember."

Harper also remembered the times Jamie had annoyingly just shown up at Ernie's or at the university to visit Grace. "Just passing though," he'd say. "Was in the neighborhood."

"I entered into the marriage with good intentions. I thought I could turn my life around. Somehow learn to be the good wife. And somehow learn how to love again." Grace touched Harper's face. "But that's far from what happened." She put her head down. "Once he took over his dad's company, he started drinking a lot, and, I suspected, started sleeping with his secretary. And others.

It was never confirmed, but a woman knows. You know?"

Harper shook her head and thought about Jamie's parents' nasty divorce; it was legendary in Scottsdale.

"But what finally broke the camel's back was me."

Harper brought Grace's hand up and held it against her cheek. "What do you mean?"

"I was so unhappy, you know?" Grace looked down again. "I started seeing this woman from the club. Her name was Suzanne. She was a VP at Simons & Simons, her office was even next door to Jamie's."

"She worked with Jamie?"

"For Jamie."

"Wow."

"I know," Grace said. "I met her at one of his Christmas parties and then ran into her one morning at the club's gym. The rest, well, I'll just say we worked out a lot."

Leaning against a huge cooler, Harper played with a rope tied to the boat's bow.

"It was a huge mess when her husband caught us fooling around one afternoon in their pool. He was supposed to be away on business."

The thought of Grace with another woman was even more unsettling than Jamie.

"Probably more detail than you wanted, huh?"

Harper forced a smile. "Maybe."

Grace, too, painted on a smile. "I knew then. Hell, I knew when we were in college. That I was different. Gay. Or something."

"Or something," Harper echoed.

"But you know…the truth was, Suzanne didn't make me happy either. I was always thinking about you."

"You were?" Harper asked, tilting her head.

"I was."

A sweet moment passed between them as they sat with this. It briefly fed Harper's soul, filling one of the numerous holes in her heart.

"So how did your mom react when all this happened?" Harper asked. "She must've freaked out."

Suddenly, without any warning, a giant humpback the size of a train car breached the surface thirty feet away and seemed to stop midair before slamming back down into the water. In slow motion, they looked at each other. A monster wave doused the boat as Harper screamed, "Oh my God!"

Grace was drenched; they both were.

Quickly, Harper dug out her waterproof camera and was ready when it came up again, with another whale this time, a smaller one with spots. She captured several great images as the pod around them fed for over an hour. Each time one breached, there was a collective "Whooooa" from the boat.

The girls, still children in their minds, giggled and strolled home in knee-deep water, relishing the memory, stopping once to look at the digital images. Their faces close together at the tiny screen. Their cheeks touching.

Neither could believe how massive the whales were. "They were bigger than I remembered," Harper said, her finger in the loop of Grace's khaki shorts.

A few strides from Seasmoke, Grace dropped a bomb. "I have to go home tomorrow."

"We probably should get back to civilization," Harper said.

"No, I mean I have to go to Phoenix tomorrow."

"What? Why?"

"I have to go home and deal with some things. Tie up loose ends. It'll just be a few days. I'll be back before you know it."

"But you just got here."

"I know. I'm sorry. It'll be a quick trip. I'll be back Friday."

Harper added up the nights. "Five days is a long time."

"I'm sorry."

"Why are you going?"

"I've just got a bunch of stuff to deal with," Grace said, a kite gliding idly above. "Lawyers, the will and stuff."

"Look What You've Done To Me"

Boz Scaggs

That night, Harper made a pot of her Sunday gravy and homemade fettuccini while Grace looked through scrapbooks. When she got to the one Harper had put together in homage to her parents, she spoke up.

"Did you make this for the funeral?" Grace asked.

Harper shook her head. "Just for me."

The album included photos from Ana and Blue's time spent in Chile, even a picture of Ana waving from the plane before it took off. Inside, there were also clippings from the paper, their obituaries and shots of Harper scattering their ashes.

"How many places did you spread their ashes?" Grace asked, focused on Harper holding the urn on a cliff.

"Four. Machu Pichu, Zion, Popina Island and Sedona. All of their choosing."

"What was that like?"

Harper peeled garlic cloves. "Surreal," she said, smashing the cloves with her knife. "It's all a blur now. I didn't cry in the first few places. Peru, Zion and the island. In those places, it was more of a rush. Not until I dumped the remainder of their ashes in Oak Creek Canyon." Harper started to choke up again. "Once the urn was empty."

Grace walked to the kitchen and put her arms around Harper. She kissed her temple. "I'm so sorry."

They left Seasmoke early the next morning to ensure Grace had time to pack before catching her afternoon flight.

On the road, Grace's phone rang as they hit the Portland city limits. She dug around her purse until she found her cell. Harper kept one eye on the road and one on Grace, who looked at the screen and hit ignore.

"Who was it?" Harper asked as Grace powered down her phone.

"Just Mummy. I'll call her once I'm at the airport."

Together, they made a quick stop at Grace's new home, perched in the West Hills overlooking downtown Portland. It was a traditional three-story house with a grand open staircase and bamboo floors throughout. The For Sale sign was still in the yard. Grace gave Harper a hasty tour before she pulled out her suitcase.

"There's still a lot I want to do," Grace said, flipping on the hallway light.

As they walked through the gourmet kitchen, Harper noticed the answering machine's light blinking. Grace did too, and just as quickly as it started, ended the kitchen highlights.

Harper made a mental note, but hadn't thought much of it until she saw Grace's wedding ring, a sparkling five-carat diamond with platinum band, in a dish in the bathroom like it had just been taken off to shower.

Harper tried to be cool and calm about things. Grace was going through a divorce and that was complicated, but she couldn't ward off the ever-persistent voices in her head.

"So, what do you need to take care of at home again?"

"We've got a meeting with the family. That stupid will crap. And I've got a bunch of divorce stuff to deal with too."

"How long until that's final?"

"It could take months."

"You've filed, though?"

"Yes, Bella. I filed months ago. Almost a year now."

"Why is it taking so long?"

Grace shrugged. "Lawyers."

As they got closer to the Port of Portland, unease continued to stir within Harper. Stopping at the curb, Harper turned to Grace. She looked carefully into her eyes before saying goodbye.

"Who's picking you up?"

"Daddy," Grace said.

"And you're staying with your parents?"

"Yes. For the third time." She gave Harper a big hug, and was suddenly in a hurry. The kind of hurry that happens at airport curbs. "I'll be back before you know it. You won't even have time to miss me."

Harper sat still, a pit in her stomach, and watched Grace wheel her suitcase inside.

Grace blew a quick kiss from the revolving door.

That night, there was nothing she wanted to watch on TV. Lying on the couch in the same position, flat on her side with a throw pillow tucked under her head, Harper fitfully surfed the channels until her eyes got droopy.

In bed, she flipped on the lamp and picked up a novel she hadn't gone back to in weeks, plowing through several chapters. A momentary escape.

Grace called around ten. "I'm just getting to bed," she said, "I'm exhausted."

"What did you do tonight?" Harper marked her spot in the book and set it on the dresser.

"Dinner at the club and then we had an event to go to."

"Why are you whispering?" Harper asked, knowing the layout of the Dunlop house, knowing her folks were at least an acre away.

"I don't know," she said, raising her voice.

"What kind of event?" Harper asked.

"A concert."

"For charity?"

"No, it was just a show. I've got to get to sleep. I'm so tired. I'll call you tomorrow?" Grace said, in a hurry again.

"Who'd you go with?"

"Mummy and Daddy. Why?"

"Just curious."

There was a pregnant pause. "I'm going to bed. I can barely keep my eyes open," Grace said, signing off.

Harper flopped around for hours, eventually watching more TV—an infomercial for the George Foreman grill and then an episode of *Three's Company*. Jack in bellbottoms. Chrissy in short shorts.

As Harper lay there, staring at the screen and then the ceiling, she fought off images of Grace and Jamie at their wedding. Grace in her gown. Jamie fucking her in their hotel suite after the reception. From there came thoughts of Grace and that woman, the one she met at the Christmas party, going down on each other in the steam room at the club.

Finally, after enough torment, Harper got up and slid her laptop out of her leather workbag. In just her panties, she walked with the small Macintosh under her arm through the kitchen and then back up the stairs.

She had e-mail to check, gallery work to get to and an airline ticket to book. Maybe. She'd just peek. And see if she could get a good deal to surprise Grace the next day.

Sitting with her legs out straight, leaning against pillows she'd stacked between her and the headboard, she checked her Yahoo account first, then opened an Excel spreadsheet—July expenses—before closing it again. She wasn't in the mood and it wasn't really why she got her laptop out.

Then, Harper searched for a flight to Phoenix. The following day, there was a two o'clock flight with plenty of seats. A summer blowout special and prices were dirt cheap.

Without much thought, she booked it and fell asleep almost immediately. Grace was going to die, Harper thought. It would be a great surprise.

On the plane the next day, Harper's second thoughts began: Was she doing the right thing? She hadn't been invited, after all, and she worried Grace would be taken aback by her just ringing the doorbell. They'd just arrived at this great euphoric place and she didn't want to do anything to mess it up.

Despite the little voice, Harper stayed buckled into her seat and read the rest of her novel.

Grace was crazy about her. And it would be a fabulous surprise, Harper kept telling herself.

Once she landed in Phoenix, she rented a car and drove straight toward the Dunlop's house. Her hands were sweaty against the steering wheel; she wasn't used to the desert heat or the nerves. A bank billboard she passed said it was 118 degrees.

When she arrived, there was no movement at the house, no activity she could see, so she pulled her rental car into the circular driveway and put it in park. Still, she wasn't sure she should be there. She looked out the window toward the front door; the large brass Irish Claddagh ring still hung dead-center on the dark wood. She'd banged that thing so many times.

Harper checked herself in the mirror, put on one more coat of berry gloss, and then got out of the car.

She stood for a good minute before ringing the doorbell. Even thought seriously about walking away, calling from around the block first. Instead, she went for it. From outside, she heard the bells chime throughout the house.

Taking a full breath, she waited. It could be Cilla. Or even Grace's dad. She prepared herself, thinking about various scenarios. Then, there were footsteps at the door, someone fiddling with the lock.

And then her worst nightmare.

Jamie. Standing with his legs spread apart, wearing a Nike visor and a matching zip-up golf shirt.

Immediately, Harper heard her therapist. "You MUST let Grace go. She's never going to be yours again."

"Oh my God," Harper said, flabbergasted.

"I'll be damned." Jamie laughed out loud. "I should've known."

Before she could ask if Grace was there, she walked up behind him.

"Harper. What...are you doing here?" From inside, standing next to Jamie and his small pooch belly, she pulled the door all the way open. Her mouth was gaping, just a hint wider than Harper's.

"It's not what it looks like," Grace said.

"You sure didn't waste any time, honey," Jamie said.

"He was just leaving. He was just dropping off..." Grace paused, got a startled look on her face. "Go," she said, pushing him out the door.

With his arrogant swagger, Jamie dug his hand into his pocket and walked out. "You girls have fun. I'll be back at six tomorrow to pick her up," he said, not looking back, still the world's biggest prick.

Harper, in utter shock, looked at Grace.

"What are you doing here?" Grace asked, looking back into the house before pulling the door shut, nearly closed.

"I just"—she looked back at Jamie again—"wanted to surprise you."

That was all Harper got out before tiny fingers, whose nails were painted bright pink, wormed through the crack of the door. Grace followed Harper's eyes to the child trying to get out.

"You should go," Grace said.

"But, what..."

From inside, just on the other side of the door, a little girl yelled, "Mommy!"

"Can you give me a second?" Grace didn't wait for an answer before disappearing into the house.

Just like before, Harper stood alone at the big wooden doors. A quail skittled in the bushes under the Joshua Tree.

A child?

Harper pushed on the door, but it was shut this time. All the way. Stepping into the flower bed, she looked through the decorative glass panels flanking the door. Craning her neck, she could see Grace inside squatting in front of a little girl, maybe three years old, who was crying. Grace held both her hands and was talking softly.

As she watched, Harper was overcome with emotion she couldn't quite decipher, a fusion of irritation, joy and love. She didn't know what or how to feel. Building like a wave crashing down on her, then pulling back out into the ocean, only to crash in again as she stood there watching a mother with her daughter. Grace with her daughter.

Standing in a bed of flowers, Harper watched Grace send the little girl deeper into the house, pointing with her long arm toward the living room. Just then, Cilla came around the corner and took the girl's hand, leading her away from the door.

Like she was sneaking out of the house in junior high, Grace slipped back outside and gently closed the door behind her. With her arms crossed, Harper stood with her weight on one foot waiting for Grace to say something, anything to make sense of it all.

"I don't even know what to say," Grace said, her face pained like she had a migraine. "I hadn't intended for you to see all this. I'm sorry."

"What's going on?"

"I'm sorry." Grace was awkward. Extremely uncomfortable. Her eyes were lowered, narrowed.

"What was all that? Was that your daughter?"

"I'm sorry. But I can't talk about it right now. Or invite you in. I'm sorry. You have to go."

"Quit being so sorry and tell me what's going on!"

"Please. Lower your voice…I'm begging you." Grace squeezed her eyes shut, on the verge of tears. "Yes, that was my daughter. But I can't talk about it right now."

Shifting her weight to the other foot, Harper said, "Why didn't you tell me about her? And what the fuck was Jamie doing here?" Grace was wearing her wedding ring and Harper looked at it as she spoke. "Are you guys really over?"

"YES. We are. But I just can't talk about any of this right now. Please. Not here. Can I call you later?"

"I don't understand. Why can't you talk about it? I mean. What's going on?"

"I just can't. Please. Let me call you later."

With that, Harper angrily turned and stalked to the car.

"Harper. Wait," Grace said. "I'm sorry."

"The Old Songs"
Barry Manilow

After calling the airlines, Harper wasted no time getting to Ernie's. She'd had enough *pleases* and enough *I'm sorry's* to last a lifetime. What she wanted were answers.

All flights to Portland were overbooked for the rest of the evening. The earliest she could get home was the following day.

Ernie's hollow door swung open easily, as it always had. The waft of smoky bar was a departure for Harper, but not a far cry from the reality she stood in at that moment.

Jamie.

The lies.

It had all started there.

At the door, she held on to the square handle and took another breath, a deeper one, and let it all come back.

The lingering looks.

The games they played.

And were still playing.

She sat at the bar. From a bartender in a Cardinals jersey, she ordered a Corona. She rubbed her temples. What a disaster.

As she sipped her cold beer, Harper looked around the room; it had seen some improvements since her last visit. The flooring was new, so were the chairs. The shuffleboard trophies were still lined up on the same shelf, probably not dusted since Harper last played. It was a trashy place, Harper thought, seeing it more subjectively now, acknowledging that Cilla had been right all those years—it was a horrible place for them to hang out. Yet, despite the silk plants, the webbed glass behind the bar, and the old ashtrays, there was something endearing about Ernie's, something comforting to Harper amidst her storm of confusion.

She set her cell phone in front of her and made sure the volume was high. Grace had better call soon.

Sitting at the bar, speckled Formica washed out from years of bleach, Harper envisioned Grace squatting in front of her daughter, their profiles so similar, their golden locks seemingly from the same head. She folded the corners of her cocktail napkin and watched traffic cruise by on Scottsdale Road.

And then, in her mind, she saw Jamie. He was still so callous, more malevolent than ever. The way he talked to Grace. His patronizing laugh.

There was no way they were still together. It was clear, Harper decided, thinking about it away from the chaos of the moment. But why was she wearing her wedding ring? It didn't make sense. She needed answers.

Harper had seen the jukebox when she came in, only a few feet away from where she was sitting now. It was also new. The unit, which looked more like a poker machine than a jukebox, had a brown casing with six embedded speakers, three on the top, three on the bottom. It seemed too small for the corner, too small for the enormous space which held the musical catalyst for the girls years ago, when they were old enough to know better and too in love to care.

A child?

An episode of *Southpark* went by and so did two gin and tonics before Harper used the restroom. She dropped the phone into the back pocket of her Lucky jeans.

Not until she began walking did she realize the significance of where she was headed. It was a dirty, grimy room, but also a safe haven, the Garden of Eden—a sanctuary of forbidden love—one with a lock, where Grace and Harper could be alone, even if for ten seconds, with no one else watching. Hard to pin a number on how many secret kisses were stolen in there. Twenty? Thirty? Maybe more. She thought of the women who pounded on the door, eyeing them after they unlocked it, wondering. That was back when things were simple, before the world began closing in around them.

At the door, Harper hesitated once more, knowing the smell of the room, just like the bar itself, would suck her deeper into the past. And it did. The grape flavored automatic deodorizer was still wedged in the corner. The stalls were in the same spot, but everything else had been replaced, repainted, recaulked. Even still, Harper felt an odd wave of safety in there. She stood with her arms crossed against the counter before washing her hands. The lock on the door was gone; there was no more hiding.

Back at her barstool, Harper pulled the bills from her stack of change and headed to the jukebox. Sure the new box would be full of Lynard Skynard, Led Zeppelin, Johnny Cash, she wondered if she'd know any of the songs. It was a dive bar, after all. Divier than ever.

Standing at the glass, the prism-esque CDs spinning in a window above the music lists, Harper scanned the albums. It had been full of records back in the day.

As she read the labels, she pressed her forehead against the glass. The music was much the same, just a different conduit. Looking at the titles, she could remember nights, moments even, she'd played so many of them.

First, she picked Phil Collins' "Against All Odds." As the keyboard reached the speakers, Harper leaned into the jukebox and closed her eyes. She listened to the whole song before playing another, this time Neil Diamond's "Hello Again," another stinger, one she'd played over and over in Europe while they were apart. She smiled when "Secret Lovers" by Atlantic Star started, remembering all the times they almost got caught. She saw Rich's face, wondered where he was in life. If he'd married. Had kids.

Things got a shade darker for Harper when she played Wynonna's "Is It Over Yet," and suddenly it was as if she was leaving Arizona all over again. In her mind, Harper drove by the Dunlop house in her U-Haul just like she had, three loops of contemplation as she decided whether or not to stop, say a dramatic goodbye before heading to Seattle. She didn't. By then, she and Grace hadn't spoken in eight months. She never dreamed the gag would last twelve years in all. The ruse still in its final act.

She wondered now, standing alone at Ernie's, if things would've been different if Grace had known she was leaving. She was done with the what-if's. Had surrendered them so long ago.

But that little girl…

Drifting off, Harper's mind went back to her, the white bow in her hair, the way her little hands clenched her mom's fingers, the same ones Harper had sucked on, slowly and thoroughly, days before at the beach.

Why had Grace kept her a secret?

"Late For The Sky"

Jackson Browne

It took Grace about two hours to show up.

Harper's phone never rang because Grace knew exactly where to find her.

Grace wore a black sleeveless dress with her hair straight—flat-ironed—a look Harper had never seen. When she walked into Ernie's, Harper had just ordered another gin and tonic. The last one, she decided. Keeping a close eye on the digital clock above the register, she was planning on leaving at eight. Grace made it in the nick of time.

All Grace held was a car key. And she was out of breath at the door. Harper, tipsy and not as agitated now, met her halfway.

"Your timing is perfect," Harper said, grabbing Grace's hand. Peaches & Herb's "Reunited" had just begun. "Dance with me. I played this for us."

Grace pulled away. "What are you doing in town? Why did you come?"

Harper tried to twirl Grace. "I wanted to surprise you."

"Harper." Grace yanked her arm away harder, aggravated. "If I'd wanted you here, I would have invited you."

"You're upset?"

"Of course I'm upset."

"I can't believe *you're* upset, when I'm the one that was lied to."

"I never lied about anything," Grace said, and she was right. She hadn't. She'd just omitted one very major detail. "It's been such a hard twenty-four hours and then you show up," Grace said, exhaling a big breath. "It totally complicates things." Her hands were shaking.

"I don't understand," Harper said. "I thought you'd be happy."

"I'm not. Abby is upset and doesn't understand what's going on."

"Neither do I," Harper said, holding her ground, and then smiling a little. "Abby?"

"Abby," Grace said, tempering too.

"That's pretty. What's her full name?"

"Abigail Junebug Dunlop."

"Junebug?"

"It was Jamie's grandmother's name."

For a moment, Harper forgot Abby was half Jamie; she looked nothing like that bastard troll.

A man at the pool table broke a rack of balls with a loud crack, startling both of them. Together, they walked to the bar and sat down.

"Why didn't you tell me about her?"

"I don't know. I wasn't ready," Grace said, scooting her stool in. "I was afraid. I thought it would scare you off."

"Scare me off? I've spent every day of the last decade pining for you and you think I'd run? Over something like this?"

Grace closed her eyes. "I don't know. I'd just gotten you back and with all the drama and trouble I caused, the timing didn't seem right."

Grace ordered a dark beer, Harper a glass of water. They each took a moment to themselves.

"I'm sorry I lied," Grace said. "Well, not lied, but that I wasn't totally honest. It won't happen again."

"I'm sorry I just showed up."

"Were you checking up on me?"

"No," Harper lied.

"You don't trust me."

"Should I?"

Again, they took another moment. Harper focused on the water, Grace on the ice sheen covering her frozen pint.

"I'm sorry," Harper said. "I thought my showing up would be a good thing. I was so excited to see your parents."

Grace put her head down, said "Christ" under her breath.

"What's she like? Abby."

Looking up, Grace's eyes brightened. "She's the greatest thing ever. She's sweet and thoughtful. And funny. She loves horses."

"Just like you."

"I guess. And she loves to play the piano. Last night, we were at her *recital* in the living room. The concert I mentioned," Grace said, "it was mostly chopsticks."

"Like mother like daughter."

Grace shook her head. "Not so sure that's a good thing at this point."

"Whatever," Harper said. "Why the hell was Jamie over?"

"He was just dropping Abby off."

"God, I hate him so much," Harper said, having never admitted it so flagrantly.

"Me too. I knew what it looked like, him answering the door. You know how he is. So invading. I was worried you'd think something weird was going on."

"I did at first, but the more I thought about it..." Harper looked at Grace's hand. The ring was gone again. "Why were you wearing your wedding ring earlier? And not now?"

Grace looked at her finger. "Well," she said, "that's the other reason I'm home." She closed her eyes as stress sucked out what little confidence she had left. She deflated, so much that there was almost a physical transformation. "I've got an important mediation with Jamie Thursday and I thought if I wore my wedding ring this week, it would go smoother. Maybe Jamie and his lawyers would go easier on me. They're like pit bulls, his legal team." Grace rubbed her temples. "I don't know."

"Is it about your settlement?"

"No. It's about Abby."

Grace, getting visibly upset, explained. "She's not with me in Oregon because I've given Jamie temporary custody."

"What? Why in the world?"

Harper moved her chair and put her arm around Grace.

"He's been blackmailing me," she cried. Rage began pumping inside Harper. "He's been blackmailing me to get full custody of Abby."

"That. Fucking. Asshole."

Grace used the damp napkin to wipe her eyes, her nose. "You don't even know what a monster he's become."

"I can imagine."

Harper suddenly felt twenty feet tall, her protective muscles expanding like the Hulk.

"Ugh, I can't stop these tears. Sorry."

"Don't be sorry. I fucking hate him."

Harper scratched Grace's back. "What could he possibly have against you? The Grace I remember wouldn't let anybody blackmail her."

"The Grace I remember wouldn't either," she said. "I don't even know who I am anymore." She took a sip. "He says he'll tell Mummy everything if I fight him on it. We're meeting tomorrow because I'm negotiating visitation rights."

"Wait, what?"

"I don't want to push him too far, there's no telling what he's capable of."

"Tell Mummy everything? What do you mean? Everything?"

"Everything." Grace said, looking around, lowering her voice. "You know. About the affair and stuff."

"Wait, your mom doesn't know about the affair?"

"Of course not," Grace said, clearly flummoxed by the thought.

"Or about us?"

"God no."

"You mean you haven't told your parents you're gay?"

"Baby," Grace said, "I can't tell my parents. Mummy would have a nervous breakdown. You know how she is. And, bigger yet, the consequences," she said, pausing and swallowing hard, "would be horrendous."

Harper sat back in disbelief. It hadn't occurred to her that Grace would still be living a lie. She, herself, had been out for so long. Grace simply wanted to pick up where they'd left off?

"Wow. I just"—Harper looked at Grace—"I had no idea you were still in the closet."

"That's a big reason why I moved to Portland for law school," Grace said. "To get the hell out of Paradise Valley so I could..."

"...hide," Harper interrupted.

"No. Be with you."

"But what about your daughter? How can you let Jamie have this power over you? And at such a price." Harper stood, herself getting upset. "Why aren't you going after full custody and fighting like hell for it? You have something over Jamie, too, remember? Like that cocaine habit you mentioned. And his affairs."

Grace sat with her arms crossed, listening.

As Harper lectured Grace, old resentment billowed up from the pit of her stomach. A new song came over the speaker, one Harper hadn't played. "Late for the Sky" by Jackson Browne.

"I want to tell them. I"—she stopped, distressed—"just haven't yet. Please, sit down."

Harper finally did. A fidgety, dismantled Grace spun the ashtray in circles as Harper's imaginary world crumbled. Life is never what you want it to be. What you think. What you expect.

"What bullshit story did you tell them about leaving Abby behind in Arizona?"

Grace sighed. "They think I left Abby so I could get things established in Portland first."

Harper shook her head, tried to contain her irritation. As the lies and deception escalated, she wondered how Grace could have not shared this with her the night before. All of it. She was a coward. Always had been. Strong as hell in some ways, but totally gutless in others.

"I can't believe you're still in the closet," Harper said, burned again.

"For now," Grace said. "I'm going to come out. I am."

Harper watched the bartender make a Spanish coffee, the

sugary blue flames charring the glass.

"You of all people understand how my family is," Grace pleaded. "I just can't do it right now. I just can't. You understand? Don't you? My whole family is crazy."

"What are you waiting for? When's the time going to be right? We all have to face this and it's never easy. The timing is never right. Do you understand that?"

"I swear I'll come out. Just let me get through this with Jamie."

"Why are you letting him manipulate you? It's pathetic. Letting him bulldoze you."

By digging into it, Harper knew she had made Grace feel small, even weaker than when she walked through the door.

"I don't know," Grace said, lowering her head. "I'm sorry."

Harper took a deep breath and, feeling bad, put her hand on Grace's back again. "I'm terrified it will all come apart," Grace cried.

"It already has."

"I don't want to lose Abby or Mummy or you. I've already lost too much. Please." She fell into Harper's arms.

Harper, sensing it was time, pulled money from her purse, paid their tab and led Grace, who was still crying, out the door.

In the poorly lit parking lot, Harper held Grace while she continued crying.

"I'm so scared," Grace whispered.

In their mostly silent embrace, so much was said again and again. The bond, the love, the patience, the loyalty. It was all they had anymore.

Harper couldn't count on a normal existence, or the life she'd dreamt about the night before, even an hour before. Their life together, the three of them.

Just like that, the water muddied again.

Just like that, they were right back where they started.

"Hallelujah"

Jeff Buckley

Harper checked into her hotel alone. Grace, sitting on a stone bench in the courtyard, waited near a cascading fountain, monotonously watching the lights flicker against the water's ripples.

They'd stayed at the Royal Palms once before together, years ago. It was during the height of their scorching affair. It was that Christmas, when everything came unraveled right before Dean died, that Harper had begun spinning into her first depression. A swallowing shadow she'd been running from ever since.

Like that night, there was still nowhere else to go. Stuck again, caught somewhere between the truth and lies. Reality and make believe. Heaven and hell.

With her welcome packet—minibar key, pool passport and spa list—Harper and Grace walked down the path lined with exotic desert plants. Perfectly manicured lantana and hibiscus. The moon, a toenail in the sky, was just above the camel's head on the mountain. It was a warm desert night, the air a dry, dusty blast.

The room was cold, very cold, a sharp contrast to outside. Harper turned off the air-conditioning and joined Grace, who'd sat down on the edge of the bed.

Harper lay back first, Grace followed and they eventually ended up facing one another in the middle of the giant California king. A bedside lamp was on. Live jazz from the hotel's bar in the distance. Mostly bass.

It was in this place that they lay for another two hours, Grace getting deeper than she'd ever been with Harper, more honest, talking in detail about the painful years of denial. The world where she was still living.

"You know I couldn't even admit that I was gay for the longest time. Even now, it feels weird saying it out loud."

"Me neither," Harper said, listening intently.

"And you remember that night? I was so angry at you when you came down from the mountain."

Harper shook her head, still seeing it clearly.

"I'm so sorry."

"Don't. You've made your peace. And I've forgiven you."

Forgiving didn't equal forgetting. They both knew that.

"That night," Grace continued, "I was really just angry at myself. I tried so hard to outrun those feelings. Like you even said. And I'll never forget it…the knowing. But it kept catching me."

Harper studied Grace's delicate eyelashes; a thin layer of mascara covered them.

"It's been such a heavy burden over the years. Not just that I was gay, but knowing I slammed that door in your face." Grace kissed Harper's fingertips. "And the lies. God, the endless lies. And all the things I've done. The sneaking around. The way I'd look at other women without realizing. The way I hid it, even from myself."

Harper understood everything she said, having experienced it all a decade earlier.

"It's a process," Harper shared, "and it's not easy. You should be proud of yourself for getting here. Finally able to admit it. It took me a long time to finally admit it to myself."

The year Harper spent mentoring queer youth in Seattle paid off in this moment. She'd processed it over and again. She remembered clearly the way she had come to terms with her own sexuality.

"At some point you have to give in to yourself," she said, "surrender to who you really are. Stop trying to be something you're not. No matter the cost. That night when I came down from the mountain. That was it for me. There was no turning back."

For her, it had taken another six months from when she left Arizona to when she was one hundred percent sure. Once she got to Seattle, she still tried dating guys, went on two or three dates before resigning from the hetero world. A last ditch-effort, she called it.

"It's crazy, I finally got to the place where my happiness, my sanity, really, was more important than losing everyone in my life. I figured if people really loved me, they'd still be there after I told them. And by that time, I was happy—well, maybe not happy—but totally at peace with my sexuality. I wasn't denying that part of myself anymore. It was truly liberating. I'd begun to love myself unconditionally."

"Is that when you told your parents?"

"Yeah, in Seattle. I'd been gone for about a year, I guess. They came for a visit and I told Mom as we stood outside the original Starbucks at Pike Place Market. A friend of mine walked by holding hands with her girlfriend and she asked if I'd ever been with a woman."

"She did not."

"She did. I couldn't believe it. At first, I stared at her blankly, and then decided to just do it. I said something like 'well actually, yes, I'm dating one right now'."

"Was that Alex?" Grace asked.

"No, it was before Alex. It was a woman named Natalie. And it was nothing serious. She was in my master's program at UW."

"What about Blue?" Grace asked.

"Dad walked up a few minutes later carrying two Dungeness crabs. He cracked some joke and then quickly realized something was going on."

"When did you tell him?"

"Later that night. We were making dinner. Mom was in the shower. You know how Dad was always in the kitchen."

"And you were always his sous chef."

"I loved cooking with him," Harper said, drifting for a spell.

Grace touched Harper's face, waiting for her to continue.

"He looked at me and said 'Baby girl, what's going on with you'." Harper recalled. "I told him right then and there. And oddly, I was much more emotional with him." She shook her head, mystified. "I don't know why."

With a serious sigh, Harper sandwiched Grace's hand with hers. "Tell me more about you."

Grace thought for a moment. "There were glints of happiness with Jamie, believe it or not. When Abby was born. Even when we first got married. But those were fleeting. No matter what I did, I couldn't escape the truth, you know? I tried everything. Therapy. Medication. Nothing worked. If I hadn't been caught with Suzanne, who knows? I might still be with him, attending company parties, crying behind my sunglasses while Abby plays at the park, just being miserable."

"I can't imagine how you did it for so long," Harper said. "The year we spent hiding was hard enough." She was tickling Grace's arm now, going over her watch and down each finger.

"I just don't know how I'm going to tell Mummy. Or the whole family," Grace said. "I wish Dean were here. He'd be easy to tell."

There was silence, a good bit of it as Harper made her decision.

"Dean knew."

"Knew what?"

"He knew about us. Right before he died, he confronted me about it. Well kind of. He never actually asked me, but it was clear."

"I don't understand. What do you mean?"

"It was so long ago. I remember he just told me I could trust him and that if we ever needed him, he'd be there."

"What?" Grace said, staring at Harper, but looking through her. "Why didn't you tell me?"

"It was when all hell broke loose with your mom. Hours before. It was the night of the winter ball. Right before he left for Mexico. And then when he died…I don't know. I just never got a chance."

"Are you sure?" Grace said, her tears now coming from a different place. "I mean, could he have been talking about something else?"

"No," Harper said, "I'm sure."

Burying her head into a pillow, Grace lay silent for a while. And Harper let her be with her private thoughts for as long as she needed.

Since their falling out, she'd wanted Grace to know. Before she let go of what-if's, she'd wonder if that, too, would have made a difference. When Grace finally came up for air, through a plugged nose, she said, "I can't believe he knew. God."

Harper moved closer and held Grace in her arms. Lying on their backs, they were both looking straight ahead when the next bomb dropped.

"There's something else I haven't told you," Grace said.

Harper braced herself. "There's more?"

Grace took one more long breath and then said, "If I come out of the closet, I lose my inheritance."

"What?"

"My great-granddaddy was a crazy man, Harp, and wrote some horrible things in his will before he died."

"He said none of the heirs could be gay?"

"He said no deviant behavior. It's in black-and-white. A list, taken from some archaic Catholic doctrine, which cites homosexuality as deviant."

Harper, completely stunned, stared at Grace. This was something she had not known. Sure, she knew the big granddaddy Dunlop was a little off his rocker, but not in a Howard Hughes meets Jerry Falwell kind of way.

"Why didn't you ever tell me this?" Harper asked.

Grace shrugged.

Harper pulled Grace in even closer, as close as she could get. "Wow. I…" she sighed. There was no immediate response as Harper let Grace's words sink in.

"I have to protect Abby," Grace said. "We've got our annual family inquiry tomorrow with Stowe." Harper listened carefully, a scowl on her face. "And I'll have to swear my life away again."

They both sat with this for a spell. Music could still be heard, a sax this time. As they both continued processing, Harper searched her soul for courage. She knew what needed to happen.

"What are we gonna do?" Harper finally whispered.

Grace spoke softly back. "I need you to be patient."

"I'm not sure I can be."

Grace's tired eyes widened.

"Please. I'm begging you. Just give me a little more time."

"I love you more than anything, I really do, but I can't be your secret again." She wiped a tear slowly sliding from Grace's eye. "I just…" she said, gently, "…can't live a lie."

"But things are different now."

"Are they?"

This made Grace cry even harder. Harper was surprised by her strength, unsure where it came from.

"I can't lose you. I just can't," Grace said. "I don't know what to do. I'm trapped." She sat up and got manic. "I'm not going to betray you this time, I swear. I swear on my life."

There was nothing Harper wanted to believe more, but the raised scars on her heart, where the knife had gone in and then come out, were too much a reminder.

The slammed door. The silence. And she knew better than anyone what a person was capable of when they're in the closet, especially under the hammer of a revocable trust. Shame and fear were shrewd players, and horrible bedfellows.

Grace smothered her face in a pillow again.

Harper didn't cry, just cracked her knuckles and stared at the clock. It was a little after midnight.

There was too much history. Too much water under the bridge. She knew Grace's patterns. Grace's weaknesses. Her own.

"I'm sorry," Harper whispered.

Grace suddenly sat up. "I'll tell Mummy everything tomorrow."

"What?" Harper said.

"If that's what it takes not to lose you, I'll do it."

Grace was standing now, pacing the room.

"Don't do something you're going to regret," Harper said, standing too. "Inheritance or no inheritance, you should only come out of the closet for yourself, not for someone else. Not even me. Especially with all that's at stake."

Grace began crying again, tormented, totally lost, still walking in circles.

Harper had said all she could say. This was something Grace had to do on her own, a decision that would shape the rest of her life.

"Are you sure you're okay to drive?" Harper asked as they said goodbye at the door.

"I'll be all right."

In the glow of the landscape lighting, Grace looked just like her mother, just like she had when Harper was growing up. Such poise and still so beautiful, even under duress.

"I'm headed back to Portland tomorrow," Harper said.

Grace clenched her fists, flexed her arms with conviction. "I'm gonna do it," she shouted, walking off into the darkness. "I'm gonna do it!"

"Love Is Everything"
k.d. lang

Grace didn't show up at the hotel the next day.

And Harper half expected it, even though she'd gotten on her knees the evening before and prayed that Grace would come back before she had to leave. Her luck had run out.

In the front drive, Harper waited at the valet stand, hoping—with what little faith she had left—that Grace would pull up as she waited for her car. But her prayers weren't answered this time. Not by a long shot.

Before getting into her rental car, Harper hesitated, looking back at the lobby one last time before shutting the door.

Should she have waited even longer, like she had so many times in college when Grace was late? Should she have taken a later flight, just like she'd put off her life in the past? Or should she let Grace go? It was an ultimatum she'd made with herself the night before. If she was a no-show, it was a no-go. They were over.

Harper wanted Grace to come out for herself—she'd insisted again at the door when she left—but part of Harper selfishly wanted nothing more than for Grace to take this brave step for her. For them. They'd never have a normal existence, especially with Abby involved, until she faced the truth. Even if they were able to skate under Stowe's radar, play on Abby's prepubescent innocence for years, Harper's heart wouldn't allow it. She couldn't live that way. Not any longer. There was no going back.

It would be the last time Harper waited for Grace, the last time she hung her happiness on Grace's next move.

She'd promised herself.

Rain trickled from the gutter to the driveway as Harper arrived home. Carrying groceries—she needed a home-cooked meal—Harper struggled with the keys. She dropped a potato and a tin of peppercorns.

There was a business card wedged into her front door, where Quincy, who'd been looked after by a neighbor, met her at the door scratching to get out. A painter, the card said. The old house could use a paint job; the lead-based green was peeling.

She was surprised once again by the emptiness inside, almost forgetting Alex was gone.

Except for Quincy's toenails against the hardwood floors, the house was quiet. He was thrilled with the company, and ran laps through the kitchen, down the hall and back through the dining room while Harper swept the floors downstairs. The empty place where the couch used to sit was filthy. Sick how much litter collects in dark, unreachable places.

After prepping a beef shoulder, Harper cut up vegetables for dinner. As she dumped everything into a roasting pan, she thought about the gallery, wondering if Mona had managed without her.

"Things are fine," Mona said, when Harper called. "We've been busy and I've been feeling good. A little slow getting around, but all's well. We've had record sales while you've been gone. You should go away more often."

"Oh yeah?" Harper said, thinking about the previous four days.

"Alex stopped by to pick up her ladder."

"She did? What'd she say?"

"Um,"—Mona was distracted—"she needed it to trim trees. Or something. I can't remember."

"Did she say anything else?"

"Hold on a sec." Mona talked to a customer in the background.

"Sorry. What do you mean?"

"Never mind."

Mona paused. "Is everything all right?"

Harper exhaled dramatically. "Not so much. I'll explain later. I'll be in tomorrow. First thing."

Harper had been dreading the cleanup, had thought of it several times on the plane, but was now finally faced with the mess upstairs. She couldn't avoid it forever. It was, after all, where she slept—the attic door just to the left of her pillow.

Her hope chest hadn't been organized in years, so she tried to see the unloaded items as a way of cleaning house. Getting rid of unnecessary clutter. It had been hard to latch anyway; too full of all she was running from.

Things were scattered everywhere. Photos fanned on the ground like a peacock tail, a display of memories, some torn to teeny bits.

Most of the stuff left inside the chest had nothing to do with Grace—family photo albums, her debutante dress, her parents' wedding bands. Alex had known what she was looking for and had carefully exhumed the relevant evidence. All things Grace.

Legs folded beneath her, Harper clutched the dusty sombrero she found in the dumpster. It was from that secret trip across the San Diego border. "*Tijuana o busto*!" it said, which they were told by a local meant, "Tijuana or bust!" They were sophomores, maybe juniors in high school. Cilla had flown into a rage when they'd returned to the Coronado beach house with tequila on their breath in the wee hours of the morning.

Harper grabbed an empty box nearby and started filling it, its flaps covered in tape and worn from overuse. This was for stuff she didn't want anymore. Crap. The sombrero went first, then the mangled ukulele, which Grace had accidentally sat on one morning in the dorm. They'd laughed about it for days.

She started piece by piece, contemplating each item before tossing it into the chest or the box. To keep or not to keep.

Slowly, Harper went through the first pile, lots of photos, dried flowers, and Gamma Kappa memorabilia.

She wondered why she'd held onto the stuff for this long; so much of it was junk. Had lost its meaning. Had seen its day. She couldn't even remember what some things stood for or where they'd come from.

As she worked though the piles, especially those which had spilled out into the bedroom, she became more and more incensed.

How could Grace think that they could just pick up where they'd left off? Was she really that foolish—to think Harper would just slither back into the closet like that? She had given Grace too much credit back in the day, Harper thought. She'd always considered Grace ahead of her in some way, emotionally and psychologically, although she'd never admitted it. Strange how time changes perspective.

With both arms, Harper scooped up the biggest pile by her ski equipment and let go without even looking.

She was done sorting through the wreckage. It was all garbage, she decided.

The items crashed into a second cardboard box she found in the corner, which used to hold an air conditioning unit. It was in that large box that she got rid of nearly everything from their past. It felt good, like washing the slate clean.

As she dumped another large load into the box, the rusted lightning bug jar slipped from her grip and smashed onto the floor, exploding into a thousand shards. Harper cursed and began picking up the pieces. The mouth of the jar, still mostly intact, fooled Harper as she reached for it. The sharp edge sliced Harper's pinky finger wide open, splattering blood on to the rough floor panels.

"Shit," she snapped, quietly to herself.

After Harper doctored her finger with gauze, she continued picking up the pieces. The glass and her shattered history.

There were a few things spared in her massive cleanout—

some random this and that's, and anything associated with her parents. She couldn't part with Dean's Ralph Lauren sweatshirt either. Very, very faintly, it still smelled like his cologne.

Once the mess was cleaned up, she dragged the boxes along the hardwood floors and flumped each one down the stairs. Two large boxes of history, mementos and dusty words which had long since faded. And many of them were no longer true, no longer extensions of herself. Scared sentences and "trigger words," her therapist called them, which no longer triggered.

Outside, the windstorm had passed, so had the rain. Harper, determined to finish the project before dinner—a roast she'd been cooking all afternoon—pulled the boxes down the damp driveway, the history too heavy to carry upright. The cardboard was loud against the cement. Grating.

She'd save her strength for the final lift into the trashcan, when it would all be gone forever.

The smell of the can, a sour mix of expired cottage cheese and dog food, reminded Harper of her dumpster dive so many years ago. The cards and the journal she'd found that morning were a part of the trash she was purging now, stuff she never should've held on to.

Standing at the trashcan, Harper looked at the sky, an ashy gray reflecting the city lights. This was it.

She squatted down and wedged her fingers underneath the first box, lifting it with minimal effort to her knee first, and then to the lip of the can.

Still holding on, she peeked inside. After a momentary second thought, she let the contents dump into the foul darkness. Water splashed as her things hit the rainwater pooled at the bottom.

The next box, torn on one side, ripped all the way when Harper lifted it up to her thigh. It was even heavier. Bigger. As it started to slip, Harper—thinking she could leverage it—swung it up and over the can, missing the hole completely. The bulk of the weight slammed against the short retaining wall lining the grass. When it landed, the box split open all the way, hurling stuff into the air and onto the lawn.

"Damn," she said, aggravated by her weakness. She bent over and began collecting the trash.

As she went along, she found a note from Grace the week after their debutante ball and a receipt from the ice chalet at Rockefeller Center with the date highlighted—Grace's eighteenth birthday. A few feet away, Grace's half of the best friend charm was lying in the crack of the sidewalk next to a homecoming picture, Jamie's face scratched out with a ballpoint pen.

Some things never change, Harper thought.

And then one picture, just beyond her reach, teetering on the limb of an Acuba bush caught her attention. It was the one she carried around, the only one, since their falling out.

For years, she'd kept its duplicate taped to the last page of her date book underneath her emergency phone numbers. It was still there. She had looked at that picture at least a million times—sitting at stoplights, waiting in line at the grocery store—the sunshine bright on Grace's face, revealing her subtle freckles.

Looking at the image, she finally understood. So much of what she still longed for was the memory of their love. The romance. The innocence, the deep stirrings. Even the pain. No one had hurt Harper since; no one had even come close. She'd done a good job insulating, keeping everyone at a safe distance.

She was certainly still smitten, yes, always would be, and certainly still physically attracted to Grace, but, staring into those young clever eyes—blue like ice, the inside of a glacier—she slowly understood her Grace, the one who'd lived on in her mind, the one locked in her hope chest, had been glorified in their years of silence. All the poison had been washed away and what was preserved was a sanitized version of Grace, a clone without the imperfections, limitations and cowardice.

"You Had Time"
Ani DiFranco

Sitting in the downtown Phoenix law office, Grace Dunlop and Jack Stowe were in a standoff. You could almost hear the western music. He pressed Grace, who had one hand on top of the Bible he was holding.

"Come on," he barked. "You know the routine. Do you comply with the provisions outlined in your great-grandfather's will?"

Her glazed over eyes moved to the window. From the sixth floor she could see across the desert valley, the opaque summer air, stagnant and blistering.

"Hello? Anyone home?" said an impatient Stowe.

"Grace," Cilla said. Slowly, Grace looked to her mother. "Any time."

"I..." Grace stammered. She looked around the room and then at the door, as if suddenly confused about where she was.

"Grace!" Cilla boomed.

"I feel faint." Grace rested her forehead on her hand and took a moment.

With a pointed directive, Stowe dispatched one of his assistants—a college boy in a starched suit—from the room. He quickly returned with a bran muffin and an ice water, setting both near Grace.

"I don't want anything," she said softly, still holding her head.

Stowe slid it closer. He looked at his watch and then at Cilla. "I've got a lunch meeting at noon."

Cilla touched Grace's arm. "Honey, eat something. Drink this water."

"I'm not hungry."

"It'll make you feel better," Stowe growled. "Eat! So we can get on with this." He picked it up and waved it in Grace's face and looked at his watch again.

"I don't want the *fucking* muffin!" Grace roared, swatting it. The muffin flew across the table, slammed against the wall and crumbled into pieces on the floor.

Cilla's eyes were huge, so were Stowe's and everyone else's at the table.

A tongue-tied Stowe adjusted his wide tie. "Well…I… thought you needed the muffin, that it would make you feel better. Apparently not."

"You know NOTHING about what *I need* or what would make me feel better."

"Grace!" Cilla gasped. "What's wrong with you?" She looked at Stowe, sorry on her face. "You know female hormones. It must still be postpartum."

"Postpartum?" Grace said. "Abby is three!"

"I was just trying to help," he said, resigned, gesturing at the destroyed muffin then sitting back in his chair.

"Help?" Grace laughed madly and stood. "Are you kidding me?" She suddenly felt reckless, exhilarated, free. She planted her hands on the table and got in Stowe's face. "You've never helped anyone in this Goddamn room! You've made our lives a living hell, you and your fucking lynch mob."

"GRACE ANNE! STOP THIS RIGHT NOW!"

Cilla was trying to regain control with her screamed command, but Grace continued the beating: "Ever since you sold your soul to that monster years ago…my dear old great-granddaddy, JW, who EVERYONE in this room has been a slave to…you've spent every godforsaken day enforcing this—"

Grace grabbed the yellow, ragged will in its leather jacket and held it up "—antiquated bullshit!"

For an old man, Stowe was on his feet quickly. He ripped the will out of her hands.

"GRACE, sit down!" Cilla ordered. "And shut up."

Grace glared at her mother, only fueled by the interference, and then leveled her stare on Stowe. "So you want to know if I comply?" She jabbed a finger at his register, which was open on the table, revealing years of compliant signatures. "Get your pen out." Grace nodded to the pen in his pocket. Stowe sat back down, sullen. "Go ahead. Do as I say," she continued. "You work for me, right? For all of us?"

Stowe, unsure what else to do, reached for his diamond-encrusted pen and took off the cap. In the room, everyone was on the edge of their seats in awe.

"Are you ready?" He placed the pen to the page, right next to Grace's name and the date. "Okay, write this…FUCK YOU and FUCK THE MONEY!"

With that, Grace stalked to the door. She couldn't believe what she'd done; she was so proud of herself. At that moment, what seemed appropriate was applause—she deemed her monologue award-winning—but everyone just stayed in their places and stared at one another in disbelief. Except for Cilla, who jumped up and was right on her heels.

In the foyer, Grace rushed past the secretary.

"Grace, STOP!" Cilla demanded.

"I'm outta here. I don't want to be a part of this anymore."

Out the door, Grace pushed the elevator button several times. "Come on!" she urged it, pulling a car key from her pocket. "Forget it," she finally said, heading to the stairwell.

Cilla moved swiftly and positioned herself right in between Grace and the exit, her black business suit like armor.

"You aren't going anywhere young lady."

"Young lady? What, are you going to give me a spanking now? Send me to my room?"

"What has gotten into you?" Cilla said, her eyes wide, glaring. "How could you talk to Stowe that way? And run out like this?"

Grace simply turned back and continued pushing the elevator button.

"Grace!" she pleaded, gripping her arm.

"I'm done. I'm going to get Abby and we're going to Portland." The elevator door opened and Grace stepped inside.

Cilla held open the door with her body. "You're not going anywhere!" she yelled, and then lowered her voice. "You're gonna deal with this and that is the end of it. Now get in here and do what you're supposed to do."

"Go to hell, Mother."

Cilla almost fell over at her words. Enraged, she struggled to speak. "What about your future? Abby's future?"

Grace stepped out of the elevator and crossed her arms. "You really want to do this? Right here? Right now?" She glanced at the front door to Stowe & Associates Law.

Cilla was sweating, holding her ground. "Do what?"

She pointed at Stowe's door. "This is a pathetic joke. All of us have been enslaved by the will for too long. Aren't you tired? Tired of living your life for someone else?"

"How can you say that? After what the trust has afforded you? The opportunities? What you've been given?"

"You mean what's been taken?"

"What about Abby? What about Jamie? This affects them, too."

Grace laughed. "Newsflash! Jamie and I are getting a divorce. We're not just taking a break. You can get off your knees and stop your prayin' because we are over. Nail-in-the-coffin over!"

"That is not how our family works. You need to stay in this and work it out."

"Jamie is a bastard. It's time you see the light," Grace said. "He's been blackmailing me for months."

"What?" Cilla gasped. "Blackmailing you?"

"He's been blackmailing me about the divorce. The terms."

"How's he blackmailing you? With what?"

Grace knew this question would come, knew she'd have to explain, but in the moment, she had no idea what to say.

"What have you done?" her mother demanded.

Emotion came before words. Suddenly, Grace softened and

covered her face. "He's a monster, Mum," she sobbed. "You've got to believe me."

"Tell me what happened." She put her arms around Grace, who was becoming increasingly unglued.

"We've got to go," Grace decided, pushing the elevator button several more times. The doors opened. "I'm going to get Abby."

Cilla blocked her escape again.

Grace broke free and aimed for the stairs.

"GRACE!" Cilla yelled, hurrying down each step in her shadow.

Cilla caught her at the bottom even though Grace had twenty years on her. She restrained her with both hands.

"Let me go! Our bags are packed."

"Stop and calm down!"

Grace wept against her shoulder, leaving a wet stain of tears, until Cilla coaxed Grace to sit down on the steps. "Talk to me. We're all alone now," she said, composed.

Fixated on the fire hose bolted to the wall, Grace tried to rein in her emotions. She thought about Dean; she asked him for help, for strength.

"I had an affair," Grace finally said. Cilla, stone-faced, waited for more. "I fell in love with someone else and Jamie found out. He's trying to use it against me."

Cilla put her hand to her mouth. "With who?"

Grace bawled, "He wants money and he wants Abby."

"Tell me... who... you... had... an affair with," Cilla commanded.

"Someone at Jamie's office. No one you know."

"How could you do that to him? He's been so good to you."

"Good to me?" Grace was aghast. "What warped reality do you live in?"

"He loves you and takes good care of you and Abby."

"Where have you been?" Grace shouted, unable to believe the depth of Cilla's denial. "Jamie is a sick, lying, cocaine-abusing, whore-fucking bastard. He's been sleeping around for years."

"A little indiscretion here and there is different than a full-blown affair."

A stunned Grace was no longer crying. "*Mother.*"

In that moment, Grace didn't even know the woman standing before her. Her mom. Her blood. The one person she thought truly had her back. Had she not held Grace's best interests all along? Had it just always been about the money? Making sure everyone stayed in their places?

"Do you have any idea what this means? For you? For your future?" Cilla boomed. "You've shamed the family. No wonder you're trying to run out of here."

Grace wept. She was being pushed to her limit again.

"How did you get caught?" It was more of an order than a question.

Grace had finally had enough. She came out swinging. "Her husband caught us *fucking* in the pool."

Cilla huffed—first at the word *fuck*, but then, as seconds passed, Grace could actually see the gears clicking, the transformation on Cilla's face as she decoded Grace's words.

Grace sat motionless, calm, suspended momentarily in the eye of the storm.

Without a word, Cilla stood and walked to the stairwell window, which faced the parking lot. She folded her arms and began to cry.

Grace tentatively approached.

Before she could touch her, Cilla spun around. "HER HUSBAND?" Cilla's voice shook.

"Her name was Suzanne," Grace said, composed, done hiding. "You can't be that surprised."

"How could you do this?" Cilla moaned. "HOW COULD YOU DO THIS?" She collapsed melodramatically onto the stairs.

Grace knelt below her. "I'm sorry."

"All these years, I've given you everything," Cilla roared. "And all I asked is that you're a good daughter."

"I am a good daughter. I've tried to fit into this mold, but—"

"No you're not. You wouldn't do this to me if you were."

"Do this to YOU?" she sneered. "I've given you my goddamn soul! Compromised everything I am to please you!" This epiphanous moment radiated in every vessel of Grace's body.

She felt it and Cilla, who wouldn't give in easy, felt it too. "It's not about you or my lunatic grandfather anymore," Grace said, pausing, exorcising the demons trapped in her soul, offering a hint of a smile amidst her diatribe. "It's finally about me."

"How dare you talk to me this way? I didn't raise you like this." Cilla had become hysterical. "Please God, please, where did I go wrong?" In bottomless agony, she pounded her thighs and stomped her heels like a child having a tantrum. "I tried so hard to protect you."

"Protect me? *Control* me. Your protection destroyed my life! I'm just skin"—she fought to catch her breath—"skin of the person I once was, who I'm supposed to be. You've sucked everything out. You and that *fucking* will."

"How could you do this to Abby?"

"This IS for her Mother." Grace sat with this for a beat. "The cycle stops here."

Grace sat beside her mother and watched her weep. Cilla pounded her thighs once more, but beyond that, there was no more moaning, no more berating, just profound sadness.

Decisively, Grace laid it all on the line. "I love you, Mum, but I love Harper too."

Cilla looked up and into Grace's eyes. She took a slow, deep breath. "Harper," she said, not even blinking at this revelation.

"I'm done lying. I've lost too much."

"What about what I've lost?" Cilla said, quiet and meek.

"What do you mean what you've lost?" Grace raged. "How can you keep turning this around on me? It's my life!"

"I drove Dean away. The night of the ball."

"What?" Grace was suddenly jarred, puzzled.

Taking a tissue from her pocket, Cilla blew her nose with the force of a lion. "I confided in him about what was going on. The rumors about you and Harper. He defended you and I yelled," she admitted, looking devastated. "I was so mad. I told him to leave."

Cilla stared into space, seeing it all again. "I killed him." She paused. "He was still in his tuxedo when he took off for Mexico."

For the first time that day, Grace looked desperately into her mother's bloodshot eyes. "What?" she said, white-faced, shocked by the confession. "Why didn't you ever tell me?"

Cilla shook her head and spoke softly. "I never told anyone."

The silence in the stairwell was long and deafening. Finally, Cilla reached out and took Grace's hand. She brought it to her face, inhaling it before kissing it tenderly. "My baby," she whispered, kissing it again, over and over, the affection becoming frantic. "My sweet baby girl."

They cried together, Grace still on her knees.

"I love you," Cilla said.

"The Glory Of Love"
Bette Midler

Grace never would come out to her family, Harper decided. She didn't have it in her. Her inheritance—hers and Abby's secure future—was too important. The money would win. The money would get the girl.

And Harper would be fine without her. She'd done it for twelve years already, what was another fifty. Or sixty if she was lucky.

She tossed the photo she'd kept closest to her heart into the box.

Crouching down in the grass, Harper finished gathering the rest of the strewn items.

Headlights lit her front yard and then her face as a taxi turned onto the street. Harper sat up and watched it stop in front of her house. Her knees popped as she stood with the box.

The interior light came on first. Harper could see someone who looked like Grace—she wasn't sure—paying the driver and a little blond head beside her.

It couldn't be.

Could it?

And then Grace opened the door.

Helping Abby out, Grace walked her to the curb and told her to wait on the sidewalk. "Mummy will be right back."

In disbelief, Harper watched Grace wave off the cab and head in her direction. Harper set the box down and closed the flaps.

Grace walked up slowly and before saying a word, threw her arms around Harper. She let out a sigh of relief and then began crying—quiet, guttural tears.

Holding Grace, Harper watched Abby who was stroking the hair of her doll. When Grace sniffed through her tears, Abby looked over. She smiled at Harper and Harper smiled back.

"I did it," Grace finally uttered. "I told Mummy everything."

"Oh my God," Harper said. "Everything?"

"Everything." Grace pulled away, looked at Abby and winked. "I told her I wouldn't lose you twice."

"Really? What did she—"

"You wanna know the best part?"

"That's not the best part?" Harper smiled.

"I finally got to tell Jack Stowe to fuck off."

"WHAT?" Harper's mouth was wide open.

"There's so much to tell. It was a long, awful ordeal, but it's over," she said, taking another deep breath. The next words didn't come easy. "My mum said she'd always known."

Despite the dark circles, Grace had, along with her independence, recaptured that sparkle in her eyes. Harper picked Grace up off the ground.

"Congratulations!"

In Harper's embrace, Grace whispered, "Abby doesn't know yet, but she will in time."

"I can't believe you did it." Harper paused. "I have to admit. I didn't think you had it in you."

"Me neither," Grace said, a slight laugh, Juicy Fruit on her breath. "But I did."

Harper could feel the relief in her grip, hear it in her words. "What about Jamie? The mediation?" She set Grace down.

"Fuck Jamie and his threats," Grace vowed, very much herself again. "He's gonna have to come up here and get Abby over my dead body."

Holding Grace in her driveway, Harper was certain he would try. And that it would be an ugly battle. One that Harper would help fight with everything she had.

"He doesn't have power over me anymore," she said. "No one does. It's my life. And I'm ready to start it with you."

Grace looked at Abby. "Sweetie," she said, walking to her daughter, pulling Harper along her. "This is my friend I told you about."

"It's nice to meet you," Harper said, shaking Abby's tiny hand.

"Hello," she whispered before hugging her doll. Abby was soft-spoken and sweet.

"Have you had dinner?" Harper asked. "I made a roast."

Grace lifted Abby and hugged Harper again. "Thank you," she said softly.

"Why don't you go inside and make yourselves at home?" she said, reaching for the can. "I need to take care of the trash before morning."

Suddenly noticing the gauze, Grace said, "What happened to your hand?"

"Oh nothing. Just sliced it open earlier. I'm fine."

Grace smiled sympathetically and touched the bandage. Then, with Abby in her arms, she climbed the stairs to the front porch. Harper watched every step they took with careful deliberation as they got closer to the door, closer to really getting that second chance.

After the screen door squeaked shut, Harper, for a moment, looked to the sky in wonderment. Grace had finally done it. She could hardly believe it.

Harper closed her eyes. She, too, was overcome with relief.

She thanked the universe, the gratitude swelling like a balloon inside her.

She lifted the cardboard box up off the ground and opened it one last time. The stolen kisses, the laughter, and the tears, they were all murmuring: hang on, hang on.

After she looked at the house one last time, seeing Grace through the window hanging Abby's jacket in the closet, Harper dumped the contents into the trashcan and rolled it out to the curb.

Just outside Harper's dining room window, where the three of them would share their first meal together, a lone firefly hovered around the dogwood tree. Its light going on then off and then on again.

Publications from Bella Books, Inc.
Women. Books. Even better together
P.O. Box 10543 Tallahassee, FL 32302 Phone: 800-729-4992
www.bellabooks.com

TWO WEEKS IN AUGUST by Nat Burns. Her return to Chincoteague Island is a delight to Nina Christie until she gets her dose of Hazy Duncan's renown ill-humor. She's not going to let it bother her, though...
978-1-59493-173-4 $14.95

MILES TO GO by Amy Dawson Robertson. Rennie Vogel has finally earned a spot at CT3. All too soon she finds herself abandoned behind enemy lines, miles from safety and forced to do the one thing she never has before: trust another woman.
978-1-59493-174-1 $14.95

PHOTOGRAPHS OF CLAUDIA by KG MacGregor. To photographer Leo Wescott models are light and shadow realized on film. Until Claudia.
978-1-59493-168-0 $14.95

SONGS WITHOUT WORDS by Robbi McCoy. Harper Sheridan's runaway niece turns up in the one place least expected and Harper confronts the woman from the summer that has shaped her entire life since.
978-1-59493-166-6 $14.95

YOURS FOR THE ASKING by Kenna White. Lauren Roberts is tired of being the steady, reliable one. When Gaylin Hart blows into her life, she decides to act, only to find once again that her younger sister wants the same woman.
978-1-59493-163-5 $14.95

THE SCORPION by Gerri Hill. Cold cases are what make reporter Marty Edwards tick. When her latest proves to be far from cold, she still doesn't want Detective Kristen Bailey babysitting her, not even when she has to run for her life.
978-1-59493-162-8 $14.95

STEPPING STONE by Karin Kallmaker. Selena Ryan's heart was shredded by an actress, and she swears she will never, ever be involved with one again.
978-1-59493-160-4 $14.95

FAINT PRAISE by Ellen Hart. When a famous TV personality leaps to his death, Jane Lawless agrees to help a friend with inquiries, drawing the attention of a ruthless killer. No. 6 in this award-winning series.
978-1-59493-164-2 $14.95

A SMALL SACRIFICE by Ellen Hart. A harmless reunion of friends is anything but, and Cordelia Thorn calls friend Jane Lawless with a desperate plea for help. Lammy winner for Best Mystery. No. 5 in this award-winning series.
978-1-59493-165-9 $14.95

NO RULES OF ENGAGEMENT by Tracey Richardson. A war zone attraction is of no use to Major Logan Sharp. She can't wait for Jillian Knight to go back to the other side of the world.
978-1-59493-159-8 $14.95

TOASTED by Josie Gordon. Mayhem erupts when a culinary road show stops in tiny Middelburg, and for some reason everyone thinks Lonnie Squires ought to fix it. Follow-up to Lammy mystery winner *Whacked.*
978-1-59493-157-4 $14.95

SEA LEGS by KG MacGregor. Kelly is happy to help Natalie make Didi jealous, sure, it's all pretend. Maybe. Even the captain doesn't know where this comic cruise will end.
978-1-59493-158-1 $14.95

KEILE'S CHANCE by Dillon Watson. A routine day in the park turns into the chance of a lifetime, if Keile Griffen can find the courage to risk it all for a pair of big brown eyes.
978-1-59493-156-7 $14.95

ROOT OF PASSION by Ann Roberts. Grace Owens knows a fake when she sees it, and the potion her best friend promises will fix her love life is a fake. But what if she wishes it weren't?
978-1-59493-155-0 $14.95

COMFORTABLE DISTANCE by Kenna White. Summer on Puget Sound ought to be relaxing for Dana Robbins, but Dr. Jamie Hughes is far too close for comfort.
978-1-59493-152-9 $14.95

DELUSIONAL by Terri Breneman. In her search for a killer, Toni Barston discovers that sometimes everything is exactly the way it seems, and then it gets worse.
978-1-59493-151-2 $14.95

FAMILY AFFAIR by Saxon Bennett. An oops at the gynecologist has Chase Banter finally trying to grow up. She has nine whole months to pull it off.
978-1-59493-150-5 $14.95

SMALL PACKAGES by KG MacGregor. With Lily away from home, Anna Kaklis is alone with her worst nightmare: a toddler. Book Three of the Shaken Series.
978-1-59493-149-9 $14.95

WRONG TURNS by Jackie Calhoun. Callie Callahan's latest wrong turn turns out well. She meets Vicki Brownwell. Sparks would fly if only Meg Klein would leave them alone!
978-1-59493-148-2 $14.95

WARMING TREND by Karin Kallmaker. Everybody was convinced she had committed a shocking academic theft, so Anidyr Bycall ran a long, long way. Going back to her beloved Alaskan home, and the coldness in Eve Cambra's eyes isn't going to be easy.
978-1-59493-146-8 $14.95